The Ghosts that Haunt Me

Tim Ford

Published in Canada by Pandamonium Publishing House™
www.pandamoniumpublishing.com
pandapublishing8@gmail.com

CONTENTS

1

Bean cake for breakfast, lunch, and dinner. Your cell is dimly lit, you never know if it is daytime, or nighttime, in fact, the only thing you know for sure is you're doing dead time. As usual, I would exercise like a fiend, basically to exhaustion to silence the demons in my head.

If anything, Charlene will be the last chick I ever get serious with. Fuck that falling-in-love-bullshit. I am never going to be betrayed by a chick again. I was meditating and extremely deep in calming thoughts, when I heard a key open my cell door. Levy must be here; fucker better get his ass in gear and get me out sooner than later.

"Hey, Strongbow, you are a free man. Let's go."

I was a little shocked to say the least, but I also know not to argue with my unexpected freedom. I jumped up and got my ass off the cold, damp floor.

The light in the hall was blinding, but if it meant freedom, then it was truly a ray of sunshine.

The screws took me down to start processing my release. They gave me a hanger with my tuxedo that I was wearing the night of the brawl. *Man, you think they will cut me a break with my late fee if I tell them why it hasn't been returned yet? Then again, with the stains of blood on it, and about a dozen tears, looks like I will be eating this one.* I was given my wallet and truck keys and was told to leave.

As I walked outside, I heard a car horn honk. I was squinting when someone yelled, "Hey asshole, want a ride?"

It was Jerry. I just stared at him; he too has been on my mind a lot lately. Fucker. Ripping off his own family member for cash over his club. I walked closer with a scowl on my face.

He gets out of the Caddy and says, "I am the reason you are out of jail, not your lawyer, Levy. Get your ass in here and quit being a bitch."

For the sake of hearing how he got me out, I will get in, only because I need a ride home.

"So, you have my attention; tell me a story, Jerry."

"As you know in our world, I can't tell you the whole story, but what I can tell you is a couple of the boys put the fear of the lord into Burns. Enough so that he has dropped all charges against you. And two days ago, he was traded to Green Bay, did you know that?"

I thought to myself *this also means that Charlene will be moving to Green Bay with him, good, I hope she freezes her cunt off.*

Jerry said for me to call Levy and he will tell me all the legal bullshit. He also informed me Levy's fees have been paid by him and no need to pay him back. Guess he feels bad for fucking me out of the weed dealing profits in Alaska. I asked how Grandpa liked Monterey. He said he liked the music, but too many pale faces acting weird. That made me laugh out loud.

He asked if I was heading for hunt camp later this week with him, Donnie, Joseph, and Uncle Jack. He said Oscar was flying them all in.

I had to ask what today's date was. I did some math in my head and said, "yeah for sure." I will be back in lots of time for McDowell's shipment of weapons.

Jerry dropped me off at my place and said he would be in touch. He then looked at me and asked if we were good. I thought about it for a second, stuck my hand out and said we are better than good, we are Strongbows.

Jerry smiled and said, "damn straight!" before shaking my hand and driving off.

***

I see someone put a ten-foot-high gate in my driveway that will keep the little pukes away. Bet you it was Donnie.

Strolled into Pamdora's where Janine looked at me with a great big smile on her face. She came rushing over and gave me a huge hug.

"Oh, Mitchell! So glad to see you. According to the papers, I thought I would never see you again!"

"Don't believe everything you read in the papers."

I dropped my hands from her back to her ass, gave a nice hard squeeze, bit her neck to see her reaction, as I was rock hard.

She started to laugh, not the exact response I wanted as she said, "This grope is your one and only freebie, I respect that you have not seen a female in a month."

I stepped back, laughed at her, and said, "Fair enough. So, let's talk business, how are things going?"

She said, "Business is good."

I asked if anyone called for me. Janine gave me a bunch of names and phone numbers. I went over the list, did a quick once over and did a priority list mentally. Mad Bill I called right away.

He answered gruff as ever.

"It's Mitch, I'm free. Can you talk on this line?"

He said no and for me to call him from a payphone to one near him. Said to give him five. I wrote down the number, asked Janine for a couple bucks change and walked to the payphone down the street.

As I went to leave, she said it was really nice to see me again, I said thanks and likewise. She then put her tongue in her cheek and simulated a blow job. I just smiled and shook my head. She has been cock teasing me for over a dozen years now, damn! Me and my raging hard-on strolled to the nearest phone booth.

Called Bill, very interesting call to say the least. Right off the bat he reiterated Joseph O'Reilly is to know nothing of our deals. He said if he smells anything that stinks like him, all deals are off. He assured me there is a lot of money to be made. He also said Stokes will be arriving with the first shipment as he wants to see Oscar and me.

Rule number two; each delivery will be a different landing strip. We will be given a piece of paper when the shipment arrives. Less chance of being ratted on. So, he said to make sure that Oscar has a full tank of fuel.

Rule number three; the cargo is my responsibility until the wheels hit the ground at the drop off point.

I agreed to all rules. The date for the ship and Stokes arriving is Thursday, October 30. I started to snicker as that is Natasha's birthday. Pretty sure there will be no birthday gifts on the freighter for her.

He asked me to make contact with him every Monday at noon or if anything comes up, he should be made aware of.

I let him know I was heading to my grandpa's place for a bit to hunt and would contact him once I get back.

After I hung up, I had a gnaw in my gut. Him saying I am responsible for the merchandise until we land, didn't sit well.

I will keep Joseph out of the loop. I totally respect Mad Bill's business decisions. But I will need some muscle, some *solid* muscle.

Will have to think about this one. Donnie would be perfect, but would it get back to Joseph? And Jerry has already burned me once for serious cash flow, mamma raised no dummies, not going to trust him that way.

Paul is more of a thief, and Tommy the Greek I think wants to keep a low profile. Fuck it, time to go back home and see what else is new in my world.

***

I went inside and the apartment had a bit of a musty smell. I opened up the windows, poured myself a glass of Jim Beam's hooch, and rolled a really tight joint. I sparked it up, had a couple sips from my drink, and saw the answering machine light flashing.

Fuck, I better check messages just in case.

Rachel left three messages, Joseph, Donnie, a couple from Jerry, Stuart sisters, Basil, and then one that made me put down my drink and the joint in the ashtray.

At first, I couldn't hear it clearly, or understand it, but then I realized it was a female crying, it was Charlene.

Well, my stomach flipped as some hard-core guilt came my way.

"You are nothing but a piece of shit. I woke up to masked men in our bedroom pointing shotguns and me and Matt's heads. They fucking asked if we wanted to meet Jesus seeing at how we are now devoted to our saviour, Jesus Christ. How could you have done this to me? I was warned by my cop friends, especially Kurt Wilson, who you called liars, guess I now know you the real fucking liar is right, Mitch? Matt says he is dropping charges against you and has asked for a trade. I swear to God, Mitch if I see you again, I will kill you myself. Then you and your worthless life can burn in hell. And that is where you belong, fucking asshole."

I took a deep breath, looked up to the ceiling, and just shook my head and snickered. So, this is how Jerry got me off the charges.

I took a couple more drinks and just stared at the phone and replayed the message again and again.

Had a pretty good buzz happening when I said enough of her. I erased her message, no regrets. Gotta move forward.

Called Rachel's house and left a message that I am free, and all charges are dropped and asked when I can see her.

Then I called Mindy and lucky for me she was at her office. I totally caught her off guard when she answered the phone.

"Hey beautiful, I am a free man, a free horny man, I really need to see you."

"Oh, handsome I will always have time to see you. Are you home right now as I can be over in twenty…"

"Yes, I am home baby, slide by."

I went and checked the freezer and still had a bottle of vodka in there. Mindy's drink of choice. Had lots of weed for us. All set.

Mindy showed up wearing a purple dress that was skin-tight and showed lots of cleavage and legs.

As soon as she got to the top of the stairs, I picked her up as she wrapped her legs around me. I was necking with her and grabbing and squeezing her ass.

I held her up until she mouthed those two words, "Fuck Me!"

Carried her into the bedroom and threw her down on the bed. I ripped open her pantyhose right at her snatch and started to finger the hell out of her wet and throbbing pussy.

Her moans and groans of lust were sweet music to my ears, fuck Charlene. Her loss is Mindy's gain.

And there was no better sight to be seen then Mindy unzipping me and putting my rock-hard cock in her sexy mouth.

She was stroking and sucking me as vigorous as I was playing with her pussy. After about ten minutes I couldn't hold back and started to shoot down her throat. Her eyes got big and sparkled as she swallowed every last drop cumming from my cock.

She then stuck out her tongue to show she wasted nothing. Not to be outdone, I slid the two fingers I used on her into my mouth.

She had the biggest smile come to her face as she said, "I fucking missed you so much, Mitch."

"I missed you big time, baby. Round two we fuck, so wanna bat you home. Till then, you want a drink?"

"You mean other than cum?" She winked and then started to laugh.

I helped her up out of the bed and went into the living room. Poured her a drink, rolled up a joint and told her to help herself.

Took me twenty minutes, or more like one drink and one joint before I was fully hard again. Mindy's teasing also worked their magic.

Mindy asked me what position, I said missionary, I wanted to see her beautiful face, sparkling eyes, and yes, seeing those tits of hers move as I pounded her hard. And after she came twice, that load of mine shot all over those beautiful breasts of hers.

We grabbed a shower, then had a great life conversation. I honestly believe the relationship I have with Mindy is exactly what I need. Great sex, fun times, and no commitment. That is my new motto.

After she left, I wanted to head down to the Drunken Leprechaun but was pretty wasted and what little energy I had, fuck, Mindy drained me, in more ways than one.

Fuck. I was even too buzzed to use the phone, so I went to lay down for a bit.

***

I woke up sixteen hours later to the phone ringing. It was Rachel, she asked if we could do dinner tonight. I said yes here or in Sacramento? She said here as she needed some authentic Mandarin food in Chinatown. I said I would make reservations and would see her around seven.

I called Donnie and asked him if he wanted to meet for breakfast. He said sounds good. I asked him if he put the gate up in my driveway. He said yes, the key for it is in my Raider coffee mug. He also said he fixed the Mustang and the truck, said the bill for both is under the mug. I thanked him and told him I would bring the cash with me.

I grabbed a long hot shower and the whole time I debated on asking him to work with me on this gun deal or not.

Even on the drive over to meet him, I am still not sure. I will know when we meet, I will feel him out, see what he says.

His bike was already in front when I pulled up. I put my bike beside his and walked in.

He waved over at me from the table, he got up and gave me a hug and said he was glad to see I am out.

Told him thanks and maybe in time I will ask who the shotgun toting boys Jerry sent over. If I know Donnie, he was one of them.

Oddly enough, Donnie sort of let me know he was one of them that night, as right off the bat he told me what a great rack Charlene has.

Just him being blunt made me burst out laughing. I thanked him and said yeah, she does.

He looked at me really seriously and asked if me and Charlene were done.

"One hundred percent done. After her being with Burns, she is now tainted meat. Even after they split, and you know they will. Done for good, man. Thanks brother, I really appreciate everything you have done for me."

"We are family, Mitchell; I know you would do the same for me."

"I would kill for you, Donnie."

He half smiled and said that day may come. I suddenly felt a cold shiver go up my spine.

"Listen, I have to ask you something. And I trust it remains just between us."

He nodded and told me to go ahead as I now have his complete attention.

"I was offered a job to make some really decent cash. The

guy who offered me the job said Joseph is not to be involved at all. Said any involvement by him, and the deal is off. You interested? That would mean no conversation getting back to Joseph."

He asked me a couple questions before committing to me and my deal. First was how well do I know this guy. I told him the whole story including him being an ex-cop. That made Donnie nervous. He asked what we had to do. I told him what the jobs entailed, and then he asked how much cash I was offering.

He raised his eyebrows and said it's good money, risky, but good cash.

He said he wanted to do a background check on Mad Bill first before jumping on board. He reminded me that Jake was thrown in prison for a gun deal gone south. I said fair enough. I let him know when the first deal was to take place. He said that was more than enough time.

Donnie asked if he could personally talk to Bill about guns for the club. Fuck, I had visions of the Alaska weed deals all over again. But Donnie has always been solid for me. I guess Jerry has too to a certain degree, if not for him I could be doing the next twenty plus years back in San Quentin.

"The main gun dealer is a guy named Kevin Stokes. He will be there for the first deal. He too is another guy I served with in Nam, also Special Ops and SOG. Best to deal directly with him, as Bill is just the middleman."

He thanked me for my honesty and said he will talk to Jerry tonight.

***

After we ate, we both jumped on our bikes and headed to Popeye's for a workout. I was greeted with hugs and laughs by everyone. So nice to feel the love and respect.

Had a killer workout, then it was off to the grocery store, a little nap and wait for the one true love of my life who never ever lets me down, Rachel.

As soon as the doorbell rang, I raced downstairs. I opened the door and gave her a huge hug.

She said I was certainly in a good mood. Just loving life and the freedom that comes with it was my reply.

This gave her an ear-to-ear smile, she said so nice to hear. She came up and we had a drink before heading to dinner.

Rachel seemed to be enjoying life too and the new man in her life, Pat Price.

I asked if she was going to head up to Hunt Camp with us. She blushed and said that Pat was taking her to Hawaii that week, as a birthday gift.

As happy as I am for her, time for the big brother to ask questions.

"How serious are you with him?"

Rachel went red faced, yeah now, she suddenly looked full blooded Sioux.

At first, she didn't answer, so I asked if she loved him. She said yes with a full smile and sparkling eyes.

I asked if he loved her.

"He says he does, and I honestly believe him."

"And what did Jerry and Grandpa think of him?"

"Jerry doesn't warm up to anyone. Grandpa said he likes him. They actually spent a lot of time together which was nice to see."

That alone spoke volumes to me.

It was a good dinner, but as we were having our post meal drinks Rachel broke down and said she loves me, but I am really stressing her to the max these days.

"Twice, since you have been released from prison, you have been charged with attempted murder. And twice you have gotten lucky and if it was not luck, I don't want to know about it. Mitch, you are my only full-blood relative left on the planet. Please, if you truly love me, try and control your temper. *Think*, instead of reacting. One of these times you will not be so lucky. If not for me, think of Katrina. One day the truth will come out and she will want to get to know you. Don't blow that opportunity."

I just smiled and shook my head no.

Rachel said, "It will happen, Mitch. Deep down in my heart, I know it will happen."

I smiled and said, "I truly hope you are right. I think she would have that calming effect on me. Fuck Rach, if Tash wasn't such a twat, Katrina would know I am her dad and then yes, I would be at peace."

Rachel didn't argue with me; she said she agrees. Normally, I would ask if she has heard from Tash, but she's another twat I don't care about.

I asked if she wants to go fishing again once I get back.

"I would love that; we had such a good time. Thanks for reminding me-I have your deed for the land on me. Pat also sends his regards and is glad you are free."

"Tell him I said thanks and I haven't forgotten about him wanting to talk business. Actually, maybe I will see if Donnie wants to take a run up this weekend. You two have plans?"

"Nothing that I can recall. There is a really nice Sunday buffet just around the corner from his condo. Maybe we can meet there?"

I told her I would talk to Donnie and let her know.

We went back to my place, Rach phoned grandpa and said someone wants to talk to him.

"Hi grandpa, I am free. Cops dropped all charges."

He was so happy and asked if I was coming up next week to hunt. I promised him in jail, that I would be there.

It was nice hearing the joy in his voice. Not sure who I feel more shittier about disappointing, Rachel or grandpa.

Rachel stuck around until Joseph and Oscar showed up.

I gave her a hug, thanked her for her concern and told her I would talk to Donnie. Told her to say hi to Patrick.

***

Joseph gave me sort of the same lecture that Rachel did. But there were no tears, and the word cunt was dropped at least a dozen times by him. I looked at Oscar who was smiling behind Joseph. He would also put two fingers up to his lips to simulate eating pussy.

"You stupid fuck, I can see your reflection in the window. Never ever mock me Oscar, understood?"

Oscar knew that Joseph meant business and apologized.

"So, boys I know you two are heading up to hunt next week, anything else going on that will take you away from me?"

What the fuck, did Donnie rat me out? I looked at Oscar who also seemed puzzled. Never let the cat out of the bag, let's see what he knows and where he is going with this.

"Oscar and I have a private job from one of my army buddies, why?"

"Baseball playoffs are happening, and I am sure not all will

10

want to pay up. I will need you two to collect some cash. Who is this army buddy and what type of job?"

I have learned if you tell a tale, this has to be some sort of truth to it.

"Kevin Stokes is his name. You hear of him?"

"Can't say I have lad, should I?"

"Not sure, he went AWOL while in SOG. He is coming here and wants a private plane to take him up north."

Joseph scratched his eyebrow then looked at Oscar and me.

"You are helping a deserter?"

"Anything but a deserter, he is wanted on murder charges. He was set up by the CIA. A couple crates of weapons went missing a couple months in a row. He had an idea who the thieves were. Shot three Laotian officers dead, and the thefts stopped. But because he did this on his own, the Laotian government freaked, they want him to be held accountable."

Joseph nodded his head with approval and said good for him.

He had a beer then left; Oscar stayed behind so we could talk about our next mission.

Now, if you are wondering about why such an elaborate story, it was the truth. But Stokes set up an officer from Laos who was also involved with the thefts.

Oscar was a bit pissed about the lack of trust that Bill and Stokes had in us. I just said their cash, their rules. I was fine with it.

As a pilot, he said it really puts pressure on him for flight charts, refuel spots and not knowing anything about the landing strips.

I respected that as I never really thought about it that way.

"Well fuck them, Oscar; it just means our wheels aren't in the air right away."

Oscar said nothing but he was still not happy. Well, cash makes me happy, hopefully it will do the same for him.

What makes Oscar happy is pussy. He looked at his watch and said at midnight there were two stewardesses are arriving at San Fran airport.

"Strongbow, both have big tits and like to suck the cock. If you are over the librarian, I say we go pick them up, take them back here and have our ways with the DD twins."

"Let's head to the airport," was my answer.

For the first time since Oscar got here, he smiled.

***

We sat in the bar and waited for the girls. Oscar said they knew to meet him there. He told them he will try and get a friend to come along. Oscar said he took the two of them on alone last time, it almost killed him.

"Strongbow, too many mountains to climb with these two. They are both insatiable in bed."

We just ordered our second drink when we saw these two buxom stewardesses come in the bar. Everyone present turned around to look.

Oscar wasn't lying. Damn both had huge boobs. Oscar tapped me and asked which one I wanted.

"The one with the black curly hair, thick lips, and piercing blue eyes."

"That is Maureen, good choice. Only thing, she doesn't take it up the ass. Lynda does, I am happy, if you are."

Fuck yeah was my answer. Something about a woman in uniform does it for me.

The closer she got, the more the uniform brought out the blue in her eyes.

Oscar did the introductions, both girls gave me a hug. Yep, Charlene who?

We had one more drink with them, then they wanted to eat.

I said I know this pizza joint on the way back to my place, we can have a drink while it cooks.

Girls said they were down with it.

Oscar jumped in the back with Lynda and Maureen jumped in the front with me. I could tell right off the bat there was a lot of sexual chemistry between us.

Once the pizza was cooked, we went back to my place. The girls said they wanted to get out of their uniforms right away.

Maureen put her index finger up to her lip and asked if she could change in my room, while Lynda was getting changed in the spare room. I said absolutely. She thanked me, went in and changed, but left the door wide open.

I was sitting on the couch watching the whole undressing.

She took off her top, then her bra, gave her boobs a rub in the mirror, looked at me and winked. I think we have a bit of an exhibitionist on our hands. Once she took off her skirt, she pulled open her underwear, did a little swipe along her lips and then once again winked at me.

She put on a pair of jeans, Levi button up top with no bra and showing more than enough cleavage.

The four of us ate pizza, drank beer, and smoked about a quarter bag of weed.

There was lots of necking between Maureen and me. You are pretty sure you are going to score, but you are never one hundred percent sure, that was until she whispered in my ear that she wanted to suck my cock, right now.

Those blue eyes and thick lips of hers told me all I wanted to hear.

I took her by the hand and off to my bedroom we went. I laid down beside her on the bed, while necking with her and unbuttoning her top. Then I just sucked on her tits, biting her nipples from time to time.

She already had my cock out of my pants and stroking me. By the time I got her pants off, and was fingering her, she was soaked.

As much as I wanted to see those thick lips of hers around my cock, I needed to fuck her as I knew she was going to cum quick.

Then I heard those dreaded words.

"Mitch I am sorry, but you want in me, you better be wearing a condom."

At first, I was horrified, and then I remembered Anita's *no glove, no love* statement.

I had two left. Note to self, buy a box.

I asked what her favorite position was. Her eyes got big, and said I was a totally unselfish lover.

"I love slow dogs to start, then I want you to pull my hair and smack my ass."

Like she said, I was unselfish, of course I would respect her wishes.

I started off nice and slow, playing with those massive tits of her, I have to say, they are the biggest set I have ever played with.

I could tell after a couple minutes her pussy was tightening up, her body muscles were starting to contract. Time to speed up my thrusts, time to pull her hair, smack her ass and bite her neck.

By her third or fourth orgasm I couldn't hold back and shot a load and half and then collapsed on top of her.

Both of us just laid there all sweaty and trying to catch our breath.

When I finally rolled off her, I laid on my back, had whatever energy I had left in me to take the condom off and put it in the waste basket beside the bed. Maureen, much like a cat, rolled into me and started to purr. We both passed out within minutes.

My subconscious, heart, and lust certainly didn't sleep. I dreamt about Charlene and me on a beach in Hawaii. And what made this erotic dream more complete, was me looking down and seeing Charlene sucking my cock. It was so real, I even heard her say, "You're loving this, Mitch."

I can't remember the last time I even had a wet dream, but fuck I am ready to cum. Just as I am starting to squirt, I come out of my slumber and see Maureen stroking the shaft of my cock hard, as the head of my cock is in her wet mouth. After about two minutes, Maureen's face is now covered in cum. She was smiling asking how she did.

"You did amazing, what a perfect way to wake up."

She thanked me and asked if it was good enough for breakfast out, and a drive back to the airport?

My turn to smile and see absolutely. She looked at her watch, yelled at Lynda in the next room, and said they have to leave shortly.

She asked if I wanted to take a quick shower together. Never been one to turn down a shower with a hot chick.

We both left the bathroom when it was Oscar and Lynda's turn to jump in the shower. Lynda grabbed me by the cock and said too bad there wasn't more time, as the four of us in the shower would be much more fun. Fuck that was a hot statement.

As the four of us were having breakfast Oscar asked how much luggage they are allowed to carry on.

I knew he was thinking of moving dope of some kind.

14

Maureen was smart, and said they have dogs that sniff for dope if that is what he was thinking. Too bad was his answer. For me I was thinking of moving cash.

I know that Donnie and Joseph have bank accounts under different names, in several different cities. A great way of hiding your income, and also if you need to lie low from the cops or feds, you will have a cash nest already set up.

But I really don't know her, or Lynda that well yet. I think I will get to know her for a bit. Then ask her if she would do bank deposits for me, of course I would pay her well.

Maureen and I exchanged numbers. I told her next time she is in town I will take her out for authentic Chinese food. She said she would really like that.

As soon as they left, I asked Oscar the lowdown on them.

Said he met both in Los Angeles at a bar. Did a threesome with them. Not much to add.

Guess not.

I drove Oscar back to his place and we discussed hunt camp and the gun deal. I told him I talked to Donnie to make sure we have some more muscle. I reiterated what Mad Bill told me about Joseph involved. He also agreed not to say anything.

***

After I dropped him off, I headed to Donnie's shop. We discussed the extra muscle and he said he would pass, but he talked to Steve and Rick, and they were in.

I talked to them myself and told them my rules. The deal stays between us and us only. I don't even want them to think out loud about it. I told them I would pay them cash once we land back in California. They would be supplying their own weapons of course.

But the biggest rule, no itchy trigger fingers. I don't wanna be shot by someone in my own crew. They both agreed, we shook hands, and I told them I would give them notice when the deal is going down.

I then asked Donnie if he wanted to meet up with Pat Price and Rachel on the weekend. He was a little surprised they are now an item. I asked what he thought of him as Rachel's significant other.

"He is a good guy. Bit of a playboy reputation. But if she is happy, why not?"

I just nodded my head as those were also my exact thoughts and fears.

"Don't worry, Mitch. Just like you're a big brother to me, she's like my little sister. He hurts her, I will put a bullet in his head. Don't matter how much dirt we ate together in Nam."

That made me laugh as I said thanks.

He said he would like Jeanie to come along, too. He said the women can go and shop as us guys talk business. I saw nothing wrong with that at all.

I thanked him and told him I would let Rach know this Sunday is a go.

I headed home. Gave Rachel a shout and told her that Donnie and Jeanie would join us. She said great and she would let Pat know.

2

Over the next couple days, I focus on the gym and figuring out my finances. My bank account I have in Boston I think I will always keep intact; in fact, this will be part of my emergency funds. It is so close to Canada I can get across the border as a "First Nations Native". I will get Joseph to get me a phony native Canadian identification.

Between my hidden safe in the apartment, the hidden safe in Pamdora's, bank accounts under my name, and Willie Hertz just here in San Fran, I had eighty-two thousand dollars. You consider I own my own Harley, GT Mustang, pick up truck. I own Pamdora's and the building it resides in, and some land.

I am doing not bad for someone with not even grade twelve schooling. My education was in the jungles of Southeast Asia.

As happy I was with all that I have done. I sit back and figure I have wasted about the same amount of cash on dope and booze and whores. Fuck, all the cash and dope I robbed and killed people for when Lucy and I were shooting smack.

I looked over at the picture of Lucy and me that was taken before we were junkies. Fuck, I would give away all my cash and toys to have her alive.

Needless to say, a bottle of Jack and a half bag of weed was polished off that night. Fuck, I didn't even make it to my bed that night. Passed out on the couch.

***

The next day, I was hurting pretty good. My head was pounding, and the doorbell kept ringing like crazy.

Fucking assholes, whoever it is they are going to take a beating. I struggled to go down the stairs, it has to be Joseph. I looked out and it was Mike Battaglia and two of his apes.

Without fully thinking I open the door and tell them to come upstairs. Then a cold sweat comes over me as I walk up the stairs. *Ella...fuck, I wonder if they are here to kill me? I wonder if she cried her head off to her Godfather, even though he wanted me to end my relationship with her.*

I am unarmed, and I know his apes always carry firearms. First thing I am going to do is to go and discreetly get a weapon out of my bedroom. So, I offer them a drink and ask if they want to smoke a joint. I have some grass in my room along with two, 9MM, fully loaded handguns.

Mike says thanks but they are in a hurry. He says he has a message from his dad and asked me to have a seat. My head and heart are both pounding hardcore.

He looks at me all serious and says, "Dad wants some of that deer sausage."

I must look totally confused as Mike asks if I am not heading to hunt camp next week.

"Yeah, heading there next week. Yeah sorry, man, I tied one on last night."

"You look like shit, Strongbow. By the way, dad says you have the most unique way of breaking up with someone, but he sends his regards."

"Well, that was not the plan, it just happened that way. Burns is a fucking creep, and now he and Charlene are engaged."

Mike frowned, shook his head and said, "What a stunned cunt she turned out to be. He would play rough with the girls at the club, had to ban him. I should have had one of the boys put a piece of lead in the back of his head, would have saved you some jail time."

"Lead, head, and dead. Spoken just like Billy Shakespeare himself."

He called me a smart ass, as he and his guys got up to leave.

18

"Once you have the sausage, let's deliver them to the old man. You in?"

"I really think I need a couple days, and more importantly, nights in Vegas. Yeah, that sounds good, really good."

I shook Mike's hand and said I would be in touch.

Well, a natural herbal cure for a hangover is weed. So, I rolled a joint and smoked it while soaking in the bath.

By the time I finished the joint, my head stopped pounding and I felt semi normal. Yeah, totally relaxed.

But like everything else in my life, chilling seems to be overrated and unattainable as the doorbell went once again. I heard a female's voice.

Well, I was also pretty horny right now, that is another great way to get rid of a hangover, a great round of sex.

So, I wrapped a towel around me and my semi, and went downstairs.

Fuck, it was Janine with a huge smile on her face looking hotter than ever. Skin-tight blue jeans, a white blouse, and I am pretty sure no bra. Black leather jacket, high cut leather boots, painted nails and wearing lots of rings, including one on each thumb.

I opened the door and smiled at her. She blushed as she looked down and saw the perfect image of the head of my cock through the towel that is now fully hard and pointing right at her. She giggled and then asked if we could go upstairs and talk as she needs a favor.

I said of course so we headed to the living room.

Also felt this huge sexual urge coming from her, the strongest I have ever felt.

The last thing I want to do is to creep her out or scare her. She is the reason Pamdora's makes money, not me. I would be lost without her.

So, I asked her what favor she needed.

"Listen, me and a bunch of girlfriends are headed to Lake Tahoe for the weekend. I was wondering if I could buy some weed off you."

"Yeah, for sure, not a problem at all. How much do you want?"

"I was thinking of a nickel or dime bag, is that O.K?"

I said not a problem. I got up and went into the bedroom where I had a quarter pound of weed in my top drawer.

As I get out a baggie to put Janine's weed in to. I see her reflection in the mirror get up from the couch and head towards my bedroom.

Just like when Mike was here, my heart was pounding hard as was my cock. I felt the dryness in my mouth and butterflies starting to flutter.

I turn around as she has now entered my bedroom. She has a serious look on her face and a twinkle in her eye. The leather jacket is now off, and I can see both her nipples are erect right through her blouse.

She walks over and starts to rub my cock through the towel. I am speechless to be brutally honest. I go to kiss her, and she shakes her head no, and rips the towel off me.

She orders me to lay back on the bed. I do as instructed.

Janine then slides onto the bed ever so gently and starts to stroke my cock. She asks if this is what I want, or do I want her to suck my cock.

"Suck my cock, Janine; I have fantasized about this for a dozen years."

Everything went into slow motion as she opened up that perfectly round mouth of her. Those thick lips looked amazing around my cock.

Like a machine in perfect rhythm she stroked, sucked, and licked.

I was once again a teen fantasizing about her, while secretly listening to her tell other girls how to properly suck cock. But this time she is not performing on a Popsicle driving me crazy, it is my cock, on my bed.

Just when I thought it couldn't get any hotter, she was able to deep throat me, as she was playing with my balls.

And when she started to moan with my cock rammed down her throat, I felt myself getting ready to cum.

I let her know this and she started to stroke me with both hands while putting one of my balls in her mouth.

Couldn't hold back any longer, I let her know I am ready to cum and that sweet mouth of hers covered my cock, as she took the full load down her throat.

Her tongue licked the last drop out of me, she then looked at me and asked was this my fantasy about her.

"This was my fantasy, but you are ten times better than I ever imagined. God damn, Janine; that was beyond hot."

She smiled and said good, it was nice to feel appreciated. A huge red flag went up when she said that. But she is going away with the girls, the last thing I want to do is ruin her weekend by asking what is going on between her and Alfie.

So, I gave her a dime bag, along with a pack of rolling papers. She went to pay me, and I said no way. She gave me a long French kiss and said thanks. She then laughed and asked if I like the way I tasted. I had to think about it for a second, realized what she meant and pretty sure my face grimacing said it all.

As I walked her down the stairs, I stopped and gave her a piece of advice. "I would never judge you in a million years, just make sure if you decided to hook up with some guy there, he wears a condom."

She smiled and promised me a condom would be worn.

Once again, a kiss goodbye, and yes once again I totally forgot she still had droplets of me in her mouth.

Man, my legs were shaking going up the stairs, felt like I just had a heavy leg day at the gym.

I headed back to my bed, lit up a joint, smoked it and laughed out loud. It wasn't from the high of the grass. It was the high of an amazing blow job from someone I have had a crush on forever.

I woke up several hours later and had to really think did Janine actually blow me or was this another deep sexual lustful dream.

It took take me a couple minutes to realize the fantasy had now, pardon the pun, cum true.

I just chilled that night, made all kinds of business and nonbusiness calls. Really interested in what Patrick has in mind for us tomorrow.

3

Next morning, Donnie and Jeannie, picked me up and off to Sacramento we headed.

Rachel and Patrick were already waiting for us at the restaurant. It was nice seeing Rachel so happy and madly in love once again.

After we ate, the girls went shopping and were told to come back in an hour. That was time enough for us to talk business.

Patrick said that he was giving inside information, that the University of Sacramento is expanding, and will need more student housing. He has a chance to buy three apartment buildings that will be right across from the spot of the new campuses.

He will have the current tenants evicted through legal action. Fix up the buildings a bit, and then flip it to the university. He said for fifty thousand cash, and more than likely some muscle to kick out the most stubborn tenants, we could all be partners. He said we will all double or triple our cash as soon as the university buys the buildings off us.

Donnie asked how long this would take. He said six to nine months max.

We both said we like the idea, but we would have to talk on our own first. Patrick said that was fine.

Before we knew it, the girls were back. Rachel said Uncle Karl and Aunt Sandy are meeting Patrick for the first time tonight and if I had any advice for him.

"Cuban cigars, good bourbon, and you will be in like flint."

He shook my hand and thanked me for the advice. Donnie and I both said we would have an answer by the time we head to hunt camp.

On the drive back, we didn't talk business in front of Jeannie, even thought it was legal for the most part.

But once back at their place, Donnie and I went into his shop, had a beer, and talked.

One of Donnie's biggest concerns was the whole legal aspect.

"You get some of those Black Panther types in those buildings, and our cash will be tied up fighting legal battles. But I also see this as a very profitable business deal. Universities are more interested in income than turning out students. It is truly a big bucks enterprise. What do you think, Mitch?"

"Yeah, I hear you; I am not sure if he needs us more for muscle or cash. Whatever you decide to go with I will do the same, either way."

Donnie said he wants to check out a few things first with his contacts in Sacramento, before saying yes or no. I said that works for me.

I had another beer before heading home.

***

Ironically, Mindy called me and asked if I had dinner plans. I said no, I also wanted to run the business deal past her. Donnie has his contacts and I have mine. I am also willing to bet the fifty grand my contact, is hotter and sexier than his.

Surprisingly, she wanted me to pick her up at her condo. I asked about her husband, she said he is away on business till Tuesday.

Now, Mindy lives in a brand-new building, real swanky place.

So, I said sure why not. Let's see how the other half lives. Ella had cash, but Mindy and her husband are two of the richest people in San Francisco...actually, in the whole Bay area.

I grabbed a long hot shower. Put on some dress pants and a nice long-sleeved shirt, as I know Mindy likes restaurants with proper dress codes. Grabbed a nickel bag of weed and jumped in the Mustang and headed over.

As soon as I walked into the lobby, I was stopped by hotel security, and asked who I am here to see.

I tell them Mindy Matheson. Yeah, the security guy is eyeing me up and down as he goes over and calls Mindy.

His eyes change on the phone. He hangs up and summons the elevator guy over and tells him to take me to the penthouse floor.

Fucking fast elevators, my ears almost pop.

The door opens and I ask which door is Mindy's. He says, "All of them. Her and her husband have the whole floor. In fact, they own the building, sir."

Well, fuck me large. I guess if I go in with Patrick and Donnie, I can also say I am a building owner. Pretty sure our buildings will be not as fancy as this though.

I ring the doorbell, and yes, it had this fancy ass chime to it.

Mindy answers the door only wearing a black see-through negligee. She has a drink in her hand and invites me in. I just stare at her and get hard. She laughs as I am still just standing there.

"Are you going to come inside, Mitchell? I will make it worth your while."

I took a sip of her drink, gave her a kiss and bit her neck. Then I followed her inside without any hesitation.

"Mitchell, how come you didn't bring me any flowers?"
I pulled out the bag of weed and said, "I think these buds are from the perfect flower."

She smiled and took the bag off me and told me to follow her.

Once again, without hesitation I followed her right to her bedroom.

It was bigger than my whole apartment. It had a king size four post bed with mirrors on the ceiling. That was very hot to say the least.

Mindy sat down in front of a dresser with a massive mirror and rolled up a joint.

I came up behind her and started to massage her neck, she smiled, but her eyes looked glazed over. I guess hubby away means partying and getting freaky in the bed they share.

After she rolled the joint, she sparked it up and headed to

the bed.

She took a couple tokes, told me if I wanted a puff, I would have to lose my clothes.

"No chance of your husband coming back, correct?"

She squinted her eyes and asked if I was scared of him.

"No man walking the face of the earth scares me. I just worry about you."

Her eyes got big as she now pulled her head back.

"That is sweet of you, Mitchell. I am deeply touched by your concern for me. And for this, you get to fuck me as many times as you want tonight."

I took full advantage of her offer that night. I shot once in her ass, once in her pussy, and once in her mouth. Then I collapsed from fatigue and was done for the night.

***

Mindy woke me up the next morning and said I deserved a nice relaxing hot tub after a hard night's work.

Outside the sliding glass doors was a hot tub and a heated pool. She had a bucket of champagne on ice beside the hot tub. She cracked open the bottle, poured us each a glass, and said cheers.

Fuck, I can get used to this lifestyle really quick.

As we were drinking the champagne, I told her about the business deal in Sacramento. She thought about it for a second or two, then said it sounds good, and for me to go for it.

We fucked in the hot tub, her price for the financial opinion. We grabbed a long hot shower then went out for breakfast.

The more I got to know her I realized she really was one of us. By that I mean street smart. Lived on the wrong side of the tracks. Her white prince rode into Vegas and took or rescued her from a lifetime of stripping, to be his trophy wife, and amazing sexual partner. But he is not a bad boy, she says he can't get her wet and horny like I can. And the best thing is that she is married. She won't leave this lifestyle. I get a steady wild fuck, with no commitment.

I told her I was going back to the rez to do some deer hunting, and would she like me to bring her back some deer sausage.

She said she has never tried it before but would be more

than willing to try it. I told her good, we would have a BBQ at my place, just beers and sausage sucking of both kinds by her.

She laughed, gave me a kiss goodbye, and said once I am home to call her at the office. Promised I would.

I headed over to Donnie's to see what his people said. His people agreed with Mindy. And with us going away tomorrow, we both agreed as promised to Patrick. Donnie called him and said we are in. Patrick said he must the cash before we left for hunt camp.

So, Donnie grabbed his fifty grand and a couple 9 MM handguns. He jumped in my car, and we headed to my place to get my cash, and yes, my own 9mm.

Even though the cash is for a legit business deal, you know if the cops were to pull us over, they would never believe us. So, you obey every single stop sign, stop light, and no speeding at all. There was a quiet and yet powerful conversation on the way over. It doesn't matter if he is Rachel's boyfriend or not, if we lose our shirts on this deal, we both agreed that he will go missing.

We walked into his office building carrying two gym bags. Both dressed in our leathers, sunglasses, and motorcycle boots. Needless to say, we turned a few heads. Checked in with the cute receptionist and told her we are here to see Patrick Price.
She had an intriguing look to her; hmm I might have to drop in a little more often.

She called Patrick's office and told us he will be right out. I stuck out my hand and introduced myself. As I was shaking her hand, Patrick came out of his office. Donnie gave me a smack on the shoulder and told me to go.

I shook my head at the receptionist, funny as Donnie also shook his head at me.

Patrick said to come into his office. He shook our hands and then asked us to take a seat. He asked us once again if we wanted to be partners with him. We both said yes. He said good then handed us pens and legal contracts to sign. Pat also assured us that Rachel's law firm drew then up.

That was good enough for me, and I signed at the bottom line. Donnie continued to read, nodded his head yes, and then signed.

Pat then signed and said, "So, the owner is a numbered company. His lawyers want fifty grand down by the end of the day, and the following one hundred thousand in a week. I try to stay away from numbered companies, but this is too good a deal to turn down. The owner has owned the buildings for about seven years now. He hasn't put any cash into the place and has had several lawsuits against him. None that have ever seen court. More than likely settled out of court. You boys have the cash on you?"

We put our gym bags containing the cash. He wrote us receipts for our cash, without even counting it.

Asked if we had plans tonight. Donnie said he is taking Jeanie out for dinner and an early night seeing at how we are heading to hunt camp tomorrow. I had nothing planned, and asked what was up.

"Rach and I are seeing Steve Miller tonight. I have a bunch of extra tickets. Thought you might be interested."

That little, or actually big, horny devil in me came out and asked would he mind, if I took his receptionist.

Patrick, smiled, did a little snicker. Took a deep breath and said, "Sorry, Mitch, but no; if you take her out, I would have to fire her."

I was shocked, told him to humor me as to why.

"Never ever mix business with pleasure. It is a company rule. We are business partners now."

Donnie had a smirk on his face. Not quite sure what Rach has said about me. But I am sure Patrick is hoping I don't lose my shit over this policy. And somewhere, somehow, Joseph senses what just took place, his one eyebrow will be raised, and those steel cold Irish eyes will be burning a hole in my head. I told him fair enough, and asked if I could use his phone.

Called Mindy at SOL records as discussed. Asked if she wanted to see Steve Miller tonight with my sister and her boyfriend, she said absolutely. So, I told her I would swing by and pick her up at her place around three.

Patrick gave me the name and address of the restaurant where he and Rach had reservations for. Oliver's steakhouse which was the place they had their first date. What a romantic sap, fuck I hope I am never like that.

Donnie thanked him before we headed back home.

On the drive back, he reminded me that Oscar said to be at the airport for ten am sharp, and asked who Mindy was.

"A married friend. Super hot, and one hell of a piece of ass"

He smiled, shook his head for like the tenth time today and asked if I needed a ride in the morning to make sure I didn't miss the flight, I said that would be a great idea.

***

I got cleaned up and felt like taking out the bike. Nothing better than the run to Sacramento on a bike. I also know I won't get so fucked up riding it. I hate flying all sucked off and hurting.

So, I brought my spare lid, fired my bike up and headed over to pick up Mindy at her apartment. On the way over I wasn't sure if she had a leather jacket or not.

I pulled into to Paul's car lot, slightly used, and yes, mostly hot items warehouse. If anyone would have a female leather jacket, it would be Paul.

Sure, as hell he did have one that I sort of guessed would fit her. I grabbed it and headed to her place.

Now, if the security guy in the front lobby didn't like me before. Wait till he sees me all dressed out in my leathers.

Yep, he eyed me up and down and then that recognition light came on.

He just looked at me and picked up the phone. Not once did he take his eyes off me. *Hmm, I wonder if Mindy's old man pays him extra to keep an eye on her comings and goings?*

The elevator guy was summoned over by him, and he told him to take me to the penthouse.

He just smiled at me, either because he didn't like the security guy, or he knows I was plowing Mindy.

I just smiled back and nodded my head, fuck, why not?

Mindy was totally shocked and seemed very grateful for my gift. She looked super hot wearing it, and if we didn't have dinner reservations with Rach and Pat, I would have fucked her right then and there. She also held up her left hand and asked if I noticed anything. When you have a hand fetish, you notice everything.

"No wedding ring, baby? Does this mean you are divorced, or just not wanting any grief?"

Mindy laughed and said, "I know how much your sister means to you. I just don't want her to think I am some married run

28

around whore."

She came over, hugged me, looked up and said she was only a whore for me. So fucking hot.

The hostess eyed us up and down and asked us in a snarky sarcastic tone of voice, asked if she could help us, even though you could tell she didn't like the look of us.

"Reservations under the name Price, or Strongbow."

She takes a deep breath, puts her glasses on and looks at the reservation list. Snotty cunt looks up, snaps her fingers and this waiter comes over and tells him to take us to our table.

On the walk over I tell Mindy, welcome to my world. She squeezed my hand and said, "Remember Mitch, I used to live in your world. I should buy this restaurant and have her scrubbing dishes. You are a good guy, pay no attention to her."

I squeezed her hand and said thanks.

Pat and Rachel both stood up to greeted us as I did the introductions.

I howl inside whenever I bring around a new chick and introduce them to Rachel. I can see the same look mom would give checking them out. And just like mom, she welcomed her with a warm smile and handshake.

I ordered a beer while Mindy ordered a vodka martini. Being the older protective brother, I wanted to see how Pat acted around Mindy. I want to see if he is fully devoted to my sister or will the playboy reputation, that I heard so much about, come out. He did the obvious up and down checking her out. But for the most part, it was all eye contact.

Eventually, Rach asked her what she does for a living. She smiled and said she was a self-made entrepreneur, that is when Pat's eyes lit up.

He asked her what exactly business she was into. She smiled and looked at me for direction. I nodded yes.

As soon as she started telling him what business she had, he looked like a little boy seeing Santa for the first time.

And then it happened, Pat realized exactly who she is. He looked at me and did a smirk.

After dinner, Pat said he had some interesting kind of dessert.

Now it was my turn to be intrigued and I asked exactly

what.

"I have some magical mushrooms, if anyone is interested." I asked Mindy and Rachel if they were in. Rach gave me that *don't tell mom* look and said yes. I looked at Mindy and asked her the same, she said if I eat some, so will she.

Put my head back, closed my eyes and said, "I have to pass. Sorry guys, long flight tomorrow. I hate hanging while flying. Don't wanna still be high when I see Grandpa. Pretty sure I have disappointed him enough lately. Looked guys, don't let me bum your trip. Please eat up and enjoy, that includes you, Mindy."

She is still not sure, so I whisper in her ear, "Hubbies away, Mindy should play." She burst out laughing, reached her hand out and asked for some special dessert.

The three of them washed down their Jibboo with their drinks and giggled like schoolgirls telling secrets. I felt pretty fucking proud of myself for passing, that was my high. No more disappointing Grandpa.

We had one more drink before heading over to the concert hall.

Parking was truly a pain in the ass. Took me about twenty minutes to find a spot that we could both park in.

Pat said we better haul ass or we will miss the beginning of the concert. Mindy is in heels. Time to adapt. I told her to jump on my back and I would carry her. Mindy burst out laughing and asked if I was serious, told her dead serious. She said she would keep her helmet on in case I dropped her. Good thing I didn't do legs today. Mitch and Mindy for the win, beat Rachel and Pat by half a block.

I put Mindy down and got out our tickets.

As I pull out the tickets, my criminal senses zone in that someone is definitely giving me the evil eye. A foe, not a friend.

As the ticket taker takes our tickets, the security guy approached us and says no entry with motorcycle helmets. By now Rachel and Pat are right behind us.

I ask the guy is there not someplace we can check in our helmets. Fucker smiles at me and yells out for "Tommy Boy" to come.

This muscle head sporting the largest, and goofiest smile makes eye contact with me the whole while asking his co-worker what's going on. He explains the helmet. Tommy Boy now clenches his jaws, makes a fist while still smiling like a lunatic.

"Next time, try reading the back of the fucking ticket. No motorcycle helmets allowed on property, you stupid fuck. They don't have schools on the rez you dumb fuck?"

It appears Tommy Boy wants to go at me. Fucking insult me in front of everyone? I take a deep breath, eye up my opponent, time for me to smash Mindy's helmet right into Tommy Boy's pearly white teeth. I start to get ready for the wind up, but my arm is being pulled back by Rachel. She pleads with me not to fight him. She reminded me that I promised her that I will start to control my temper, no more criminal charges.

I stare at Tommy Boy, while Rachel keeps repeating, he is not worth going back to jail, or prison.

She is right, too many witnesses, and way too many coppers around. In fact, I see a cop now talking to Tommy Boy. Not sure what all was said, but it was enough for him to lose the smile on his face as he looked serious now.

I told Mindy, Rachel, and Pat that I will meet them at our seats. I wink at Rachel and promise no fighting when I come back in.

But you know I am going to get the low down on Tommy Boy. He will pay for his ignorance and bravado, just not sure how much.

I made it back to my seat with no issues, no idea where that goof disappeared to. Mindy said I only missed two songs, but as far as I am concerned, shouldn't have missed any.

Mindy, Rachel and Pat were pretty stoned, nice and mellow, all smiles and giggles. Too bad the row in front of us are not high.

About six drunks are now starting to fight with each other. I swear trouble has a way of finding me. So, I find myself getting ready for the battle. Security is doing a shit job getting there in time.

I try my best to shield Mindy and Rachel. Not sure how good a street fighter Pat is, not going to take a chance of the girls getting hurt.

Two of the fighter's wrestle themselves right on top of us. They knock Mindy and Rachel back. I still have the rage from

Tommy Boy brewing inside me, these two will now pay.

I grab both by the hair and smash their faces into each other, then I kick both dazed fighters back to their row.

Eventually security gets the drunken scrappers out. We sit back down when suddenly about four security guys lead by Tommy Boy, and three cops are standing in front of us.

Tommy Boy sporting an ear-to-ear snaggle tooth smiles says, "Strongbow, you and your friends are out of here for fighting."

"Are you fucking serious? I never threw a punch."

"I saw you smash those two guys heads into each other."

"How about next time instead of watching, haul your steroid injected ass, and deal with those fucks, you pussy."

That wiped the smirk off his face, "Get the fuck out of here now or I will break all your heads open."

Oh, it's go time. This time, Rachel doesn't have a hold of my arm. But what gets my attention is the three cops now getting in front of Tommy Boy.

The one guy, a sergeant, says in no uncertain terms, "Strongbow, you guys leave now, and I will make sure no charges come your way, deal?"

My eyes are shifting back and forth between the sergeant and Tommy Boy. But my ear catches a sweet and sassy voice, "Mitch if we leave now, my ass is all yours tonight, please don't fight," said Mindy.

Rachel now speaks up and says to take the advice, let's just leave. Pat also says not worth going back to jail.

I clench my jaw. Nod my head to the cop that we will leave peacefully, as long as Tommy Boy keeps that big trap of his shut.

The cop now points at him and tells him to find something to do.

We were peacefully escorted out even though I was burning with rage.

As soon as we were outside the gates, Tommy Boy did a mock Indian battle cry, flexing his lats and arms before pretending to be a cowboy and doing a pistol draw. Tommy's security guys thought it was pretty funny. But those cops that escorted us out, they looked at Tommy, shook their heads and walked away from him.

Cops know I am a scary guy; I know one hundred percent that they told Tommy Boy who I was. Two things come to mind: number one, coppers knew not to fuck with me, secondly, coppers knew exactly who I was. This is Sacramento, not the Bay area. This is truly a bad thing that I am even a heat score out here.

On the way back to my bike, Rachel kept telling me how proud she was of me. I kept saying thanks. But the whole walk I am plotting and planning the extent of Tommy's Boys injuries. He will die. Slow death at that, he earned it. Once I meet up with everyone tomorrow, I will see if they know anything about him. If not, I am sure someone in the Sacramento Hell Hounds will know who he is.

Once we got to my bike, Rachel said to tell Grandpa she loves him and misses him, safe travels and to call her once I am home.

My turn to show concern. Can't say I liked the look of either one of their eyes. I asked Pat if he was okay to drive home. He smiled ever so slow and said no. They would grab a taxi and will get his car tomorrow. Of all the madness and anger tonight, that made me smile knowing her cares that much about Rachel's safety. I gave them both a hug goodbye, as did Mindy.

I gave Mindy a long, wet kiss and massaged her boobs before jumping on the bike and firing it up. I told her maybe she will get lucky, and the ride home will numb her ass a little. She smiled rather seductively and said, "I like the pain."

My bike couldn't get us back to my place fast enough.

As Mindy promised, it turned out to be a great night. Man, she knows how to keep me happy. The shrooms seem to make her wetter, and hornier than even after her snorting coke. And yes, I pounded her ass as if I was pounding Tommy Boy's face. I bet you by the time I come back from hunt camp, she will still be tender, not able to sit.

Before I passed out that night, I could see Tommy Boy mocking me. There is revenge, and then there is a Strongbow revenge.

***

The alarm clock woke me up and I had no clue why. Eventually, I had butterflies reminding me I was heading to see Grandpa and going to hunt camp. I rolled over and gave Mindy a morning kiss, a long kiss. Next thing you know we are doing our morning exercises of in and out dick thrusts. Perfect way to start the day.

A quick shower, a cup of Joe and some bacon and eggs and the morning rise was complete.

Before I knew it, the doorbell was ringing. I went downstairs and it was Donny. He asked if I was ready to go. Said all set, just have to drop Mindy off on the way to the airport.

I threw all my hunting gear, rifles included in the trunk of the car. Off we went. Mindy was really hanging off me. Holding me really close. She would look at me and I saw sadness in her eyes. I just smiled and had this uneasy feeling inside. I promised myself after Charlene I would not get serious with anyone again. I think Mindy might have other ideas.

She asked when I was going to be back. I said in five days.

"Please call me at the office and let me know you made it home safe and sound."

I promised I would. Gave her a kiss goodbye. She stood there and just stared at us as we drove away.

Donnie commented, "Nice digs for her."

"Yeah, she owns the building."

He laughed at me and said, "Just the condo you mean."

"Dead serious, man; she owns the whole fucking building," was my response.

"I assume she is married, right?"

I nodded my head yes.

"She has fallen for you large, be careful."

I thought about what he said, never really thought about that. Here I am worried about falling for someone else, and yet it seems someone has fallen for me.

I then told Donnie about my hassles at the concert last night. He said he would ask some of the Sacramento Hell Hounds about Tommy Boy.

Oscar had the plane out of the hangar, I also saw Jerry's Cadillac parked. What I did not see until we got out of the car, was George and Ruby wearing hunting clothes, and not leathers. Still scary looking guys.

Both came over and gave me a hug and asked how I was. I said good, will be nice to get some fresh clean air.

Oscar came over and said we can load up all our stuff. We have the green light in twenty minutes to take off.

He went back to check the plane. Ruby turned to me and said he still doesn't trust Oscar. I once again reiterated that he is solid, just don't trust him alone with your woman.

Ruby nodded yes, then brought up Burns and Charlene as his face turned red with anger. "You say the word and I will put a bullet in that cocksucker's head. I fucking warned him about calling the cops on you. He must think I am full of shit. I see this as a slap in my face; cocksucker should pay for insulting me."

"Thanks, Ruby. Maybe in time, but right now, the cops would come after me."

He agreed and just shook his head. Fuck, he is angrier about it then I am.

One thing is for sure, Burns is a lucky man. And I don't just mean being alive but being with Charlene. But Charlene is not lucky to be with a creep and two-timing asshole like him, what the fuck she was thinking, him over me?

Thank God Jerry brought a cooler of beer for the flight. Needed a couple right off the bat to take the edge off. Fuck, still pissed about how everything went down.

The first half of the trip was smooth sailing. Blue skies, beautiful.

We refueled, and Oscar said before we took off that we will be coming into some bad weather. Just be prepared and to wear our belts. He also let everyone know he has flown in typhoons and monsoons before.

Sure, as fuck we were twenty minutes into the second leg of our flight and as I looked out the window it was like we were flying into the apocalypse. The sky was jet black. The plane was starting to rattle. Oscar yelled back and told us all to put on our seat belts.

Suddenly the voices that were loud, were now silenced. You could sense the fear coming from inside the cabin.

Uncle Jack, Donnie, and I all served in the Airborne. We all know how to jump from the clouds. But there were no parachutes on this flight.

And as I looked out again, well, the only time I could see anything was when there was a lightning strike.

The earlier plane rattling had now become more like an out-of-control roller coaster ride.

I was handling things pretty good until I heard Oscar say, "Holy mother of God."

I looked outside and needed sunglasses as the lightning strikes were once every five seconds.

We hit air pockets and would drop fast; Oscar was swearing and trying to get the plane to climb again.

Well, I have been in two horrific helicopter crashes, should have died in the last one. One airplane crash that claimed the life of Caleb Dalton. If this is to be plane crash number two, it too will be horrific. Maybe claiming all our lives. Time to meditate. So hard with the air pressure changing in the cabin.

Trying my best to control my breathing with my eyes closed. The strikes outside are lighting up the inside of my eye lids. I somehow manage to get into a zone when I heard a temple bell being rung.

After the third ring, a loud bang rang through the airplane. We now started to free fall.

I yelled up to Oscar and asked if he needed help. He said one of the engines took a direct lightning strike.

After about thirty seconds he had the plane levelling off. Then I heard that one word from Oscar I truly hoped I'd never hear.

"MAYDAY, MAYDAY, this is flight 811 from Nevada. We are down to one engine. We need to get this bird on the ground as quick as possible."

Oscar frantically called me to the front and said he needed help. I un-clipped my belt and raced to the co-pilot's chair, buckled up and was horrified at what exactly we are into. I looked to the right and saw a dead propeller.

"I trust you can still find longitude and latitudes on a map?" he asked.

"Like it was taught to me yesterday, what am I looking for?"

"If my instruments are correct, we need to find San Luis Valley Airport. It is a smaller airport. I will keep calling maydays. You figure out a plot for us."

As I worked on the map, Oscar kept calling mayday,

checking his instruments, and doing his best to keep us from slamming into the side of a mountain.

Of all places to lose an engine, surrounded by mountains in an intense thunder and lightning, a monsoon rainstorm with heavy down drafts. Yeah, not good at all. As mentioned, I can hear monks chanting after the temple bell being rung, really loud. I can also smell smoke.

"Well, it seems our only working engine just caught fire," said Oscar as he looked over at me.

He just stared ahead, deep in thought for a couple seconds.

He said, "Fuck it. Prepare for a crash landing!"

He handed me the radio and told me to keep calling mayday as he was looking for a place to try and land.

Oscar managed to get us out of the Rockies, there might be hope for us after all. As I looked at him, he was so intense, total undivided concentration. Then I saw a glimmer of hope.

He smiled and said, "What airport is that off to the right?" I looked on the map and nothing showed any airport. He told me to get back on the radio and call in a Mayday.

I did as instructed and no response. Oscar was now treating the plane like a glider. But for every movement of the plane, the storm and lack of engine power made it one hell of a fight.

He said we will get one chance and only one chance to land there.

Oscar said, "Here goes nothing," and lowered the landing gear. "Mitch, when we land, I need you to help with the brakes."

"Not the first time we have been in a jam. I am ready, brother."

Oscar yelled to the back and told Donnie as soon we stop moving to get the door open and everyone get out as quick as possible.

"Assume the crash position, nothing sharp in your hands. Two minutes or so till we hit the tarmac."

For me, fuck, I have had this death vision so many times. I flash to all my family members alive and that have passed. The one that always gets me, Katrina of course.

The lightning strikes and wind were still strong as ever. I knew better then to talk to Oscar. He was singing in Syrian, once again, no interrupting him.

The closer we were getting to the ground the more unstable the plane was becoming. Just when Oscar would straighten it out, a gust would lift us or have the wings teeter totter.

As we hit the runway hard, a lightning strike blinded me. Oscar yelled for me to hit the brakes. All these heavy leg workouts better pay off now.

Suddenly we heard a loud bang and the plane almost flipped over.

"Blown tire, keep squeezing those brakes, Mitch."

You could see sparks shooting from the rim that we were riding on. We were slowing down but were also running out of runway. No idea what is ahead, but in twenty seconds we will be finding out whether we want to or not.

Another loud bang and now the plane was level, certainly more unstable and now sparks from both sides, left tire blown.

Oscar told me to keep the brakes on, but to protect my head as the end of the runway is in five-four-three-two-one. He counted down.

The nose of the plane went into the ground really hard as the ass end went up in the air. I thought for sure we were going to flip onto the roof, but we landed back down really hard.
It literally stuns you. You are physically shaking, and you can't thank your lucky stars, or God as you know that you are still in danger.

Oscar gets out of his seat and tells Donnie to get the door open as the cockpit, and body of the plane are filling with smoke. He yells at me to go. Donnie is using all his strength to get the damaged frame of the door open. I go over and help him as Oscar is helping to get everyone else out of their seat belts. It took every ounce of strength, but we managed to get the door open.

One by one, we all get out. Oscar is the last one. The rain and fresh air are refreshing as we all run to get away from the plane that has now gone from smoldering to visible flames starting to engulf it.

Jerry yells to get into a building entering from a door he just kicked in.

Uncle Jack is the last one huffing and puffing pretty good when we heard the plane explode. He grabs his chest and collapses to the ground.

Jerry is now freaking, asking if he is all right. He is nodding his head yes, but he is turning this greyish color.

I tell Ruby we need to get help. We leave the building. The plane is fully engulfed, and we can hear bullets exploding. *Why has no one come to help us? How can they miss a plane explosion?*

Every door is locked. Not a soul around. I don't have a clue where we are. But we have to get Uncle Jack help.

I tell Ruby we have to get into the control tower, it is the communication centre. So, while dodging our own gun fire we head to the tower. It's locked. I try and kick the door open, but it is solid.

Ruby says to move aside and shoots the door handle. It falls off and we are in like flint.

I pick up a phone and the line is dead. Must be from the storm.

We haul ass up to the control tower main area and we try all radio communications, but nothing. We both look at each other with frustration and no solutions until we see what looks like a fire truck coming our way.

I tell Ruby to head back to where everyone else is and I will flag down the fire guys.

We both race down the stairs, I head one way and Ruby the other.

I can hear all the ammo now starting to off more frequently. Can see the bullets hitting metal objects. In combat you try and juke, so the enemy won't have a bead on you. This is all out madness. Nothing safe in what I am about to do. But he is my uncle. And I would die for family.

So, it is an all-out sprint to the direction the emergency vehicles are coming.

Bullets are whizzing past me. Beside me and behind me. *Just keep running, Mitch.* Tet all over again. Total besiege, total out of control madness.

Instinctively, I run from one cover position to the next. If I don't get out and warn them, they will be basically driving into an ambush and there will be no help for Uncle Jack.

I am now up to my final cover position. I wait to catch my breath as I see the vehicles are about two hundred yards from me.

I say those two magical and mystical battlefield words,

39

"Fuck It" and ran like the wind to meet the emergency fire trucks.
I am out fifty yards in when I feel a sharp hot pain on the outside
of my shoulder.

I know this feeling all too well. I have been shot. But I
think I am just grazed. Only my stride is affected for a couple steps
and before you know it, I am hauling ass once again.

I head right down the middle of the road while waving my
arms. At first, they don't see me. They are not slowing down. I
keep running and waving my arms. No sense yelling as they won't
hear me.

Suddenly, those headlights beaming right at me drop, and I
know I have their attention.

I am doing my best to tell them about the ammo going off,
but I am so out of breath.

Then a bullet goes flying through the windshield, now their
eyes get big, and they understand exactly what I am trying to say.

As they start to back up. I tell them my uncle is in the one
building having a heart attack, he needs help.

They ask what building exactly. The fire chief says he
safely can get to the building coming from the opposite end of the
airport.

It was like riding a tank into battle. So much power as we
raced down to save Uncle Jack.

A couple fire fighters raced inside and started to evaluate
him.

They said he needs to get to a hospital right away. They
took him out first, and the rest of us jumped in the second fire
vehicle.

They raced Uncle Jack and Jerry to the hospital while the
rest of us drove to a safe enough location.

They called in the state troopers to block off anyone
coming to the airport until the plane was completely burnt out.

They had a look at my shoulder and said a bullet did in fact
graze me. They cleaned me up. Gave me a couple stitches and said
I would live. No shit.

Eventually, the state troopers came by and took down all
our names. Asked where exactly we were heading. Oscar also gave
them the flight path and his pilot bullshit.

You could tell as soon as the one trooper left his patrol car, he knew exactly who we all were, I am sure his dispatcher warned him.

Oscar and I were fairly recently released convicts and we were the least of their concerns. Jerry is the Oakland Chapter President; Donnie is the Sergeant at Arms and California main enforcer. George is the head guy for all of Texas and new chapter recruiter. Ruby is now the national enforcer from Texas to Florida.

They didn't believe our story at all. So, I said phone my grandfather and ask was he expecting visitors. And to also let him know that his son is in the hospital.

Well, you know if you tell a cop it is dark out tonight, he will refuse to believe you. Can't tell them anything logical or suggest anything.

"I will call the reservation police, then your grandfather and see if your story checks out. Till then, no one moves at all."

We just look at each other and roll our eyes. Not even sure where the fuck we are. I then have that moment when your gut flips and you realize *now what?*

"Oscar, we have no plane, and we have a big job in less than two week's time."

He just looked at me as if to say *really Mitch, now of all times?* He shook his head and walked away.

Ruby looked at me and was laughing; he asked what I said to piss Oscar off so bad. I have been taught no one outside my circle gets told anything.

"I told him he makes a better stewardess then a pilot."

Ruby now squinted his eyes and looked around, "I still don't totally trust the guy but looking at mountains all around us. He did a great job flying and keeping us alive."

Ruby then asked the one state trooper where the hell we are exactly.

"Cortez, Colorado," was the trooper's response.

A huge smile came to Ruby's face as he said I knew it. "I sensed we were in Colorado. I am actually one quarter Navajo. I have relatives not far from here. You ever hear of the missing Anasazi Indians?"

I told him can't say I have. Now Donnie and George were also paying close attention to him.

"When I was just a rhubarb, my grandpa would take me to

41

Mesa Verde Park with my dad to hike. Eventually, as I got older and stronger, we explored more of the land that included where the Anasazi would live. Mitch, they lived in the side of the mountains. Then one day they all disappeared. Vanished into thin air. I know you get a lot of visions and spiritual stuff. I would like to hike with you and see what vibes you get."

His story sounds fascinating and as stupid as this sounds, buried very deep inside my soul, I can clearly envision what has happened to these people. The more he would talk, the more I was there.

And speaking of people, in less than a couple weeks I have a huge shipment of arms coming in from southeast Asia. And right now, my back is against the wall as I see the still smoldering remains of the plane, we were going to use to move these weapons across the country.

"I promise you, my friend; I will come back here with you and spend a couple days on the ground, and in the mountains just exploring. Right now, I have some stuff on the go and on a tight time frame." I truly meant what I said to Ruby, every last word.

About ten minutes later, the state trooper said our story checked out.

Then the fuck said he wants all of us out of his state, sooner than later.

Donnie pointed to the pile of wreckage that was our ride and asked how are we supposed to get out of his state exactly?

"The guy who was having the medical emergency needs more advanced medical treatment. His son is paying for a private plane to take him to a Denver hospital along with a nurse. Must be nice to have that kind of cash, I guess crime does pay after all. Speaking of crime, I think it would be in your best interest for all of you to be on that plane."

We all looked at each other and smiled. For me I was thinking this fucking goof state trooper must come home after a shift to cheese spread sandwiches. I am sure all of us combined have more cash on us then he makes in a year. Now that is criminal.

I called Grandpa and let him know what is going on. Told him as soon as we land in Denver, I will call him, as he was not sure if he should make his way there or not.

We saw a DC 3 plane arrive at the airport and within ten minutes an ambulance showed up. This must be our ride.

Uncle Jack and Jerry were the last ones to board. Jerry using his legs and Uncle Jack in a hospital bed. He was hooked up to a couple IVs, and oxygen to help him breathe.

As they were strapping him in, he looked at us and gave us the thumbs up.

I asked Jerry how he was.

"He is still alive, that is a good sign."

We all offered him cash to help with the cost of the flight and he said all good.

He told George to call Val and let her know what is up with her dad.

Once again, as we are heading down the runway, I am nervous until we hit our altitude setting.

Once we leveled off, I started to breathe normal again. I may have a string of good luck when falling from the sky, but that doesn't mean I don't get nervous.

Eventually, the boys were all thanking Oscar for his piloting skills. Even Ruby was laughing and patting him on the back.

While everyone was surrounding the hero of the day, I made my way to the back of the plane to see Uncle Jack.

He looked just as scared as he did in the building we hid in. He also seemed to be kind of doped up as I asked how he was feeling. He blinked at me and gave me a thumbs up. The nurse told me he really needs to rest. So, I told him to take care of himself and I will make sure I bag a couple bucks for him. I saw his eyes get big before they teared up. I just nodded and walked away. Fuck, he looks so much like my dad, or what my dad would look like if he was that age.

I closed my eyes and tried to pick up any vibes of Dad on the plane, sadly none at all.

Before I knew it, the co-pilot was telling us to get ready to land. Palms were getting sweaty as I fastened to my seat. I closed my eyes and started to meditate.

Within a minute, I opened my eyes wide as my heart felt like it was ready to jump out of my chest. Once again, I can hear a temple bell ringing, and can smell incense being burned.

Automatically I think another engine fire. But as I look out, I see nothing. I also notice everyone else is calm. Fuck, I wonder if the nurse back there can give me some of the meds, they have given Uncle Jack to get mellow.

The landing was smooth as a baby's ass, zero issues.

Uncle Jack was the first to be taken out of the plane and into an awaiting ambulance. Jerry went with him. I have to say for the first time that I can recall Jerry showed some serious emotion on his face.

That left Donnie, George, Oscar, Ruby and I heading into the terminal.

George said he was not going with us to Grandpa's. He is going to call Val and wait for her to fly up. He too showed some concern. I guess he and Uncle Jack had a good father-in-law/son-in-law relationship.

As the four of us tried to figure out what airlines came close to flying near Grandpa's, Oscar's turn to drop a bomb.

"Strongbow, I am not going with you guys."

I was totally shocked and asked why not. Fuck we talked about hunt camp back in Nam, and in San Quentin.

"I need to find us a new plane. We have business next week."

Once again at a loss of words. I stuttered and stammered and eventually asked him where one finds a new plane while checking out an arrival and departure board.

Oscar has his hand going up and down reading the board and talking to himself out loud, "Ah ha, Miami. Dade county to be exact. All kinds of illegal planes just ready to be stolen."

I felt bad and asked if he had any help down there.

"No help at all. Just need a couple weapons, just in case."

"Look Oscar, I would help you, but no way can I bail on my grandpa."

He smiled and said all good, no worries.

That is when Ruby stepped up and really showed me, he now has trust in Oscar. He pulled out his black book. Rifled through some pages and picked up a pay phone.

"Hey Spider Monkey, its Ruby. I am sending a personal friend down. His name is Oscar. He is flying in from Denver. I want you guys to give him whatever assistance he needs. Thanks, much appreciated."

After he hung up the phone, he wrote down an address on a piece of paper.

"Look Oscar, here is the address of the Hell Hounds Fort Lauderdale chapter. Ask for Spider Monkey. You need weapons, wheels, muscle- whatever you need they will give you. This is my library card. Show it to Spider."

Donnie smiled, I guess the calling card for the unknown in the Hell Hound world is a library card. Different to say the least, and what else was I thinking? If you said Charlene, fucking right, fucking cunt.

We all thanked him and wished him luck. I asked Oscar if he was heading straight back home.

"I have a guy in Dallas that will change around all the plane info for me, I will make it legit then I will head home."

I gave him a hug and told him I would give him a shout as soon as I get home.

And then there were three.

4

We looked at the boards and saw at least one board that showed Rapid City.

We headed to the carrier and were lucky to get three tickets. We had a forty-five-minute wait till boarding. I called Grandpa and let him know as promised, as to what was up with Uncle Jack.

He once again asked if he should come up here. I said no sense until the docs know exactly what is going on. I also promised Grandpa that if he needs to come once we are on the rez, I will fly up with him. I told him the time we were scheduled to land. He said he would be there to pick us up. He thanked me, and said he appreciated it. Then, yes then I felt my dad's presence. I can picture him giving me a nod of approval for this.

This time before getting on the plane I did a couple rounds of beer and shots of Jack. Fucking nerves are shot.

This seemed to work as I passed out as soon as I buckled up. Next thing I know Donnie is shaking me saying we are descending.

I rubbed my eyes and tried my best to wake up. Even as we were departing the plane, I was still half asleep. But you know what woke me up and made me smile, seeing Grandpa in the terminal.

He smiled and walked towards us. My pace picked right up. I met him with a great big bear hug. He was laughing and said I was hurting him.

I put him down, then it was Donnie's turn for the bear hug. After Donnie put him down, I introduced him to none other than Jack Ruby.

Grandpa had a puzzled look on his face, it wasn't so much the name, but Grandpa asked him what his family background was.

He laughed and said, "If you mean native wise, I am one quarter Navajo."

"I thought so. On behalf of the Oglala Lakota Tenton Sioux nation, welcome."

Ruby was very touched by my grandfather's kind gesture.

Before we left the airport, Grandpa looked right at me and told me to honestly tell him how Uncle Jack was.

I would never lie to the most important human in my life. I told him everything I knew and reassured him that right now he is in the right place.

He said he believed me and sadly said he doesn't want to bury another child. They should have all been burying him.

What can you say or do?

I sat in the front beside Grandpa, but he and Ruby did most of the talking as Grandpa was telling him about certain famous landmarks along the way and how they were important to the Sioux people.

Once we arrived at Grandpa's house, I did what I always do. I head right to the graveyard to say hi to Dad.

Everyone came but Grandpa. I think right now the phone was his focal point.

Fuck, this is my first hunt camp in over two years. Two years of my life I will never get back. I think of Lucy and how fucked up we both were, addicts right?

I think about what Grandpa said even more as I am

standing over my dad's grave. I was there to bury both parents. But Pam was buried with my mom, and Jake died a year or so later.

I am lucky, very lucky that I was able with the help of Grandpa and the great Sioux warriors to beat the heroin addiction. Or it would be just Rachel left.

So, I told Dad here I am, safe, semi sound, and clean. Thanked him for all his guidance. Told him I am glad I decided to live even if it was in pain, then to join him and the rest of my family doing the fourth of July picnic. One day I will be a full-time figure in Katrina's life. That vision I can also see clear as day.

Donnie patted me on the shoulder and said the old man would be proud of me.

I thanked him; Ruby looked at the date of his death, shook his head and said his name will always be associated with Kennedy's death.

"Your dad died in Nam?"

I just took a deep breath and nodded yes.

"My Dad was killed in Korea. Who did your dad serve with?"

"He was full time army reg, 101st Airborne."

"No shit, same as my old man. I bet you they ate the same dirt."

"I bet you they did." I felt really close to Ruby. There was always a bond. I wonder if both dads are smiling down at us now. I bet you they are.

We went in the house to see Grandpa as I suspected hanging around the phone.

You could see the strain on his face. I asked him if he would like me to call the hospital and see how Uncle Jack is doing.

One of the jobs that guys did in the army, that there is no way I would even attempt, is defusing a bomb. The engineers saved a lot of lives. Brave, but if you asked me nuttier than fuck. I always wondered if they cut the wrong wire, and they knew the bomb was going to go off what they would think. You know the last second of thought before the boom.

Well, yours truly had that millisecond scare of his life. I was a nose hair away from picking up the phone to make the call when it rang. I jumped and swore out loud. This made everyone laugh, and me, fuck, I think I grew my first gray hair.

Grandpa said he would answer the call. I just stood off to the side and tried to slow my heart down.

As soon as he said *hi Jerry*, I focused on the whole conversation.

Grandpa had a smile come back to his as he thanked Jerry before hanging up the phone.

"The doctors think Jack didn't have a heart attack. They believe it is just angina. But they want to keep him for a couple days and run tests."

Grandpa then thanked Wakan Tanka for not only Uncle Jack, but for all of us surviving the plane crash. He passed us each an ice-cold beer; we tapped bottles and said cheers to life.

Grandpa said he doesn't have any clothes for us to wear. Me and Donnie are tall solid guys, where Ruby is shorter, but really stocky.

So, tomorrow morning we will go into town and get some clothes. He did have enough weapons for us to use. Make no mistake about it. Every reservation in the USA always has a well supply of weapons.

For me it will be even more special as Grandpa said I can use my dad's .306.

That night, Grandpa cooked us a fresh turkey dinner. I mean he killed it, cleaned it, and cooked it today. Don't get any fresher than that.

And for once I didn't feel like kicking it down. My brain was really tired. Been one hell of a long and eventful day. By the time my head hit the pillow that night I was out cold. Fresh air, fatigue and about a million adrenaline rushes throughout the day will do that.

***

The next morning, I woke up to the smell of bacon cooking and fresh coffee being brewed. Grandpa was up early and making sure we were ready for the day.

I knew I would be, but as I looked at the empty bottle of wild turkey, I figured Donnie and Ruby would be moving mighty slow.

Grandpa smiled and said three turkeys killed last night. I asked what time the boys went to bed. He looked at his watch and said a couple hours ago.

"Well, just means more food for us." And right now, I was really hungry.

Man, I love being here on the rez, I feel so alive. So full of energy.

Grandpa and I talked for a bit. He wanted to make sure I was not as angry at the world as I was the last time, he saw me. I was honest, told him I still have my moments, but I am working on it.

It was almost ten when I decided to wake up the boys. I reminded them we have to go and buy some new clothes as I will not go hunting with them wearing the same clothes the whole time out there.

Both were hurting pretty good; Ruby's face was beet red, and his eyes looked like something in a horror film while Donnie's afro looked like birds where nesting in it.

What an ugly looking pair. Was kind of nice not to be the one hurting. Well other than the stitches, I felt great.

Grandpa looked at his watch and told the boys to eat up as he has to pick up one of my cousins at the bus station in less than an hour.

I was totally shocked and asked which cousin.

"Your Grandma's brothers' son, Freddy. He was just released from the army and has decided to take a job here on the reservation."

"Cool, I don't think I have ever met him. Or have I?"

"I don't think so. His parents live on the reservation in Minnesota."

"Looking forward to meeting him. What type of work will he be doing on the reservation?"

"He is going to be a police officer here."

The boys stopped chewing their food. Fuck, pretty sure I am not in such a hurry to meet him anymore.

Grandpa picked up on us and said, "Don't worry, boys. He is not here to arrest you; pretty sure he is not contagious."

But for us career criminals, we are allergic to cops.

The low down was that Fred just served a five-year stint with the army, well to be more specific he was a M.P. Was discharged a month ago. And was just hired here on Pine Ridge. He will also be staying at Grandpa's until he gets his own place. I really don't know anything about my grandma, or her side of the family. She died of cancer just after Rachel was born. Yeah, she was fighting the disease like a true warrior. She held on long enough to see Rachel, then died a couple weeks later.

Grandpa never remarried. He totally got into helping his people on the rez after she died.

The boys ate, threw some water in their face and then we all jumped in the station wagon and headed for town. The ride in was a lot quieter then yesterday. Yeah, they were both hurting pretty good.

Once in town, we headed to the department store while Grandpa went to the bus station.

The folks in Rapid City all gave us the up and down as we walked the streets. Especially with Donnie and Ruby wearing Hell Hound sweatshirts as their leather jackets were open.

We went into the one department store to get normal or normal clothes for normal people. Socks, long johns, underwear, and t-shirts.

Then it was off to Cooper's sporting goods. As we walked

in, the guard that was on duty was slouching. He spotted us when suddenly he went right rigid and bright eyed. Almost like Barney Fife. Kind of funny actually.

We were all like little kids in a store full of toys at Christmas time.

Checking out handguns, rifles, shotguns, crossbows, different hunting knives. Man, some of them I would have bought and brought them back to San Fran, but I know with all the latest plane hijacking and the look of us, there was no way would they lets us bring them on a plane, and I know how stuff always seems to go missing once you check items.

I kept going back to this Remington 700 series rifle. After the second time picking it up, I felt this weapon and I were meant to be together. So, I bought it knowing I will be leaving it at Grandpa's when I go home.

Donnie and Ruby ended up grabbing a Remington 760 pump. Ruby also grabbed a shit load of shells, and a new knife.

With Grandpa on a pension, we hit the grocery store and grabbed all kinds of grub and beer. And also hit the liquor store to replace the bottle of Wild Turkey the boys killed last night.

We headed back to the car and noticed this guy sitting inside, but Grandpa was nowhere to be found. As we walked over, we caught his eye as much as he caught ours.

He just stared at Donnie and Ruby's sweatshirts. I asked if he was Fred.

He seemed a bit perplexed and said yes.

I stuck out my hand and introduced myself. In my world he is family first, and a cop second.

He got out of the car and shook my hand. I introduced the rest of the boys. No smiles, just steady eye contact as they shook hands.

I asked where Grandpa was. He pointed to a restaurant and said he had to go piss.

As we all looked over, we saw Grandpa leaving the

restaurant all flustered.

And within two seconds was some guy right behind him, yelling at him and calling him a drunken Indian.

We asked Grandpa what was that all about.

He said nothing, let's go. Like fuck it was nothing. I could also tell the way Grandpa was doing a little dance he still had to pee.

"Did that loudmouth fuck deny you from using the washroom?"

"Mitchell, he is not worth you going back to jail for. I have encountered his type all my life."

"Well, he has never encountered me, lets go boys," much to the chagrin of Grandpa.

My blood was boiling, brings back memories of me trying to get some coffee on our way home from a hunt camp when I was a teen. Redneck fucks tried to take my leather jacket until Jake came in and ball batted all of them.

I stormed through the front door and sought out the loud mouth. The place was empty, so I yelled, "HEY!"

The fuck came out of the back and asked what the problem was.

My fucking problem is you, asshole. Why did you not allow my grandpa to use your washroom, is it because you are so fucking busy?"

His face now matched his white shirt. He was starting to stammer as he saw exactly who he was missing with.

"I should nail your feet to the floor and then burn down this fucking dump. Would you like that you racist fucking bastard? Come on and tell me I can't use your bathroom, fuckhead."

Ruby now stepped up and called him a fucking goof, and that brand new hunting knife he just purchased, he now held it against his throat as Donnie grabbed hold of the guy.

"I am so sorry, I thought he asked something else. Please forgive me. By all means, he can use the washroom."

Then a double piss happened. Yep, a double piss. I told Grandpa to use the washroom as the manager had now pissed himself. How ironic wouldn't you say?

I then walked over and lectured him about native rights.

The cook was must have been taking out the trash, came in and asked if he should call the police. Then I heard the words that told me that *blood is thicker than water*.

Fred now spoke up and showed his badge and said, "What seems to be the problem?"

The cook pointed to Donnie and Ruby.

Fred walked over to the manager goof and asked if there was an issue.

"No issue, all good."

I swear I can now smell shit. I believe Donnie and Ruby also smelled it as their lips curled and they let him go.

Grandpa now came out of the washroom and said let's go home.

I pointed to the manager and reminded him I know where to find him, as we all left.

As soon as we started to drive away, Grandpa thanked all of us, and he said he was proud of me for not using violence.

On the drive back, Donnie asked Fred if he really was a cop. He said yep, he then asked Donnie and Ruby if they were really Hell Hounds. Same response as him, yep. He then asked me.

"No, I am just a civilian with some really bad ass friends."

That statement made all in the car laugh.

With Fred serving five years as a Military Policeman. I told him all the units I was in, including SOG. We both said we looked familiar to each other. I am sure at some point we ran into each other. As long as he wasn't one of the assholes who would throw me into the crowbar hotel in one of my drunken blackouts.

As soon as we got back to the house, Ruby said he would make his famous Texas chili for us. Donnie helped Grandpa put the groceries away.

Grandpa suggested I grab a couple horses and take Fred for a ride around the property.

We rode and shot the shit. He asked what I do back in San Fran. He may be family, but he is still a cop. I told him about the t-shirt store and working part time as a bouncer, assistant manager at the Drunken Leprechaun. That reminds me that I have to get that private security and bodyguard business up and running legitimately when I get back.

I asked him why he didn't stay in Minnesota and be a cop there.

"I have always loved the Black Hills. My parents would always talk about them. I have been here like maybe half a dozen times now. I would dream about here, especially the badlands when I was in Vietnam. And not near as cold as Minnesota. I was spoiled with the heat in Nam."

I totally get where he is coming from. The Black Hills have mystical and magical powers. This is truly my home away from home. Maybe one day I will say fuck the rat race society and move here.

By the time we got back, the chili was done, and Ruby, Donnie and Grandpa all had a nice glow. They were all sitting at the table laughing. Not too often do I ever see Grandpa drink.

So, Fred and I served everyone. I gotta say, this chili was the best I ever had. Spiciest also; man, you were never without a beer.

Fred cleared the table and did the dishes as the four of us went out back and lit a fire.

Ruby broke out the Cuban cigars once Fred made his way out. All of us just stared at the night sky, admired the twinkling and odd shooting star. Watched the fire dance and you found yourself forgetting about all of life's worries, miseries, and who was on what side of the law.

I didn't stay up too late as I know it can be a long ride to hunt camp. We were all heading there right after breakfast. Much like yesterday, I turned in first.

***

I was woken early the next morning and not by the smell of Grandpa's cooking. But by the sound of a temple bell ringing. It seemed so close; the vibrations went right through my body. I went downstairs to see if anyone else heard it. But I was the only one awake.

I put on my boots and went outside. Couldn't see shit as it was really foggy.

I heard the horses being spooked. So, I went back inside, grabbed my new rifle, and headed to the barn.

Thick as pea soup and damp, really damp. I got halfway to the barn and I heard a voice in Cambodian say, "Avenge my death." It was crystal clear. It stopped me in my tracks. It had to be Donnie or Fred; no way Ruby knows Cambodian.

I said out loud, "Funny guy, good way to get shot." Heard nothing back. The hairs on my back went up. "Show yourself now." I heard nothing but still sensed I was being watched. Not impressed. Just like in the army, time for a bed check.

Well, if the voice didn't freak me out…never mind everyone still fast asleep in their beds had me scratching my head. Fuck, I wish I had some weed to smoke right about now. All mine went up in smoke with the plane.

I took a seat at the kitchen table and stared at the barn. Did necking with Mindy who was high on mushrooms have some residual effect? I have been kind of fucked up since the concert. Something, or someone is really trying to get my attention.

Donnie and Grandpa were the next two up. Donnie looked at me and asked if I just saw a ghost.

I shook my head and said, "Something like that." Grandpa stopped pouring the coffee and looked at me. I mean he really looked at me. Then he walked outside into the fog. Donnie followed behind him. Like me they just looked around before coming back inside.

Grandpa asked what I was hearing. I went deep into thought and just shook my head no.

"Mitchell, you are here with family and friends. You are on hallowed and mystical land. What did you see, hear or sense?"

With Ruby still sleeping, I don't want him thinking of me as some fucking nut who needs to be put away in a padded room in the mental ward.

"I didn't see anyone. But I am hearing stuff."

"What kind of stuff Mitchell?"

"Stuff I thought left behind in Cambodia. I have been hearing the odd temple bell being rung. I heard a voice in Cambodian earlier this morning."

Donnie asked me what the voice said.

"Avenge my death."

Speaking of death, there was now dead silence.

"Look guys, I know the fog can play tricks with your eyes, and voices can carry not knowing exactly where they are coming from. But I can't see there being many Cambodians on the rez, right Grandpa?"

He smiled and said, "None, but I have heard of spirits latching onto people. But when was the last time you were in Cambodia? And why now, Mitchell?"

I flashed back to my time at the Khmer temple in Laos. It was such a peaceful and positive place of tranquility.

I always try and think logical, perhaps the events of the Khmer Rouge and the genocide currently taking place in Cambodia is making its way over here.

I closed my eyes and drifted back to my time at a Khmer temple in Cambodia, 1970 to be exact. *Here goes nothing.*

"While most yanks in Southeast Asia were celebrating the fourth of July. I was pulling a special ops mission deep in Cambodia. An F4 Phantom was shut down and we had to haul ass and get the pilot out before the Vietcong captured them. We also had one hell of a rainstorm to contend with. The winds and sheets of rain forced the slick to drop us off five clicks from where the pilot's last SOS coordinates were. The jungle had turned into a river. One wrong step and we would have been washed away to lord knows where. Visibility was down to maybe ten yards. So there went our eyes, the drops were the size of elephant dung, so our hearing was also lost. Making us prime for a perfect ambush. But these pilots had all risked their lives for us when we needed help. They were always there for us. Sometimes saving us when we were seconds of death. So, we valiantly moved forward, determined and without fear. I say it took us about two hours to find the downed jet. Normally, pilots are trained to head to high ground, get as far away from the jets as possible as they become a prized trophy for the enemy. Lucky for our pilots, the weather slowed down the Vietcong more than us and we were able to find them near his downed jet. One had a broken leg and was starting to go into shock. We tried to call our base to say we had recovered him, but our radio was not working due to the weather. We knew we had to haul ass to higher ground and hopefully get a better radio signal. I was the holding up the rear, when we were not even fifteen minutes away, when I noticed the foliage in the jungle starting to move. I tapped Tucker on the shoulder and told them to keep moving and I would lay some Claymore mines and catch up to them. I laid two mines when suddenly, I heard that specific sound that only an AK47 makes. I hit the ground with the intentions of returning fire, when the drenched ground gave way, and I slid out of control in a landslide down the side of the mountain we were trying to climb. I was totally out of control. Ass over tea kettle. I didn't know which way was up, and which way was down. I had to close my mouth as I was gagging from the mud stew and rain that was intent on burying me alive in the side of the mountain. After what seemed to be an eternity, my free-falling slide, roll and tumble to middle earth had stopped. That was the good part, the bad part, I heard what had to be at least a dozen VC soldiers maybe ten feet from me. I could smell the raw rat they ate for dinner. I was buried so deep in mud and tree branches; all I could do was just lay still. Lord knows where my rifle was. The one had his boot touching my buried foot when suddenly the Claymores I had planted were starting to explode up top. Then all kinds of yelling started, and they all double timed themselves away from me. Thank fuck, I struggled to free myself, I also realized I am not the only predator unearthed as I felt something slither between my legs. Once again, I was totally still as I knew it was a snake, and most snakes around there were poisonous. And then I felt the hot sting in rapid strikes. The snake was biting my calf. I struggled to free myself, but a huge branch had my right arm pinned. My heart started to race which would only send the venom through my bloodstream even faster. I reached down with my left hand and pulled out my Fairburn Sykes knife from my leg that was being attacked. This was a do or die situation. The snake attacked my hand, and I almost became serpent food. I closed my eyes, used my other senses, and managed to get the razor-sharp knife out. As I opened my eyes, I was face to face with a King Cobra ready to strike my throat. Talk about bottom of the ninth with two strikes on me. I thought, *bring it you fucker*! His head with his venomous fangs were coming at me what seemed to be a hundred miles an hour. He wanted to finish me off once and for all. Fuck him; I swung my blade with all my force and hoped for the best. I instinctively closed my eyes as his head was still coming at me. I suddenly felt his slimy head hit my cheek, but I didn't feel the sharp and painful sting that I felt on my leg. I open my eyes and saw that I had decapitated this serpent of death. But was it too late, I knew he had struck me several times already. One thing was for sure, I had to get out of there before the poison he was able to infect me with, took my life. Like Paul Bunyan I chopped the branches that prevented me from getting up. Because of the hard rains, my grip on my knife was not very tight. A couple times I dropped it because of the hard impact on the wood. Then again, slicing open a major artery would also be lethal. After about ten minutes of hacking and whacking I was able to free myself. I stood up and looked to the skies to cool me off. For once I was not cursing the rain, it was a blessing. Decision time, I knew the poison was moving through my body even faster when I tried to free myself. I should have headed up the hill to see where I was. But I knew I was on borrowed time and would run out of strength. Yeah, my joints and muscles were really starting to ache, big time ache. So, I looked east, then west. Flipped a coin in my brain and east it was. I was about three hundred yards into my life-or-death march when I heard voices. I tried to see where they were coming from, but my eyes were unable to focus. This is not good, not good at all. My inability to think logically much like the landscape around me was then washed away. Started to get dizzy spells, and it felt like the ground under me was moving. I looked down, looked back up and I felt like I was on a ride at Disneyland. My legs gave out on me, and I fell to the muddy grounds. I couldn't get back up as I had no muscle control. Fuck I couldn't even open my eyes as the whole world was spinning out of control. The voices were coming closer, couldn't even reach for a knife. I felt myself go in and out of consciousness. The voices were in Asian I might add and were standing over me. I couldn't see shit; *fuck, was this how I die? So much for going down in a blaze of glory. No extreme fire fight, or hand to hand combat. A serpent who weighs one tenth of my body weight takes my life.* I could hear Crazy Horse laughing at me in the other world. You know what? Fuck him too. Darkness was all around me. I must have passed to the other. I could smell something burning. It must be the burning of the sweet grass, the same ceremony we had for dad. But why did everything still hurt like a bastard? I was actually scared to open my eyes as perhaps the smell meant I was in hell. Afraid or not, I struggled, but eventually managed to open my eyes. Things were still blurry as fuck, but I saw the silhouettes. I heard a temple bell chiming and then chanting. I saw billows of thick blue smoke going up into the damp air. My mouth and lips were parched.

Even though I didn't speak fluent Cambodian, and to be honest I could barely speak English at that point, they knew exactly what I desired. They gave me a cup of water and told me to drink slowly. I still felt really nauseous and had no idea where I was and how I got there. After I sipped the water, I laid my head back down, closed my eyes and tried to recall anything, anything at all. Blank, nothing came to me. And for some strange reason I had this vibe that you, grandpa, were near me. I sensed you all around me. Within seconds I drifted back here to your house. I could smell the horses really strongly. Next thing you know, you and I grandpa, are riding our horses around the reservation, it was a fall day. The brisk air was actually very refreshing. The colors of the leaves were starting to change. It was beautiful. You could see the steam from the early mornings sun rise from the grass and lakes. We didn't speak. No words needed to be spoken, your strong smile and piercing eyes said it all. We rode for hours and hours until the sun started to set. The brisk air had now turned bitter cold. I started to shiver and ache as we approached the barn. Inside I could see the shadows of a male, he was holding a shotgun. I know this figure, it was my dad, I just knew it. I looked over with a smile and told you we should go see him. You had a tear roll down your cheek. Your mouth quivered and you said, "It is not my time yet, Mitchell. You and your horse have been summoned." I looked at the shadow that seemed to be staring right into my deepest secrets and fears. I stared back and watch as he pumped the shotgun that would be used to usher me in. As much as I felt this shadow had control and power over me, I looked at you and asked if I had to go. "That is up to you Mitchell," you told me. I pet the mane of the horse and told you that I still wanted to ride. Your smile warmed me up. The bitter cold that made my joints ache had left. A bell rung. I was confused and said I have never heard that bell before; what was it? "It is your life bell. Your new spiritual healers will lead you down the right path." The bell chimed again, and you smiled at me. You gently kicked your horse and off you rode. I tried to follow, but my horse wouldn't budge. Again, the bell chimed, and I opened up my eyes and could finally see. I was no longer in Pine Ridge. I was in a temple wearing just a robe. I looked down and saw the fresh marks left by the serpent. I went to get up but was still really weak, and that was followed by a big-time dizzy spell. I broke out in a cold sweat and felt myself falling helplessly off my cot. I was caught in midflight by a monk. He spoke Vietnamese and asked what I was doing. I looked at him and really had no logical answer. He told me to sit back down as I had been perilously drifting between life and death for the past seven days. I needed to rest and get my strength back. The temple was beautiful. It was built during the Angkor empire and made of sandstone. Over the next couple days, my strength was slowly but surely coming back to me. The monk who stopped me from doing a major league face plant was name Tamalinda. It was as if he was my own personal nurse. We had developed a good rapport. He was truly a kind soul. I wonder what he thought of me and my soul. I also noticed we would be watched from time to time by an elder monk, not sure why. As I walked around to get my strength and stamina back, I would watch them meditate and chant. Perfect harmony with an amazing flow. I could feel the energy coming from them. Truly hypnotic. One night, I asked Tamalinda if he could teach me how to meditate. He smiled and said my soul truly needed it and he would be more than happy to help me find calm waters of the storm I sail in. The hardest thing at first was my leg was still tender, and being sedentary for so long, my muscles were seized. So, he worked on my getting my muscles to become limber again. He was calm the whole time, but the stretches made my muscles burn harder than in basic training and LRRP School. Breathing was the key to stretching and meditation. I just couldn't relax enough to shut out the outside war. But Tamalinda was patient and understanding and after two days of trying, I was actually able to dismiss the war outside the temples and the battles raging inside of me. Words cannot describe that feeling when I was able to reach a spiritual form of enlightenment and shut out the evil energies of the outside world. I was never allowed to meditate with the others, but I would keep my distance and meditate when they did. A couple days later, the older monk with the different color robe approached me and asked for me to go for a walk with him outside the temple. I was totally shocked as he spoke broken English. He asked how I was feeling. I said much better. I also thanked him for saving my life and for nursing me back to health. "That is what we do," he said with a bit of a laugh and a smile. He asked if I felt strong enough to head back to my unit. My turn to smile. "I guess I can't stay here longer?" "No, it is time for you to leave. The Vietcong are due to make an inspection of us. You caught here would only bring death and destruction. We are peaceful people." I nodded my head yes and agreed the last thing I would ever want to do is to bring harm here. He said very well. Then he pointed to the right, and I saw my knife that saved my life, my thermos, and a bag full of cooked rice. He also gave me a map and showed me how to get to my base. So much for us being covert in Cambodia. I asked if I could say thank you to Tamalinda and say goodbye. Forced smile by him as he said no, it would be best if I left now. Fair enough, I shook his hand and said thank you. I took one last look at the temple. I truly hoped the statues out front truly will guard them from their enemies. It took me almost two days to stroll back into base. And in case you were wondering, yes, I took meditation breaks when I felt weak and needed strength to carry on."

My grandfather smiled at me as he nodded his head in support of my epic tale, I knew deep down he believed every word I spoke.

Donnie said, "Holy fuck, what an ordeal."

My cousin Fred who I have known for twenty-four hours or so said, "You seem to have the same gift, or I guess curse, that Grandpa has."

"Mitchell, next time you hear this voice, ask who they are and why revenge," said Grandpa.

Ruby came downstairs and the whole kitchen went silent. He picked up on it and asked if everything was all right. He even checked to make sure his fly wasn't open.

"I heard some voices coming from outside. Went out there and no one. Just making sure it wasn't that asshole from the diner that's all."

We ate breakfast, gathered up all our gear for a week's worth of hunting, food, ammo, weapons, knives, and garbage bags to carry the cut-up meat. The morning sun didn't seem to get the memo to wake the fuck up. This was going to be one long foggy ride.

5

Grandpa reminded everyone that bears and wolves are still very active, same with the mountain lions. We should have our rifles ready, seeing at how we have poor visibility. The last thing you want is to accidentally run across is a pair of cubs and their mamma. I truly felt I had to take the lead. Grandpa stayed back with Fred and Ruby seeing at how this was their first hunt camp here.

Donnie was a couple horse lengths behind. Not sure if it was to keep an eye on me or try and hear what I have been hearing and spook me. A fog filled forest and hills, even for a combat vet like me, has my nerves on edge. Yeah, like Grandpa said, it was the wildlife, but with what I have been hearing lately, I expected a whole platoon of Vietcong over the next ridge.

The fog not only played tricks on our vision and hearing, but for me, all my battlefield injuries were really starting to ache. I truly felt like the tin man in the Wizard of Oz. Can't wait to sit in front of the fireplace and warm up my bones.

We were about a quarter mile from the longhouse when the sun finally started to break through.

A couple hundred yards out Donnie held up his hand for us to stop. He pulled his rifle out of the saddle holster and pulled back the breach. I looked to where he was staring and pointed my rifle looking for anything.

Whisps of fog were still dancing through the tree line. I couldn't recognize anything.

So, I whispered to Donnie, "What do you see?"

"Don't know. A human for sure. But as if he was floating. Fuck Mitch, I think your Cambodian story is fucking with my head. Yeah, a floating monk, robe and all."

After a couple minutes we continued and finally made it safe and sound to the longhouse.

Grandpa, like a drill sergeant, had us bring in all the supplies including firewood and making sure the horses were given water.

Fred and Ruby being the newbies and were giving the task of sweeping out the longhouse. They opened up all the windows to air it out. They checked the fireplace to make sure no animals have made nests in it. All together it takes about two solid hours.

All has to be done before the sun goes down as there is no hydro or running water in the longhouse. And you know what? Even though I live in a big city and have everything, I just love getting back to raw nature, makes me feel so alive.

After we were all set up, we all went out to fire our new weapons. A couple freshly drained beer cans would work just fine.

As I loaded up my rifle, I was just as excited as when I was kid and opening up a new Christmas gift.

After four shots, I adjusted my scope and sights till I was 99.9%accurate. Nothing in life is a hundred percent, other than the Government fucking you for taxes.

Then, that little boy in me, picked up my dad's rifle and fired a few shots to also make sure the sights were also bang on.

All three shots landed exactly where I was aiming. The smell the gun powder made coming from dad's rifle brought back some mighty fond memories.

I think I am going to carry both rifles with me this hunt.

Fred was also a damn good shot. Ruby? Well, I think the deer won't be too afraid of him. Let's hope he is good at gutting and cleaning deer.

We had a quick lunch and then off hunting we went. Now, all of us but Donnie, had native blood running through our veins. But I have no doubt that the elders would welcome him into being a tribal warrior. I am sure he and Crazy Horse would have nothing short of respect for each other.

So, because of this, we don't sit up in a tree. We track and hunt our prey, old school. The right honorable way, the Lakota Sioux way.

A light snow began to fall after about an hour along with the temperature. Sioux or not, I live in California and really felt it getting into my bones. Same as Donnie, and Ruby the southern Texan.

Grandpa and Fred just laughed at us.

As much as I was pissed at seeing snow, I also know it would be easier to track the deer and within an hour we found a couple sets of hooves.

Fred was also a really good tracker. After about forty cold minutes, we found a bedding area.

We were about a hundred yards out; the area was really thick with brush. Deer are smart, these areas they use for bedding are well thought out by them.

Fred once again showed what a great hunter he was. He started to grunt and snort and wheeze.

It took everything in me not to burst out laughing as Ruby's face was priceless. Yeah, he didn't have a clue what was going on. But when this huge buck and a couple doe came out to see what was going on, he smiled and like the rest of us, raised his rifle and zeroed in on our prey.

Grandpa spoke very quietly and told us on the count of three to shoot. Each one of us had a specific target. Ruby and I were to take down the buck.

And you know I was going to use dad's rifle. Fucking right, I had to.

3-2-1 fire. The two-does dropped. The buck was hit, but he was a fighter and took off.

I had no time to celebrate as the wounded buck now headed back into the woods.

I jumped back on my horse to track it down. Partly because he is my prey, partly because dad always taught me never to let a wounded animal suffer.

So, we raced across the open field; the snow was almost blinding from the speed of the horse. Once we got into the thick forest, we came to almost a snail's pace.

The fresh pure virgin-white snow was splattered with thick rich red blood. I might not be able to see the wounded buck. But the fresh trail of his lifeline would lead me right to him.

I don't get mad not having a visual on my prey. I respect and know firsthand what this magnificent beast is going through.

He knows once I catch him it will be the end of his life. Judging by the amount of doe around him, I am sure he lived a good life. Man and beast are the same when it comes to being shot and fleeing to save your life.

Your heart is pounding, you may have a million things going through your mind, but the one focal point, make that your main focal point is to live, to elude and escape those wanting to take your life.

I have been there many times. And by far, the first time being shot was the worst.

May 13th, 1969. I had a seventy-two-hour leave. This was also my twentieth birthday. Myself, AJ, Louie, and Mad Bill McDowell were supposed to be heading to Saigon to celebrate my birthday. Insane amounts of alcohol were to be consumed, truckloads of weed to be smoked, and a year's supply of condoms were to be used. That was until General Melvin Zais moved my birthday party to hill 937. Otherwise known as Hamburger Hill. The good General started to attack and capture the hill on May 10th. He was getting nowhere fast. Casualties were piling up at an alarming rate. But the good General wanted to put an American flag on the top of this evil piece of dirt, no matter the cost. So, that morning, instead of taking a slick into Saigon, we were choppered to the base of this hill. This was not our first fight in the A Shau Valley. But up to then I had been really lucky. Some minor shrapnel, the typical twisted knee, ankle, from hauling up and down the side of mountains. But they say every time a Viet Cong puts a round in his magazine, it has a predesignated American's name on it. But I am a Strongbow, I am a Sioux warrior. I have proven myself time after time whether it be in a close-range fire fight, in the valleys, mountains, or Elephant grasslands of southeast Asia. On the ride over, Mad Bill told me we would be in Saigon by sundown, then the party would happen. Too bad Charlie was a real party pooper. We landed in a hot LZ. Gun and mortar fire raining down on the slicks. Eventually we made it to a temporary base camp. I looked into the face of our commander, Lt Col Stan Levely. Even he showed stress, very unlike him. He came up to me and asked why I was not celebrating my birthday in Saigon; he personally authorized my furlough. I looked at AJ, Louie and Bill and said, "I don't want to party alone. We will have this place mopped up and be drinking in a Saigon bar in no time." He forced a smile, shook my hand, and said, "Get er done, soldier." The four of us were then called to meet LT Miller. "You four are my best scouts. We captured a high ranking NVA who had these documents on him. They showed that the 29th PAVN regiment were somewhere in the valley. These were hardened and battle tough troops. They were involved in the TET offensive in Hue. Find them before they find us. Once you make contact. Give your coordinates and we will call in air and artillery strikes. Hundreds of American lives are in your hand's, boys. Happy hunting and may God be with you." Well, fuck me, if that isn't one fuck of a guilt trip, then again, not the first time we have been on missions like this. But this is the first time since TET I sensed fear in our officers. So, we loaded up with extra ammo. As much as we could carry to be honest. Jumped on a slick and headed towards the Laos border. It was a very quiet ride. I recall the TET offensive and how it affected me. I can still recall Herman and I having a conversation while high on LSD, next thing you know his brains are splattered all over me. That night I became a man by taking my first human life. And for my sins, I have never been the same. I also have this habit that I was taught to time how long we are in the air before we hit the LZ. Tells me how long it will take if we have to hoof it back on foot. Thirty-eight minutes in total. Not the longest I have flown out. But with so many enemies below us, a hell of an extremely long and very dangerous way back. And why did I know there were a lot of enemies below us? Steady being shot at the whole flight. It was also a hot LZ, we roped down and hit the ground hard. You are so worried about breaking an ankle or fucking your knee up, as you know the enemy will be salivating at the wounded chicken. Can't fly away little birdie. All four of us hit the ground and ran a couple hundred yards away and set up a cover position. Bill got the map out. In red was the route and grid area we were supposed to search. I was to take first lead. Yeah, throw the Native in front. Actually, the adrenaline junkie in me didn't mind. We were about a click from our LZ when a light rain started. We were still a couple weeks away from the rainy season. The rain really affects your sight, and hearing. And for me, I rely on both. I hear rustling in the tall grass on a calm day. I know it is my enemy, either human or animal. And over here, the animals are just as lethal and unforgiving. So, you move slower than normal. Every step is an important step. Bill was right behind me with his binoculars scouring in every direction. After about three clicks we took a breather, drank some water, and went over the map and asked each other which way we would head to the hill without being detected. Normally I don't, make that none of us believe in Army intelligence. But we all agreed, the route we were on was the route we would take. I also offered another angle, suppose those papers captured were used as a diverse tactic. Almost like Patton before D-Day. The boys also nodded their heads in agreement with me. But we had our orders, and until they called us on the radio and told us change of orders, we continued on our seek and report mission. Louie asked if I wanted him to take the lead. I said no, I wanted to find the fuckers first. We stood up to continue our mission. I didn't even take my first step when I heard the sound of several AK47s being fired. Everything went into slow motion, much like Herman's brains being sprayed all over me during TET. What was not in slow motion was the searing heat feeling just above my belly button. The pain and jolt my body felt knocked me to the ground. I felt the most intense pain I had ever felt in my life. My brain just couldn't compute what exactly was going on. I tried to arch my back to get up when I saw a river of blood flowing from my gut. My legs were now starting to shake, and my breathing was becoming very erratic. Bullets, *hundreds* of bullets were now whizzing past me in both directions. And yet I couldn't move. I tried, but the pain had me in a comatose state. I hear Bill calling my name and asking me if I am all right. I try to answer but my jaw and voice is shaky. Fuck, I've seen hundreds of soldiers shot. I always said, or believed, that I would remain unscathed my whole time here. I also said I would go down in a hail of bullets, firing away until I ran out of ammo. After a couple minutes that seemed like an eternity the shooting stopped. Louie stood over me and started to swear as he jabbed my thigh with a morphine needle. He grabbed gauze and told me to apply pressure and not to let up.

My shaking hands did as he said. What I couldn't understand was he and the boys now took off away from me. Did they leave me here to die on my own? I tried to get up but between the wound, and the morphine, I was too shaky. So, I just laid back. Looked up at the dark rain clouds and thought this by far, was the shittiest birthday ever. Not sure how much time had passed when the boys came back. Bill said, "Look Mitch, that was just a scout patrol much like us. We have three confirmed killed. Not sure if any of them got away, or called in that they made contact with us before the shooting started. I know you are really hurting, but we have to bug out. And what I am to ask you, well you may think I am fucked, but I called in a medical e-vac for us. We must head about a half click to this clearing; we will not leave you here. Now is the time to bring out that Sioux warrior in you. We MUST move you. Just keep applying pressure to your wound. It is not that bad, seen worse, way worse. Do you understand me?" I nodded my head yes. He smiled, slapped me on the face, and said, "Wait till the nurses hear it is your birthday." Louie and AJ, both helped me to my feet. With each of them taking turns grabbing me under my shoulder we headed to the LZ. Bill kept talking to me the whole time to stop me from going into shock. I tried my best to answer his questions the whole time. Eventually I couldn't talk or think, I just did what comes naturally when being wounded and the hunters are on your trail, I just kept moving my feet. By the time I saw the slick approaching us in the distance, I truly felt like I was watching a movie, a movie high on the bombers we would eat at Dubrowski's. Just so fucked up. I felt so helpless. So weak and no longer a Sioux warrior, no longer a Strongbow. I felt like some cherry getting hit on his first day in combat. I truly don't fear death, I miss Dad, Mom, Jake, and Pam. I am more ashamed of getting shot and fucking up our recon mission. We were told hundreds of American lives are counting on us, I let everyone down. I was stretchered in the slick, an IV was set up. That was the last thing I remembered until waking up in Saigon five days later.

I will tell you one thing; Saigon was not as cold as it is here. And that little snow flurry has now turned into a blizzard. Fuck me, even the blood trail is getting harder to find.

Then out of the corner of my eye I see movement. I see the wounded buck making another escape to save his life.

I fire the shot and kick the horse to chase him. Then everything goes into slow motion. Just like in the A Shau Valley. I feel a severe pain at first in my head, then neck as I am now falling backwards off the horse.

My finger is still on the trigger of my weapon, and I let off another round as I fall backwards onto the hard snow-covered ground.

I hit it with such a thud I feel the wind taken right out of my lungs.

My right eye feels three times bigger than itself, but right now I am trying my best to get air back in my lungs. A dreadful feeling, I have to say.

I see a shadow. It is Tamalinda standing over me with his hand stuck out. He says in Cambodian, if he helps me once again, I must help him and the other monks that have been murdered.

Before I had a chance to answer I heard Donnie yell for me. I turned my head in the direction of his voice, answered him. Looked back up at Tamalinda and he was gone.

Donnie got off his horse and ran over and asked if I was all right.

"You see any Asians around here?"

Donnie looked at me and said I must have whacked my head really good.

"Look, all these different voices and bell chimes, I know who is doing it."

He just nodded his head and looked at my eye.

"I am more concerned about your eye. Pretty sure you have a concussion."

Once Donnie helped me up, I looked all around for Tamalinda. Then I heard Donnie say, there! Fucking right, Donnie now sees what I have been talking about all along, I knew I was not having some trippy flashback.

"Jesus, Mitchell. This has to be at eight-point buck, good job. Now let's tie it to my horse and drag it back to the longhouse. Do you think you can ride?"

My head was spinning, partly because of Tamalinda, and partly because of the branch I nailed full force. If dad was here, he would blast me for admiring my shot, and not looking out for the dangers surrounding me.

"Yeah, I can ride as long as my horse comes back."

Donnie called for my horse to come back, surprisingly, it did. Then he helped me to get back on it, he made sure I was sturdy in the saddle before tie the dead buck to his horse.

We eventually met up with the others, I still had blood coming from a gash above my eye. Grandpa came over and asked what happened.

I looked down at my horse, as much as I wanted to blame him, I couldn't. I told him the truth. He said he would have a good look at it once we are back at the longhouse.

It was a long cold slow ride back to the longhouse. The snow was still really coming down…make that sideways, at us. With the trauma to my head, my neck was getting really stiff, almost to the point it seized up on me.

That fireplace will be my best friend.

By the time we made it back to the longhouse, I needed help getting off my horse. I couldn't move my neck at all. I was even tearing up with them helping me.

I went inside and poured myself a glass of whiskey. For fuck sakes, I couldn't even open my mouth enough or move my head back far enough to take a drink.

Grandpa told me to sit down. He started a fire then wrapped me in blankets while massaging my neck.

I felt like I was letting everyone down. They are outside cutting up the deer and here I am acting like George Wallace, a fucking cripple, sadly self-induced at that.

But Grandpa, the mystical Shaman, also seemed to have healing hands. I would say after ten minutes my neck released. He then focused on my gash. Handed me that glass of whiskey and told me to drink up.

He then went rooting through a drawer and brought out a darning needle and some thread. He poured some more whiskey in a glass and dropped the needle in it.

While waiting for the needle to sterilize he cleaned my wound. I asked how bad it was. Eight stitches was his answer. Stitches in my shoulder, soon to be over my eye. Good thing needles don't scare me.

The cleaning of the wound also hurt like a bastard, but I've seen guys in Nam lose limbs over infection.

I took another glass of whiskey before Grandpa started to stitch me up.

Yep, the booze hit the spot, I didn't move as he sewed me shut. After he was done, I went and looked in the mirror. Well, another battle wound, no purple heart this time.

I went outside and saw the boys just finished up the rumen and where now into the reticulum on the buck. Fresh berries partly digested, won't be putting them in my oatmeal tomorrow.

They looked at my wound, asked how I felt. Just a really good headache was my answer. After a couple minutes I decided to come back in. That cold wet snow is not my friend today.

***

That night we had venison steaks, baked potatoes, and salad, all fresh from the reservation. Doesn't get any better than this.

The boys stayed up till the wee hours of the morning cutting up the deer and buck.

My headache made it impossible for me to stay awake past eleven. And every two hours they would wake me up.

Normally I wouldn't be pissed as I know they are doing it because of my concussion. But at one point I was having a threesome dream and Mindy and Charlene. Maybe I was talking in my dream, not the first time I had an impure dream here. I remember having one about Rhonda Ryan.

No one woke me, well I woke myself with cum all over my leg. I was so embarrassed, I snuck outside, jumped in a frozen lake to clean the mess, to get rid of the evidence. Almost froze to death. I have often wondered what Rhonda looks like these days, I also wonder if she ever looked at the north star and talked to me like I asked her to do.

That morning my neck was pretty stiff, eye was swollen shut and I still had a pretty good headache. With my shooting eye closed shut, and this headache, I think I will just hang around here while the guys go out hunting. Maybe I will make a nice deer stew. Yeah, the least I can do.

After they all left, I washed the dishes then decided to go for a walk. Bad eye or not, I still brought my rifle with me. You just never know.

We actually ended up with about four inches of snow last

night. The sun glistened off it. Every direction I looked was covered in it. So peaceful looking. And you know what would make me happier than anything in the world right now? Building a snowman with Katrina. She would love it; all the hills would make for amazing tobogganing. I remember the four of us Strongbow kids having so much fun here, was such a big part of our life. And I honestly blame Natasha as much as Stan as to why Katrina has never been here. Fucking dicks. I'd like to hunt them here instead of the deer to be honest.

The guys came back around eight; they bagged two more deer, and judging by Ruby's huge smile he must have taken one of them down.

He was laughing, telling, and then retelling how he took the shot and the doe fell.

Ruby was just like a teen finally getting laid. Nice to see another friend falling in love with the land us Sioux call holy.

My head was still buzzing, my eye was still swollen shut, but I was able to help them cut, clean, and package the deer.

We also told Ruby that we share our meat with the elders on the rez, the ones who are financially distraught. Just like the Sioux have been doing for hundreds of years.

I helped Grandpa with the dishes that night; he asked if I would go with him back to his house. He wants to call the hospital and see how Uncle Jack is doing. I said that is not a problem.

6

The next morning, I woke up actually feeling pretty decent. Neck felt almost normal. Little bit of a headache, not sure if it was from the concussion or from the beers. And I now had a slit in my eye; yep, it was finally starting to open.

We told the boys we would be sleeping at the house tonight, it is a long cold ride, and Grandpa is getting up there in age.

Wished them happy hunting and would see them tomorrow around lunch time.

It was a really bright day, had to put on the shades, nice to feel the warmth on my battered body.

On our ride back I could tell that grandpa was really worried about Uncle Jack. All he did was tell stories about him, dad, and Aunt Rita as kids.

I felt my heartstrings pull when he told me he had already buried a wife and two children. He doesn't want to bury his last living child.

I told him what a tough bird Uncle Jack was.

"Yes, he is tough, Mitchell. But your dad was by far the toughest person I have ever met. He was the smartest of my children. The best hunter I ever went out with."

Grandpa looks at my head, shakes his own then says, "He knew how not to get knocked out by a tree branch."

What a smart ass.

"When your mom called me to say Iggy was killed, I never would have believed it if I didn't see his body with my own two eyes. And your Aunt Rita. I always worried that asshole husband of hers would kill her. He got what he had coming to him."

Now this was the first time I have ever heard Grandpa speak of him. I remember what Jake told me about him going missing out here. And it was so unlike Grandpa to be angry, especially towards another human.

"So now I worry about your Uncle Jack." Grandpa then looked up to the sky, paused and said, "Wakan Tanka I am an old man. Spare my son his life and take mine."

"He will be fine Grandpa, and I need you around. Who is going to show Katrina how to ride a horse, fish, and hunt?" What else could I say?

Once again, he looked at the gash over my right eye, looked up to the sky and said, "At least let me teach my great granddaughter how to hunt, and also her dad." He then started to laugh and kicked his horse to giddy up.

I mumbled smart ass, did the same with my horse.

"I heard you, Mitchell."

My turn to look to the sky and say *really?*

We were about a thousand yards from Grandpa's house when the glorious sun rays were covered over by dark ominous skies.

Before I knew it the cold air was sending shivers all up and down my body.

I had this feeling of impending doom come over me. That wicked headache had returned. About a hundred yards from the house, I was hit by Deja Vu. And it was a bad vibe. Really bad, my gut flipped, and I could tell my breathing was becoming erratic. I know danger is out there. I just can't see, smell, or hear it.

I pull back on the horse and trot while pulling out my rifle. I am scanning everything now.

Grandpa looks back and sees what I am doing. He now stops his horse and pulls out his rifle.

I pull up beside Grandpa who is also now looking around.

"What do you see, Mitchell?"

"I am not sure exactly. Something is not right, bad ju ju."

"Ju Ju? What is Ju Ju, Mitchell?"

"Bad shit is going to happen. I would normally get this feeling before the Vietcong would attack us."

He looked deep in my eyes. "I am sure this helped to keep you alive. Let's get the horses in the barn in case there is a mountain lion, bear, or pack of wolves."

We trotted towards the barn. We passed all the family graves when suddenly my horse was spooked. He was really fidgety. I am trying to calm him down while looking all around. He must sense what I sense.

Then I am drawn to the barn like a magnet. A fear magnet. I flashback to that nightmare I had. The barn, something evil in the barn. I fucking know it.

The big barn doors were now open, and Grandpa was standing right at the entrance telling me to come in.

"Nothing inside here is going to harm you or your horse." Grandpa reassured me.

How the hell does he know I am scared that there is something evil in the barn. I told no one about my nightmare dream.

I look at him and realize I trust him with my life. I always have. He rid me of my heroin addiction. He is truly a healer, not just for his family. But for all that come into his life.

So, I dismount. Whisper in my horse's ear everything is good and start to walk towards the barn. Not going to bull shit you, fucking nervous energy was oozing from me. But I trusted Grandpa.

Once inside I looked all around, I also sensed nothing bad. Yep, just a barn, a stinky horse barn.

Grandpa said he was going to go inside and make some calls. He asked me to feed the horses and give them some fresh water.

I did as instructed, and yes, my head was on a pivot the whole time.

When I came back inside Grandpa said that Uncle Jack was released from the hospital early this morning.

He looked at his watch and asked me if I thought they would come here.

I told him I think it depends on how Uncle Jack is feeling.

So, we stayed in with Grandpa hanging by the phone. He

gave my stitches a thorough cleaning, it burnt pretty good, but he said no infection.

Grandpa broke out the family album after dinner. And the picture I stared at the longest was the six of us in our family. I think I was around seven, I remember coming here for a week or so one summer. Jake and I were shit heads chasing Rachel and Pam around with snake we caught.

Dad told us to stop scaring the girls. Especially Rachel who was crying her head off. Well, later that night when we were sleeping in our tents, Dad put a couple snakes in the tent Jake and I were sharing, he also hid outside and shook a rattle. I am sure we were even more scared than Rachel, and when we bolted from the tent, there were all the females laughing at us. Payback, Iggy Strongbow style.

The phone rang as I was looking at the photos; I could tell by the smile on Grandpa's face things were good. The conversation was short, but his last words were *I will see you tomorrow.*

"Good news, Mitchell; everyone is coming here tomorrow. I have to pick them up at the airport. Not enough seats for you to come. So would you mind waiting here for us?"

"Not at all, I am so happy." So, Uncle Jack didn't have a heart attack after all. Just angina. But he has to see his family doctor once he gets back home. The doctor also told him no hunting or booze as he is on medication.

That night, Grandpa and I went through every single photo album in the house. He explained all the pics I knew nothing of as if the picture was taken yesterday.

Grandpa turned in early that night. I wasn't that tired. So, I went out back, lit a small fire and just stared at the stars, thought about life. Mostly the woman in my life. Past, current, and yes even future. I really enjoy my time with Mindy, I think she is amazing, sex is incredible. But I am also still hurting over Charlene and the way it ended. You know with Mindy being married, no good will become of our affair. One of us, or both of us are going to get hurt bad, really bad. I honestly hate overthinking as all it does is fuck me up. And then there is Lucy. I still have guilt over how she died. And Tash, fucking Kurt Wilson and Liz O'Malley really fucked up that relationship.

As the flames died and just embers were left. I looked up to the North Star.

"Dad, can you let Katrina know that I am her biological father, and that I love her?"

Sure, as fuck it twinkled back down at me, made me smile. I kicked some snow on the fire and like a magician, I disappeared into the night air.

As much as I love roughing it at the longhouse, nothing better than a soft cozy bed. I slept in till after ten, and I was in no hurry to get my ass up out of bed.

Grandpa was watching Concentration. He asked me to watch it with him as I ate my breakfast. Before you know it was a contest between Grandpa and me. And of course, we would make fun of the contestants who fucked up royally.

After the show he had to leave to pick up everyone at the airport. He asked me to put a roast in for us. I told him no problem. I drank another cup of coffee, put on some Miles Davis and just chilled.

To say I really love this place would be a huge understatement. I could really see in time once I make enough cash, moving out here. Maybe taking care of Grandpa. Find me a solid female that could handle the lifestyle out here. So far, can't say I have found one. Other than Anita, but she has a steady man in her life. I still haven't been with a Sioux chick.
I did as instructed and put the roast in for us.

Around two thirty, Grandpa pulled in with everyone. I went out to the driveway to greet everyone. Val came running over and gave me a great big hug.

She looked me up and down closely, then said, "I am so happy that you are healthy once again. I was so worried for you honey."

Then came the guys, Uncle Jack looked tired and frail to be honest. I gave him a hug and asked how he felt.

"I have been better, Mitchell. I understand you risked your life to save mine."

I felt humbled, very humbled. Lately I have been taking lives, not saving them.

"I know if the shoe was on the other foot, you would have done the same for me."

He smiled and nodded his head. Jerry and George came

over and asked what the fuck happened to my head.

I really wished I could say it was another mountain lion attack, a bear, or a pack of wolves. I sheepishly said *tree*.

They both looked at each other, then Jerry asked deer? I shook my head and told them the whole story. Then the razzing started. Too bad the Vietcong didn't use that secret weapon known as the "The Tree" against me.

Yep, for the rest of the night I was razzed really good, even Uncle Jack jumped in.

Grandpa asked me for a favor that night while eating dinner. He said seeing at how my eye would still be affected for hunting, would I mind bringing back what deer the boys had cleaned and packaged. Then if I could bring back the meat and help him deliver some of the meat to the elders on the rez. He said winter is coming and those that are no longer able to hunt, they really miss the taste of Sioux deer.

Without hesitation I said that would not be a problem. This made him and Uncle Jack smile.

After dinner, Jerry asked if I wanted to smoke a joint with him and George.

Now that made me smile, big time smile.

We went for a walk, sparked up, and after a couple tokes that my hurting lungs and brain needed, I asked if he ever met our cousin Fred Hill.

Jerry said he know a bit about him, never met him…why?

I told him the whole story, especially about him becoming a rez cop.

Yours truly told them that for a copper he seems really solid.

"He is still a cop, Mitch. Don't ever give him an excuse to bust your ass, solid or not."

They both thanked me for giving them the heads up.

***

next morning Grandpa and Val cooked us a kick ass meal before we headed to the long house.

A cold light rain fell the whole ride out. Thank God the boys had a fire going as I had to dry my clothes off before heading back.

Right down to my boxers with my clothes beside the fire.

The only thing colder than me right now was the tension between Fred, George, and Jerry.

I know that Donnie and Ruby don't seem to have any issues with him, or they hide it really well. But Jerry is a chapter president, their loyalty would not be questioned and the whole pack mentality would be in full rage.

I had visions of Fred ending up like Aunt Rita's husband, disappearing without a trace.

I really like the guy, he served his country much like me, and fuck, the bottom line is he is family. I have lost four family members, nice to gain a new one.

Almost as a test, Jerry pulled out his ounce of weed and threw it on the kitchen table. He asked Fred if this bothers him. Fred looked at the weed, looked up at Jerry said it doesn't bother him, it is Jerry's lungs not his.

"How about you roll us up a bunch of joints. Or are you a cop 24-7, even around family?" said Jerry in a very serious voice.

"I am not very good at rolling joints to tell the truth. Let's hope it never comes to you finding out if I am a cop 24-7, even around family."

Fuck, the air was thick with tension. Too much tension for me, fucking bullshit actually.

I went over and felt my clothes, they were dry. I looked at my watch and told the boys I am out of here. I am taking the meat back.

Fred said he would go with me. Jerry said he thought that was a great idea.

Both just stared at each other. I have no idea if Fred knows exactly who Jerry is, I mean really is, if he does, fuck he has big balls.

Donnie just nodded to me as I was starting to pack up the meat. He knew I felt awkward.

Once everything was ready, I came back in and said goodbye to the boys while Fred waited for me outside.

Jerry said to me, "He is a pig, don't trust him with nothing."

I told him I wouldn't, I know better.

Back into the cold misty fog we rode. The only thing I said was, "Lots of wildlife will be smelling the fresh meat. Keep your rifle ready."

He mumbled something, pretty sure it had to do with Jerry, but I figured I'd give him some time to cool down.

After about a half hour of riding, both of our horses seemed to be spooked. We both pulled out our rifles and after some extensive looking, Fred pointed to a ridge about a hundred yards away. There was a pack of wolves just staring at us.

I know some stuff about wolves, but I figure with Fred living on a reservation up till he joined the army, that he would have more knowledge than me.

"You think they are rabid and will attack us?"

"They all look pretty plump, not like they are starving and desperate, I doubt all of them would be rabid. Never heard of a whole pack of rapid wolves. I think they are curious. I think they want to see what kind of foe we are. Hang onto your horse, Mitch."

I did as instructed as Fred took out his rifle and fired a shot their way. They all took off. Hopefully for good.

After a couple minutes I felt I had to clear the air with him with what happened at the long house, or at least my point of view.

"Sorry Jerry acted like a dick to you, don't take it personal, it is not Fred Hill, it is you being a cop."

At first there was silence, a good couple minutes, then Fred said,

"You know I almost didn't get the job because of Jerry. The FBI red flagged me because of him. They asked about my relationship with him. Said I never met him before."

"No shit, they ask about me?"

"Your name was not brought up at all. You're not a Hell Hound, are you?"

"Fuck no, my brother Jake was. A guy in the club ratted him out, and because of it, Jake was killed in prison. I like being my own person."

"Good for you, Mitch. I assume the other guys are also Hell Hounds?"

I respect what Jerry said to me, I didn't answer, I just smiled.

For the rest of the trek, we both kept our eyes roaming and talking about Nam. I asked him if he knew a meathead named Kurt Wilson.

"Never heard of him, should I have?"

I told Fred the whole story including me doing a deuce for Lucy's death in San Quentin. How Grandpa cleaned me up, got me off the heroin. Unlike Jerry, I have nothing really to hide, well almost. But what I do have, that will remain hidden under a steel curtain.

We made it back to Grandpa's safe and sound and in one piece and I firmly believe I have not only got to know a long-lost cousin, but I made a solid friend.

We brought in all the meat, some went in the fridge downstairs, some went in one of the two huge chest freezers that Grandpa has in the basement.

Then it was time for hot shower and clean clothes.

By the time I was cleaned up Fred was sitting at the table all smiles with Uncle Jack and Val.

Funny how the five of us that night had laughs, told stories.

***

The next morning Grandpa asked me and Fred to help deliver the deer meat to the elders on the rez.

Grandpa showed me off as the big strong son of Iggy. And Fred as his police officer grandson. If only they knew we were both polar opposites when it came to crime. Then again let's hope none of them ever find out.

We had one more delivery when Fred said he wanted to pop into the police station and get his official start date.

Even though I have done nothing wrong here, I had zero interest in going in and waiting for him, so I told Grandpa we'd make the last delivery and swing back and pick up Fred.

On the drive over to drop off the meat, I remember what Jerry said about telling nothing to Fred.

And a little bit of paranoia made me wonder if he was telling his cop mates about who all is on the Strongbow property. Maybe run a background check.

Perhaps some payback for Jerry being such a shithead. He knows Jerry had some grass. Maybe see if anyone was on parole and not allowed to bother with anyone that would fuck up his parole.

Anyways, I realized that is Jerry's problem, not mine. Having said that, I also hope Fred is not that stupid.

7

We showed up at the last house. I grabbed the last box of meat and followed Grandpa.

He knocked on the door and when it opened, I was pleasantly surprised. It was a really cute chick. Long jet-black hair. Beautiful brown eyes, a perfect smile, and one fuck of a figure. Not what I was expecting at all.

She invited us in and judging by her smile, I was not what she was expecting as we had the most intense eye contact the whole time.

I asked her where she would like me to put the meat in a rather suggestive sexual innuendo. Was kind of hoping she said between her legs.

She definitely picked up on what I was saying as her smile got even bigger, twirled her hair, and asked me to follow her. With her killer ass that was not a problem at all.

She had a freezer in a spare bedroom. As I was helping her put some of the meat in the freezer, I noticed no wedding ring at all. Just a couple turquoise rings. She kept out one package and carried it to the fridge.

She asked if we would like a drink. I said a beer. Grandpa just wanted a coffee. She joined me in also having a beer.

I am pretty sure Grandpa picked up on chemistry between us two. When he introduced us, he said, "Mitchell, this is Veronica, our single, middle school teacher. Veronica, this is Mitchell my *single* grandson Mitchell, who hails from California."

We both looked at Grandpa and laughed and then shook hands.

She asked what happened to my eye, I just rolled my eye and told her the whole story, she laughed which made me laugh.

There was definitely something between us, she asked what I did, and whereabouts exactly in California I lived. Told her San Fran, told her about Pamdora's and working at the Drunken Leprechaun and bounty hunting.

If her beauty wasn't enough of a turn on, her self-confidence totally blew my mind as I really respect a venturous female.

"So, I guess in San Francisco you must see all kinds," she asked.

"If only you knew, I've seen just about everything."

"I would love to visit one day. Just seeing if it is the groovy city I have read about."

"I have a two-bedroom apartment, you find your way there, you have a place to stay. I would love to take you around, Haight Ashbury, spent time there as a teen. Fillmore, all the cool places. I have partied with Jim Morrison."

"No kidding, wow, I might just take you up on that, Mitchell."

"Mitch. I think Grandpa, and my boss Joseph, are the only two people that call me Mitchell.'

"Very good, Mitch." She then squinted her eyes, acted kind of nervous, and asked if I had plans tonight.

Totally shocked once again. I looked at Grandpa and asked if we had plans tonight. He smiled and shook his head and said no.

"I hope you don't find me too forward. But there is a movie playing in town this weekend and this weekend only. I really wanted to go and see it tonight but couldn't find anyone to go with me. Mitch, would you like to see it with me?"

"Absolutely I would be honored to join you. What movie by the way?"

"Rocky horror picture show, you hear of it back home?"

"Never heard of it, is it good?"

"It's groundbreaking, bit comedy, bit musical."

I didn't care what the movie was, no way would I turn her down. Never in a million years would I think I would be going out on a date during hunt camp.

And even more bizarre, I never would have thought Grandpa would be my wingman. But he rocked it.

Seeing at how I really didn't have wheels, Veronica said she would slide by and pick me up. I asked if she would like to go to dinner first.

Her eyes were dancing, and she said that would be great.

I finished my beer, shook her hand and she said she would be by around five.

Total eye contact with each other as we left, I felt like a teen.

86

Grandpa patted me on the back and said Veronica is a good woman. The exact kind of woman I need in my life.

She was fucking cute that is for sure. And a full-blooded Sioux, a teacher. I think it is safe to say Mom and Dad would both be smiling down at me for once. I still think Jake would like the Charlene and Mindy types better.

As we pulled up to the cop shop, Grandpa asked if I would go in and get Fred. Reluctantly I said sure. I really didn't want to, but Grandpa was my wingman, I at least owe him this.

So, I walk in and right away the cops inside just stare at me. And not a *welcome can we help you*? I guess they can spot a criminal as much as I can spot a cop in uniform or not.

Fred spotted me and told his guys he would see them Monday.

We both walked out of the cop shop together. Nice to actually leave one without charges or hours upon hours of questioning.

I asked how it went trying to get any unusual body language off him.

"All good, I start on Monday. Really looking forward to it. Good guys."

As long as he thinks they are good, I certainly don't.

Grandpa told him about my date tonight, he seemed to be quite happy for me.

Once we got home, I got cleaned up and waited for Veronica.

Five on the button I saw her lime green pickup truck driving towards the house.

I walked outside to meet her with butterflies in my stomach. I am pretty cocky and more than self-confident when it comes to dating.

Perhaps not being on my own turf, a rather self-assured female, and me not know if it is horror, or whore in the name of the movie.

Her eyes lit right up seeing me, I got a massive hard on and felt normal all of a sudden.

She told me to jump in and when I did, well, another first for me; Veronica had a gun rack in her truck with a thirty odd six in it. A total turn on. See, this tells me I better behave myself as I am sure she knows how to use it. Yep, can't say I ever dated anyone who brings a rifle on a first date.

As she drove, I just stared at her, she was so pretty. I was also trying to recall if Jake ever dated a Sioux or any native Indian.

I have an awesome relationship with Mindy, I truly do. But she is also married. I am truly a single guy, with a solid fuck friend.

We pulled into Rapid City and parked right in front of the restaurant where I had the altercation. I asked Veronica if we were eating here.

She said no and told me to take her hand and trust her. Who am I to disagree?

We walked a couple blocks to an American Legion of all places.

"Trust me, Mitch. They have this amazing fish fry every Friday night."

Once again who I am to disagree with a local? She would know.

She signed me in as a guest which kind of made me snicker seeing at how I was the veteran, and not her.

I paid for a pitcher of draft beer and the meal. Then we took our seats. I looked all around and saw how packed the place was. Both whites and natives.

I noticed all kinds of military plaques on the wall, and I asked if she would mind if I looked at them.

She said not at all as she joined me. First plaque was for locals that served and died in WW1, second one for WW2, Korean Conflict and finally the Vietnam War.

Sure as fuck which name jumped out at me? Sargent Major Iggy Strongbow. I smiled and nodded my head. Veronica clued in and asked how he was related to me.

"He was my dad."

Her hand went over her heart as she gasped and said how sorry she was.

I thanked her and said Dad died as a Sioux warrior, in battle.

She then asked if I also served. I smiled and said yes, as our dinner was now being put down at our table.

I will say one thing, the fish fry was amazing. Nothing better than fresh caught lake trout. I swear I ate a school worth. I was stuffed by the time we were done.

We finished off another pitcher before heading to the show.

Hmm, Rocky Horror, not Rocky Whore Picture Show, it said on the marquis. The poster was a set or red lips and teeth, very strange indeed.

As we walked in the theater part there were maybe a handful of people. A little shocked by that, well at least we could choose our seats. Veronica wanted right in the middle of the theater. Normally I am back row, no one can sneak up on me there.

We held hands and waited for the show to begin, both looked at each other, she giggled, and I smiled. I leaned in and gave her a long slow kiss.

When we both came up for air, she said sorry, the show was now starting, but to keep my lips moist for after the show.

Show starts off normal, pack of bikes passing the couple, yeah, I like where this is going. Hmm, flat tire, true start of bad things to come. A castle, who the fuck can afford a castle? And if that is where the bikers were coming from, sounds like a Hell Hound club bash.

Holy fuck, a mutant that answered the door. Veronica is once again giggling. That makes me happy. So does seeing Janet in just a bra and panties, man I hope they show her tits, what a nice rack.

I've got a hot chick beside me that I will try my best to score with, pretty horny right now. I wonder if she would stroke me or blow me in the theater?

I go to put her hand on my throbbing cock when I suddenly lose my hard-on as if it was shot.

What the fuck is a Doctor Frank-N-Furter? Seriously? This movie can't end fast enough for me. I've seen some pretty fucked up shit in my lifetime, this is right near the top. Not one soul will be told I actually sat through this whole film.

If we were back home, first date or not, I would bail and hit a bar.

But she has the wheels, and also a rifle.

So, I pictured myself banging all the maids and Janet, that Eddie guy should have killed them all.

The only thing I found enjoyable was some of the songs were really catchy. I'll also deny that if ever asked.

Once the movie ended, she stood up and clapped, if body language says anything, my arms were folded. She looked at me, pouted, and asked if I liked the movie.

I was really hoping to get laid so I don't want to throw a hand grenade.

"It was different, I certainly liked the music."

She smiled and said she would make it up to me. My turn to smile, as I asked how.

"Let's go back to my place, phone your grandpa, and tell him you are not coming home tonight. That's how."

I leaned in and kissed her and said that was a brilliant idea.

***

On the drive to her house, I started to rub her leg as I leaned in. It was met with no resistance.

So, I started to rub her through her jeans a little higher and higher. She let out a slight moan. By the time I got around her crotch area, you could really feel the heat and moisture coming from it. I started to rub her pussy lips. I looked up and she seemed to be in heaven.

After a couple minutes she moved my hand away and asked me to please stop. I am a very confident lover and I asked if she was sure.

"I am having a hard time concentrating on these back roads. There is way too much animal movement at nighttime."

Damn, never even thought about that. I sat up straight and told her I too will be looking for any animals.

We arrived safely at her place. We necked all the way to the front door. She put the key in, opened the door and I picked her up off her feet and asked which way to her bedroom.

She was busting a gut laughing when she said call your grandpa first.

I actually felt like Grandpa, as it seemed to take forever to dial the numbers.

Fred answered the call and said *Strongbow residence*. At first, I snickered until I realized Grandpa is on a shared line.

"Can you let Grandpa know I won't be home tonight?"

At first there was a second of dead air until he clued in and started to laugh and told me to have fun. I intend to was my answer before hanging up the phone.

Veronica, sporting the sexiest smile asked how good a hunter I really was.

"Pretty damn good," was my answer. She then raced down the hall and said to find her if I could.

Well, I let my cock find her, better than a bloodhound at finding pussy.

I stood in the doorway and saw her sitting on the bed swinging her feet back and forth.

She almost started to blush as she tapped a spot on the bed beside her.

I did as she asked, put my hand behind her neck, moved her hair off to the side and pulled her in and started to neck with her, tongue action of course.

After a couple minutes, I started to undo the buttons on her blouse. Once it was open, I started to bite her neck and worked at undoing her bra.

Once I had her bra off, I was shocked as she hid her breasts quite well. Solid D cup with really dark nipples, they were hard and as I started to suck on them, as I made my way to her pants.

Veronica lifted her ass up off the bed and slid her pants and underwear off.

She had a perfectly trimmed bush, can't wait to dive in there tongue first.

I started to finger her pussy while tonguing the top of her clit.

She was moaning away and grabbing my hair.

After about fifteen minutes or two female orgasms, my tongue needed a rest, and my cock needed some intense pussy exercises.

I stood up and took my clothes off and showed Veronica exactly what weapon I was using for this hunt.

She eagerly spread her long legs in preparation of me penetrating her.

I kept one hand on my cock to glide me in, and one hand playing with her breasts.

Her pussy was soaked, the first time my cock touched bottom inside her my pubes also became soaked.

I started to thrust harder and harder inside of her; once again she became vocal as she yelled out *yes, yes*.

Both my hands were like a magician, always moving around, up and down her thighs, playing with her breasts and nipples.

The beer that we had drunk earlier was now starting to sweat out of me. The stitches were starting to burn, the pain made me fuck her harder and harder.

I was now starting to bite her nipples.

Once again, I felt her whole-body contract; her breathing was erratic as she started to cum again.

Fuck she was loud, but it turned me on. So much for the meek schoolteacher.

I was squeezing her ass cheeks hard as I started to feel myself getting ready to cum.

I asked if she wanted me to cum in or out. Her eyes were rolling in her head when she said out.

I pulled my rock-hard cock out of her drenched pussy and started to wank it.

She laid back and played with her breasts as I started to shoot.

My cum had quite the distance as I saw her close her left eye, as she swore fuck, at the same time.

My ejaculation seemed to go on forever. My head and the bed started to spin.

I collapsed on the bed beside her, grasping for air, fuck that was good.

Veronica got up right away and headed to the washroom. She was mumbling something, but I was breathing too hard to understand her.

She came back into the room wearing a housecoat and one very nasty looking eye. She had a washcloth on it. She was not happy.

The one working good eye told me that.

"Did you do this on purpose?"

I was totally confused. She should be pleased that she got me that horny.

"I can't control where I piss, never mind where I shoot. I was aiming for your tits to be honest. Remember, you are the one that asked me to pull out."

She just shook her head in disgust. I have never really had post sex hostility, unless I moaned out the wrong chick's name when fucking, or cumming.

Well, I certainly worked up a thirst, not going to sit beside her as she sulks.

"I am going to grab a beer, you want one?" She shook her head no.

Fuck, this is going to be a long night.

So, I sat at her kitchen table and had a beer, then another beer, and a couple more. I had a nice little buzz happening. Fuck after seeing that freak movie and Veronica turning into a moody cunt. Beer was my salvation.

Around eleven she came out and apologized.

"Look, Mitch; my last boyfriend was really aggressive, and he would make me do thing I never wanted to do including, well you know."

I accepted her apology and said sorry to hear this.

She came in for a hug and all of a sudden, my stomach flipped, damn greasy fish and the beer are not mixing, plus I am sure my guts are rolling from Rocky Horror.

I broke free of our conversation and raced to the bathroom. The hairs on my arms were standing up. I was running and tightening my asshole all at once.

I lifted the toilet seat lid, plopped my ass down, and it was like the shit damn burst open.

I was spraying like crazy. It was coming out like water, acidic water.

My butthole was having contractions as the steady stream sprayed out.

The smell was gagging. Veronica came in to check on me.

"Oh my God!" Was her horrid reaction, her hand went over her mouth and next thing you know she is puking, not in the sink or the bathtub, but on me.

This was a first for me, maybe payback for me setting up David Rothstein and him puking over Jane Cooper so I could seduce Natasha. Then like something from a Three Stooges flick, Veronica now tries to puke in the sink but loses her footing and falls on the ground. She really hit the floor hard and is now crying. I go to get up to help her but round ten of cramps kick in and I have to sit back down and free base the toilet.

The smell hits her hard again and she pukes all over the floor.

Pretty safe to say, worst first date in all of mankind, and I even fucking scored.

Eventually she stops hurling and is crying and curled up in a ball. I stop shitting but feel totally physical and emotionally drained.

She is as pale as can be. I ask if she needs medical attention. She cries, so I don't know.

The whole bathroom is a disaster, we really both need to take a shower, but I have to clean up the mess first.

So, I gently pick her up and put her in the shower. I ask where she keeps her paper towels and mop.

She tells me, I go and get them and start to clean up. If anything, I want to show I am nothing like her ex-boyfriend, and I am also Fred Strongbow's grandson.

It is not spotless, but it is clean. I then jump in the shower with her. She is still shaken; I hug her and tell her all is good.

I have to wash my hair twice. I cleaned her, got her out of the shower, and then I towel dried her. Then I help her walk to her bed.

I cover her up, go to jump in bed beside her, but my gut has other ideas, I tell her to stay in bed as I race to the washroom. I swear I can't have anything left inside me.

Eventually, I struggle to make it back to the bedroom. She is out cold; I pull back my side of the bed and within seconds I am out cold.

***

As I woke up the next afternoon, yes afternoon, I had to think did I have one fucked up dream or did what happened in the bathroom really take place?

I roll over and kiss Veronica on the cheek and ask how she is feeling.

"My back is killing me, oh my God it hurts. There is no way I will be able to drive you home."

"Why don't I call Grandpa to come and pick me up?"

She tears up and says sorry.

"Hey, all good, hon."

She then thanked me for everything I did last night.

I ask if she needs anything before I leave. She just wanted me to help her out of bed so she could take some aspirin.

So, I did as instructed, called Grandpa and tell him how Veronica fell and hurt herself. There was dead air at first, I could only imagine what is going through his mind. He then agrees to pick me up in twenty.

I offer to make her something to eat before I leave, but she says she just wants to sleep.

Grandpa pulls up, comes to the door. I let him in, and he asks Veronica how she is feeling. She says her back is sore, she also has a bloodshot eye, not bruised or blackened, just red.

Veronica then tells Grandpa what a wonderful person I am helping her out, moping the floors and helping her to bed.

She came over ever so gingerly and gave me a kiss on the cheek. I guess if Grandpa had any concerns that I hurt her, all doubts were now sealed.

I gave her my phone number before we left, told her to call me if she makes it to San Fran.

On the drive back, Grandpa said he was proud of me. Made me feel really good as I know I have let him down so many times.

When we got back to his house I asked if he minded if I headed back to the longhouse. He said not at all. I want to bag him another eight-pointer.

Fred came out to the barn and asked how the show was, and if I scored.

"The only thing I can say about the movie is that it was fucked. Maybe if I was high on LSD, I might understand it. And yeah, I scored."

He smiled and said good stuff. I told him I would see him in a couple days.

Fred told me happy hunting. I gave him a nod and then hopped on my horse and headed to the hunt camp.

It was a crisp but clear day. The sun feels amazing going right through my bones. I feel so alive out here, I feel useful, like I am supposed to live out here. San Fran is beautiful, but I miss all four seasons changing. Haven't done Christmas out here since I was a kid, you know I think as soon as I land back home, I will call Rachel and make plans to spend Christmas here.

Every once in a while, gun shots go off in the distance. Hopefully the boys are having fun.

I got there and the place was empty. Seeing at how Veronica said what a helpful guy I was, it was time to help out the boys. I started to make dinner for everyone.

Then I went out back and was target shooting. My eye was no longer an issue. Still a little tender but for vision, all good.

I heard the horses approach, so I went outside. Four more dead deer. Good stuff.

At first, they were making fun of me, asking if any of the grandmas on the rez came onto me. I smiled, stuck out my chest and told them quite proudly that I fucked a schoolteacher, a hot young schoolteacher.

Ruby smiled and said bullshit. I told him Grandpa picked me up this afternoon from her house.

He looked at Donnie to see if I was a bullshitter.

"Trust me, Ruby, if Mitch could slither, he would be banging snakes."

For the next couple days, we hunted in the daylight hours and partied pretty damn good as soon as the sun went down.

By the time we left hunt camp and headed back to Grandpa's, our horses were weighed right down with deer meat. Most I have ever seen, same as Jerry.

We all rode back mighty proud. True hunters and warriors.

We spent the majority of the last night making deer sausage, using Grandpa's famous recipe.

He took the stitches out from my arm and eye. I asked if he would like some company for Christmas. He asked who, I told him me for sure, I would ask Rachel once I get home.

He sported an ear-to-ear smile and said he would really like that.

We had one hell of a scarf that night. Still no love between Fred and Jerry.

The next morning, grandpa had to make two trips to get us all to the airport.

I decided to bring home my new rifle. I kept my receipt. As I was checking in the guy at the airport counter was more concerned about my one heavy gunnysack bag that was actually my dad's.

He asked what was inside. Fifty pounds of deer sausage, steaks, roasts, and ice, lots of ice.

The gun was checked in as was the gunnysack. All of us except Uncle Jack and Val had the same cargo.

The flight to Minnesota proved interesting as Maureen was the stewardess.

She spotted me as I was sitting beside Ruby.

He goes, "Fuck that is hot," as she walks by us.

Then Maureen backs up, and goes "Oh my God, Mitch! How are you, handsome?"

"I am good, beautiful. Damn, you look sexy in that outfit."

She smiled and softly asked if I would like to join the mile high club.

Ruby burst out laughing, I guess Donnie heard her also and said to Ruby, "Remember the snake story."

She made sure we were fed first, she even gave us a couple airplane bottles even though this was an early flight.

I asked where she has been, she said now doing central mountain flights. No west coast flights for a bit. I told her to call me if she is in town. She said she would for sure.

Once we landed Ruby, Val and George had a two-hour layover before they headed back to Texas.

For the rest of us, three hours till our next flight. Might as well find the bar and have a few beers. Those little booze bottles from Maureen were just a tease.

Now, if running into Maureen was a fluke, what happened next was totally bizarre.

I noticed a mother with her two little boys. They looked all prim and proper wearing suits. The mother was wearing a lime green dress with a hemline past her knees that seemed to hide her figure. She didn't need a lot of makeup as she had this natural beauty, thick lips, and strawberry blonde hair.

I knew her from somewhere, but I couldn't place her. When suddenly I had butterflies fluttering as she stopped and stared at me, not in a creepy kind of way, but I knew she was thinking the same.

It wasn't until this guy in a suit called her Rhonda, I knew exactly who she was.

I said, "Rhonda Ryan?"

She covered her mouth. Tears came to her eyes as she said, "Mitchell Strongbow?"

The guy in the suit just stared at both of us as we now hugged each other.

Her face now matched her hair as she was tongue tied and tried to introduce me to the guy in the suit.

Finally, I stuck out my hand and introduced myself.

He said he was Digby Jones, Rhonda's husband, and their twin sons John and Michael. He then asked how I knew Rhonda.

"Mitch's Dad and my dad served together in the Airborne. And he was actually my first boyfriend." She went beet red after saying that.

Now Digby was a suit, glasses, pencil nose, sharp features. He looked at me, the rest of the boys wearing Hell Hound sweaters, and must've felt like a hero rescuing and marrying Rhonda before she was corrupted and made into a harlot of a woman.

The boys said they would meet me in the bar, I just nodded my head.

I then reached down and shook her sons' hands. They called me sir, yeah, their dad has trained them well.

I asked Rhonda where they were going to all dressed up.

"Back to Kansas, my mom just died."

I said I was sorry to hear this, but inside I still remember how she kept Rhonda away from me. I hope the cunt suffered. I bet you all the deer meat I was traveling with, that she never gave Rhonda the letters I wrote to her after they moved away.

She then asked about my family.

"Rachel is the only one left alive."

She just shook her head no and started to tear up as I told her the whole story.

Even Digby, who listened to every single word I spoke, was in shock.

Rhonda came in and gave me a hug, Digby patted me on the back and said that is awful.

He seemed to relax a little. I asked what they do for a living these days.

Digby sells life insurance and Rhonda is a stay-at-home mom.

I used my standard cover line- t-shirt store, doorman, bodyguard, and bounty hunter.

We talked for a couple minutes and then said they had to head to their gate.

I shook his hand as well as their two sons'. Gave her a hug goodbye, told them if they ever find their way to San Fran, drop by Pamdora's.

Funny, as they walked away, I still could recall our goodbyes when she and her mom were starting their new life. Fuck it, beer time.

As I walked into the bar Ruby is shaking his head and smiling, "Ok buddy, tell me all about her."

I laughed and said she was my first girlfriend, then her dad was killed in Vietnam, and they moved away. I haven't seen her since we were thirteen.

Yeah, while drinking the whole beer, I was recalling my first kiss with her, beating up Harry Swanson. Even though she is pretty square, she still turns me on. I think she would look hot in a tight pair of jeans and a tank top, some makeup on, nails painted, and a couple shots of tequila to loosen her up.

Before you know it, Val, George, and Ruby had a plane to catch.

Ruby said I have to pay him a visit in Texas soon and I better keep my word about camping in Colorado. I promised him I would do both.

I gave Val and George a hug goodbye, said I would come see them. They said I should bring Rachel along. I said I would ask her.

We had another beer then it was our turn to jump on our final flight.

The whole flight all I could do was embrace my time spent with Rhonda.

It was a good feeling. I wonder if she is thinking about me right now?

Jeanie picked us all up at the airport. Oddly enough, we just happened to be pulled over before we dropped off Jerry. And we are not talking about a single cruiser; we are talking about a half dozen black and whites and a couple detectives.

Uncle Jack was the only nervous person. The rest of us were used to it, even Jeanie if you can believe it.

We were all taken out of the car by gunpoint. Patted down and put in the back of cruisers as they went through the car.

8

We may be criminals, but we are smart criminals. All of us kept our receipts for our rifles. No crime about the amount of deer meat one could have.

Within say forty minutes or so we were all cut free. A real eye opener for Uncle Jack I have to say. A reality check to keep me in line. You just never know.

I was dropped off next. Janine was just closing shop and locking the door as we pulled up.

I asked how she was as her face turned red seeing me.

"Um, I am all right, where did you guys go?" As she looked at my gun case.

"I was at my grandfather's hunting. Can you give me a hand and help me get my stuff upstairs"?

Her eyes got big, real big.

"Are you O.K?"

She forced a smile and she said she was not sure. So, I said give me a hand and tell me what is going on. She said that would be a great idea.

She opened and held the door for me as I ran everything upstairs.

I asked if she wanted a beer. She said no thanks.

I put most of the deer meat in the freezer and the rest I put in the fridge.

Grabbed myself a beer, sat on my Archie Bunker chair and

said talk to me.

Right away she teared up. This was not good at all. Something told me to stay seated and hear her out.

"Mitch, my stomach has been rolling ever since I got home from Vegas."

This time the waterworks burst open.

Once she composed herself, she said, "I have been a horrible wife. What we did was wrong, and what I did in Vegas was wrong, really wrong."

Fuck, I feel like shit all of a sudden. I just nodded my head and said sorry. Really what else can I say? Maybe find out what all went down in Vegas, so I asked her.

"I don't even know where to start or where to begin. I acted like a whore. I slept with a different guy each night we were there. And I couldn't control myself, guys were giving me all this attention, something Alfie stopped doing. I don't know if I did it to hurt him, or to please myself."

"Maybe a bit of both. You are beautiful, you are a wonderful mother. And is this the first time you ever crossed the line?"

She was wiping away the tears as she nodded yes.

"You obviously still love Alfie as it is breaking your heart. I assume when you had sex with these guys you your drunk and high correct?"

"Yes, but I was not drunk when we fooled around."

"I wasn't lying when I told you I have had a crush on you for the past twelve years or so. I am sorry, it was lust on my part."

She took a deep breath and spoke, "I too am sorry that it ruined our working relationship. I would like to give my two weeks' notice. I promise I will not leave you empty handed."

Holy fuck, I was not expecting this at all. I am in shock, total shock.

"I will give you a raise, you name the price. The reason the shop is successful is you, not me. I promise no matter how horny I get to not come on to you."

"You are making this hard, Mitch," she snickered. "Then again, you being hard is what got me in trouble."

"Let me give you some more advice and a deal. Have you slept with Alfie since you been home?"

"No, I feel so dirty, he knows something is up, he is just not sure what."

"Good, go to the free clinic. Get tested for any diseases. Not scaring you, but some many STDs are on the rise right now. And if you decide to stay with me, I will give you and your whole family a three-day pass at Disneyland, I will even pay for all of you to stay there."

And then I saw a faint light open in her eyes.

"I have already been to the clinic. I am clean. You do care about me don't you, Mitch?"

"I swear to God I do. You are that lifeline to Pam; I feel when we talk, you keep her memory and spirit alive."

Huge smile now as she nodded her head yes.

"I swear on my kids Mitch, I planned on giving my notice, this was never about a pay raise of generous gift for me and my family. But knowing that you really care about me changes everything."

"So, you have reconsidered and will continue to work for me?"

"Does the three days at Disneyland still stand if I say yes?"

"Of course, it does, if you get naked right now."

Her eyes got big, and I started to laugh and said just kidding.

"Ok. I will stay, but no more flirting, alright?'

I stood up and shook her hand, told her thanks, and to let on to Alfie she is paying for everything.

She smiled large once again and said I was a great boss, I said she was a great manager.

After she left, I took a deep breath and blew it out slowly. I meant every word I said to her. She is also smart, she knows I do legit business, she also knows I do illegitimate business and plays the game so well.

I went in and grabbed another beer before checking my answering machine as I know more grief is coming my way, I just feel it. Chugged it right back and then pushed play.

Five voice mails from Mindy, the first three she is full of life, says she is thinking of me. Fourth one I believe she was drunk or stoned; she also told me she was going to play with herself and tell me the details in person. The fifth voice mail she had some pain in her voice, she said she really misses me.

Rachel checked in and just wanted to make sure I got home safely. Joseph asked me to call him when I got home. Mad Bill reminded me to call him once I get home. And Oscar who said I should really give him a call. So, who do you think I called first?

Mad Bill of course, too much money to be made. It was a pretty positive conversation. He said he would land in a week, gave me the time and flight number. Said I would pick him up.

Next was Oscar, just like talking to Mad Bill, you have to watch what you say over the phone.

"Oscar, I just walked in. How did your fishing trip go, any trophy fish caught?"

He laughed then said, "Of course Strongbow, I am quite the fisherman. Good, let's meet tomorrow for breakfast."

Oscar said he would meet me at the Drunken Leprechaun, kill two birds with one stone.

I then called Rachel at her office. I still get a kick when they transfer me to her secretary who of course screens all her calls.

Well, whether or not she was actually in court, who knows for sure. I left a message that her brother is home alive safe and sound to call me.

Called Joseph next and told him I would slide by for breakfast in the morning.

He seemed to be all right with it. Something was up as the whole conversation was pretty one sided with me doing all the talking.

And finally, I called Mindy. Now, don't get me wrong as I was horny as all fuck, but I know Mindy has full-time man in her life, well even if he is really part time, regardless, he is still her husband.

Just like Rachel, her secretary said she was out of the office. I left a message to give Mitch a shout once she gets back.

Well, I'm not sitting around and waiting for people. I needed to go for a ride on my bike.

As much as I love being on a horse, opening the throttle full along PCH1, still gives me goose bumps.

My ride lasted for a couple hours. Once I was back in the city, I stopped off at Electric Ladyland. I wanted to let Mike know

I had some deer meat for him and to also see some of the new talent.

I asked Rocco if his boss was in. He said not tonight.

So, I had a drink, watched some of the girls then headed home. Too much shit on the go tomorrow to get all fucked up. Time to recheck the phone messages as the light was flashing. Rachel and Mindy. Mindy said she was so happy to hear from me. Sadly, her hubby is around, and they have plans tonight and she would call me tomorrow.

Basil also called and said he would like to see me at some point tomorrow as he has a business deal for me. Rachel asked me to call her at Pat's. I looked at the time, it was almost midnight. Was starting to get a bit tired, will try playing the phone tag game all over again tomorrow.

This has to be one of the reasons why I really enjoy taking off to the reserve. Not worrying about the phone, business, and grief. On the reserve I just do what the fuck I want.

I rolled a joint, had another beer, and envisioned myself sitting around a fire and just staring at the stars in the night sky.

The next morning, I woke up and wished Mindy was beside me. Super fucking horny, yeah, I think I will stop by the record studio, and like my breakfast meetings, kill two birds with one stone.

I grabbed a long hot shower, some deer sausage and jumped in the mustang and headed out to meet everyone.

Oscar was already seated. I scanned the whole bar making sure no cops, or anyone I didn't know was seated.

I shook his hand and asked, "How did Florida go?"

"It went better than expected. Strongbow, I now own a jet, a fucking jet. A 25B Lear Jet. No more props. It will be faster than ever."

"No fucking shit! That is amazing, Oscar. And you know how to fly a jet?"

"I am learning as I go."

Now this made me kind of nervous, Oscar picked up on this when I asked if he was serious.

"I am just fucking with you, of course I know how to fly this style of jet. Listen, your friend that steals all the cars, the Negro, do you think he can forge some documents for us? I also need a forged plane documentation, my guy ended up in jail."

"Only one way to find out, let's go and see him after we leave here."

A couple minutes later, Donnie showed up as did Joseph. We all ordered our breakfast, then Joseph had a little lecture for all of us.

"I give all of you space; I have no problems with you making extra cash. But when I need you guys and none of you are around, I am losing money. I am not happy."

"Joseph, you knew we were going to the reserve to hunt. You said that was fine and as promised. I called you as soon as we got back. What's going on?"

"Zack Glickman, the long snapper from the 49ers. He put fifty grand on Fraser versus Ali a couple weeks back. Go to collect while you boys are gone, and he has disappeared into thin air. 49ers also cut him, and he bolted town. He is from Montana; no one else seems to have any information on him."

"I know the strength and conditioning coach for the 49ers, let me talk to him and see what all I can find out," said Donnie.

Joseph thanked him, said as soon as we get the information on him, we are to get our asses in gear and find him. Joseph was pissed.

"I also want you to find out exactly when he knew he was being cut from the team. That cocksucker always showing off his two Super Bowl rings he won with the Packers. Well, fuck him; those rings are now an interest charge for him not paying his debt. He either gives them willingly, or you cut his fingers off." Joseph was beet red in the face.

And for yours truly, I remember when I was rolling on the ground with Burns, Glickman gave me a couple shots. I think I will cut off his pinkies out of pure revenge and principle.

After the Glickman conversation, Oscar brought up that he has a new plane, or make that *jet*. This made Joseph smile, ear to ear smile, which I found strange, as he is not a great flyer.

Donnie asked when we could take her for a spin. Oscar replied after he gets it registered. Hopefully Paul can hook us up.

After we ate and the business meeting was over, Oscar and I headed to see Paul at his shop. I forewarned Oscar to play nice with Paul. Oscar is such a racist, and we need Paul's help.

When we pulled in one of Paul's guys, Abdul, was wearing one of those African dress things and a white wool hat on his head.

Abdul just eyed me up and down, called me by my last name and curled his lip. He then walked over to Oscar and called him his brother.

"I am not your brother; Strongbow is my brother."

"You are African, we are all brothers," said Abdul now with his back up.

"I am not African; I was born in Syria, which would make me Asian. But I consider myself American if you really want to know."

I just patted Oscar on the back and said let's go see Paul.

Paul welcomed me with open arms. He asked what brings us.

"I need legit documentation for a jet."

Paul looked at both of us with a smile, and then laughter. "Only you, Strongbow, would ask for a request like this. I actually know a guy in Nevada at the plane graveyard. Give me a day or two and I will have all your documents." He shook his head and started to laugh once again.

Oscar asked if I wanted to spend the day with him in San Jose, said I had too much running around to do.

I dropped him off back at the Leprechaun, and then I headed to Summer of Love records.

I parked my car, got out and walked in with a nice little swagger in my step.

As soon as I was inside, I could smell Mindy's perfume, right off the bat I get hard, and had butterflies fluttering.

Fuck Basil, I headed right for her office. I saw her door was closed, really hoping she is around.

As soon as I asked the receptionist if she was in, she had a scared, almost confused sort of look on her face. Before I asked if everything was all right, Mindy's door opened up and out walked Mr. and Mrs. Matheson.

He looked at me trying to figure out where he knew me from. Mindy's eyes went huge, and her face went beet red. Time to think quickly as he is walking towards me. He rubbed his hand on his chin and said he recognizes me from somewhere but can't put his finger on it.

Inside I am dying laughing as my finger has been in his wife's pussy and ass. But I better not tell him that. I really don't want to bring up the last time was at the 49er Burns brawl.

"I actually supply your company with t-shirts. Just on my way to see Basil. I thought his office was somewhere around here."

He eyed me up and down once again, "And do you give us a good deal?"

"You get the best bang for your buck through me."

Once again, he's just eyeing me until he tells me exactly where Basil's office is.

I just nod my head and say thanks, then head to Basil's office. I guess that is why she didn't return my call last night. What a fucking square stooge he is.

Basil's door was open, and his secretary asked how I was doing.

"I am doing good, baby. How are you?" She always blushes when I talk to her.

She was so shy and such a geek, but in a kind of sexy kind of way.

"I am groovy now; do you need Basil?"

"Unless you have other plans for me?"

She had to actually had to put her head down as her face went redder than Maureen O'Hare's hair, pardon the pun.

She got up and knocked on Basil's door and told him I was here to see me.

Basil came right out, looked at his secretary, me, then told me to come in. He closed the door, jokingly told me to stop flirting with all the woman around here.

"I is who I is, because I eat my spinach."

"Funny, Popeye. Speaking of which, have you thought more about the bodyguard service? I have a friend at the state department who will help get you set up all legal. And yes Mitch, she is cute."

"Count me in, give me her name and work number. I have a bunch of guys lined up."

"Glad to hear, make sure you get a lawyer to go over all the paperwork. You will be able to write off all kinds of expenses and you can launder other drug monies from us also."

I told Basil I had some deer sausage for him when there

was a knock on the door. By the time Basil had a chance to answer, the door opened, and it was Mindy's husband.

"Hello, Basil. I am glad this young man found his way to your office. I understand we buy t-shirts from him, is this correct?"

"Yes, that is correct. Mitch will also be providing our artists bodyguard service."

"The bodyguard service sounds more like it. I can't see you behind a press machine all day long." He stuck out his hand and said, "I am Marvin Matheson; I didn't catch your name."

What a sneaky fuck.

"Mitch Strongbow." I then passed him a Pamdora's business card and gave his hand a little tighter squeeze than most.

He looked at the card, smiled, and said he is looking forward to my t-shirts, and protecting his artists. He went to leave, stopped, turned around and asked if I also provide personal bodyguard service, not just artists.

I wanted to tell him I am providing one hell of a service to his wife, sometimes three times a night. But my gut tells me, I already make him nervous, or maybe jealous. The guy has to be close to sixty. I never asked Mindy about their sex life. A wrinkled soft old man on top of her is not a turn on at all.
"Of course, I do. I am all out of business cards for that. But you can call Pamdora's and one of my girls will get a hold of me."

He said very well, he would let us continue our business, then left the office.

"Now, let's get back to business. I need some blow, some H, speed, uppers, downers and in-betweens. And yeah, weed, lots of weed. Can you come through for me?"

"As I have said before. I can get you whatever you need. But I will deal with you and only you. I don't want any strangers present. Nothing over the phone at all. Cash of course."

He said deal and handed me a shopping list of exactly what he needed. He asked how much. I told him to give me to the end of tomorrow and I will have a price. I asked if he wanted a price for everything individually.

He said that would make better business sense. The weed I knew the price of for sure. He had no issues with my prices at all.

I shook his hand and told him to meet me at my place tomorrow, say eight o'clock, He said eight it was.

As much as I wanted to make contact with Mindy, I know better. Plus, she knows how to get a hold of me. Marvin is suspicious, not sure of me, or me and his wife. I have to trust my gut instinct here.

So, I jumped in my car and headed to see Donnie at his shop. I have purposely stayed away from the hard-core drugs, as Jake would say, "Don't do anything, little brother, that will kill your soul." Fuck, my soul has been to hell and back with heroin. I am strong, but every once in a while, I get the cravings.

Yeah, I want nothing left at my place, will do the business deal. Get rid of the dope, just weed, hash and oils I trust myself around.

"You know I am a club executive and dealing dope is a no-no. Steve, come on over. Mitch, you two do what you have to do. I don't want to know anything about it. And Mitch, you stick another syringe in your arm, I swear I will put a bullet in your head."

He was dead serious, no laughter.

"Just business, Donnie. Swear on Katrina and Rachel."

He stuck out his hand and we shook on it.

He went back in the shop and started working on a bike.

"Hey, Mitch! What's up, man? Heard hunt camp was cool, we barbecued some of the sausage today for lunch, was incredible."

"Thanks, man. Listen, I have a dope grocery list. Can you give me a price for everything but the weed? Actually, everything needs to be itemized."

He was looking at the list when he asked if it was for me personally.

I was honest with him as I trust him and his brother Rick.

"Not for me, a business deal. I figure no sense being too greedy as I can see a lot of business from this guy coming our way."

He said makes sense. He asked when I needed to know the prices. I told him I would drop by here tomorrow in the afternoon. He said cool, he would have all the prices for me. I shook his hand and said I would see him then.

Jumped in my car and headed home. Once I was there, I grabbed a beer and headed for the answering machine.

Sure as fuck, Mindy called me. She apologized for last

night and not returning my call and apologized even more for Marvin and her heading to Palm Springs for a couple of days. She said she will be thinking of me and will contact me once she is back.

I looked at my watch, I don't have any plans tonight. So, I packed up some deer sausage and roasts in a cooler full of ice, and of course a couple joints and headed to Sacramento, and Rachel's work.

As soon as I was out of San Fran and on the highway. I sparked up a joint, put Pink Floyd "Wish you were Here" in the 8-track player and enjoyed the drive. What a fucking cool album. I really hope they cut an album at SOL; how wild would that be? Would like to meet them all and shake their hands.

Once the buzz was in full force, I really listened to the lyrics, fuck, so many people I miss, so many people I wish were here. The list would be longer than the number of miles from my house to Rachel's work.

***

As I pulled into her parking lot at her work, I saw her Porsche in her own personal parking spot.

I headed to the receptionist who was nowhere as cute as the ones at SOL and asked if Rachel was in.

She politely with a smoker's voice asked who I was. I said Rachel's older brother, Mitch.

She then laughed and said she can see the resemblance. She called Rachel's receptionist who within seconds came out to get me and take me back to Rachel's office. She asked if I would like a coffee or beverage. I said beer, she laughed and said she might be able to find a root beer.

I said just water. She then went in and got Rachel who came out and brought me back into her office.

This was my first time at this building, pretty nice digs if I do say so.

Rachel gave me a hug and asked me how Grandpa is, and how hunt camp went.

I said Grandpa is really good, told her my idea about us spending the Christmas holidays there and what she thought about that.

She went into her calendar, smiled, and said as of right now she has no court dates leading up to the 23rd. She would have to be back by Monday the 29th.

She worried about us being able to get a flight last minute as airports during Christmas are always a disaster.

"My buddy Oscar, he just bought a Lear jet. This will be the least of our concerns." She raised an eyebrow and said my friends never cease to amaze her, she shook her head and started to laugh.

We talked about the whole hunt camp, plane crash, Uncle Jack and then I remembered about the meat in my car.

She asked if I had any meat for Pat and Uncle Karl. I said yes to both. She asked if I felt like dropping by and seeing Uncle Karl and Aunt Sandy tonight as they invited her and Pat for dinner. I said sure.

She then called Aunt Sandy to let her know I was going to be joining them and sorry for the short notice.

Rachel hung up the phone and said Aunt Sandy didn't have a problem with me coming too.

"So, tell me about you and Pat, you seem so happy."

"Mitch, I am madly in love with him. He treats me like a princess, just knows how to keep me happy. I really believe he will be the one."

"No shit, wow. Nice to see you so happy, sis. I like the guy so far."

I truly meant what I said, I just worried about his playboy reputation. He hurts Rachel by fucking around on her, or if he were to ever get physical, I would take his life, then bring him back, then Jerry would do the same as would Donnie.

We both took our own vehicles. And for us Strongbow's, the race was on.

Rachel's Porsche against my 390 GT Mustang. Who do you think won?

Well, it wasn't even close, Rach was on the front porch and halfway through her beer by the time I got there. Home street advantage to her, if this was San Fran, I would have downed a six-pack while waiting for her.

I grabbed the cooler and brought it inside. Gave everyone a hug and said it was good to see them.

They were more than happy to see me and the meat I

brought them. They were also happy that I am keeping the Strongbow family hunt alive. Uncle Karl said my dad would be proud. He also said both parents as well as him and Aunt Sandy are proud that I am drug free and have turned my life around.

I stuck around till just after nine before heading home. And yes, I smoked a joint along the way. I am at least heavy drug free; I *would* say needle free, but the best way to use steroids is through a syringe.

The next morning, I got up and hit the gym, had a killer workout and picked up my six-week cycle of steroids aka "Juice" and a whack of 22-gauge syringes off John Kantonescu.

I went home and put away my goods and then headed down to see Steve at Donnie's shop.

He didn't let me down; he gave me a per item breakdown of everything. He told me how much I should get for all the dope. I was surprised how much profit I was going to be able to make. I asked how much time he would need to get the goods to me. He said an hour or so. Once again, very pleased.

I told him I am meeting with someone later tonight, if I call him and say *drop by*, that will mean for him to bring all the dope. He said not a problem.

Then I headed to another business adventure, this one was legal. Stopped by to see Levy and get started with the bodyguard service.

He suggested I go and see his cousin's husband Ted. He is just starting off and is a business lawyer who deals with the Government on a regular basis. He called him and said he would see me right away.

Now, you might be wondering why I didn't hire Rachel. I really want to keep Rachel in the dark about my business affairs. More so protecting her than anything else.

Ted's office was as small as Pamdora's. His secretary looked kind of familiar.

Older twat, she gave me the up and down when I walked in.

I said Levy sent me over. She told me to have a seat and she would let him know I am here.

She came out ten seconds later and said Ted would see me. She wouldn't move out of the way as she eyed me up and down and this time she shook her head, what the fuck, really?

I walked in and there was the guy wearing a yamaka, an ugly lime green shirt, and a knitted checkered wool vest. His head was down, and he was writing away.

He tells me just a second, looks up and holy fuck. It is none other than quick shot Teddy Barone.

He stutters and stammers at first as he sticks out his sweaty palms for a handshake.

"Teddy Barone, how the fuck are you, man? Long time no see!"

"I am good, Mitch. How are you, haven't seen you since high school. Hey, do you remember my mom? She is now my receptionist."

Oh yes, she gave me the same evil eye when me and Jane Cooper visited his house back in the mid-sixties.

"Yeah, I sort of remember her."

"So, I understand you are starting a new business and need some legal services, is that correct?"

"Yes, I want to start up a bodyguard and bounty hunting business."

He smiled and said he would expect nothing less from me.

Ted said to go and pick up the papers and he would help me fill them out and notarize what needed.

I told him tomorrow I would go and pick up the papers and drop them off.

Once business was over, he asked what I was up to, if I was married, how work was, small talk stuff like that.

I gave him a quick, and I am sure frightening, run down of my life.

Wow was his answer. He took a minute to reflect and then showed me a picture of his wife, Levy's cousin. Now, that was frightening to me and in my mind, I went wow. She looks just like Teddy, but in drag. They could pass for twins. The fugly twins to be exact.

We shook hands once again, and before I left, Teddy's eyes shifted side to side, he whispered, "Do you ever see Jane Cooper around?"

I shook my head no, as I pictured Fagan going into the ice water.

"Can you possibly get me some weed, Mitch? I know that

you were always the guy back then."

I started to laugh and said, "Teddy, you animal! How much do you need?"

"I was thinking maybe just a joint or two. Sometimes life is so stressful. My mom and Bernice expect so much from me. I can't wind down sometimes."

"I will hook you up, Teddy. I will bring by a couple joints for you tomorrow."

A huge smile came to his face. "Thanks so much, Mitch. I really appreciate it. How much for the doobies?"

"Nothing Teddy. I remember you doing my homework for me. I am curious about one thing. I never knew you were Jewish."

The joy in his face left, his shoulders dropped. "I wasn't. This is the only way that Bernice would let me marry her if I converted to Judaism. My mom was ready to disown me, Mitch. Even now Bernice and my mom fight whenever they are together, especially when wine is involved."

"Teddy, now you know why I never married. And my daughter's mom is Jewish. Fuck that shit. Anyways, I promise to take care of you."

He smiled and said in a sincere way, "thanks."

As I left his office, I truly felt sorry for the guy. All his brains and what has it got him in life? I am sure an ulcer is brewing, more than likely going bald under his yamaka. I would rather be living my life than his.

I headed to the place to get the papers to officially start my business.

I pulled out the info on the chick I was to ask for, and the one clerk went to the back and said she would get her.

I sat down and out of the back came this tall, curvy, and busty black-haired girl who made a bee line for me. She looked like one of those pinup girls from the fifties. For an older chick, she was smoking hot.

She asked if I was Basil's friend. I said yes. She shook my hand and said her name was Janice. She asked me to follow her. The walk she had gave me a massive hard-on. Her hips and ass all moved perfectly together.

The whole time I am thinking to myself, *Janice if I have to fuck you to get my state licenses, I am more than willing to do that.*

In her office, she asked me to take a seat. As I went to sit down, she stared at my crotch area and smiled a little, fuck she knows how to tease.

She asked what type of business I wanted to start, I told her, and once again the same smile as when she stared at my cock. She then got up and went into a filing cabinet and got out all kinds of paperwork. Of course, she had to bend over for the one set, slow and graceful like a ballerina.

When she stood back up, she just stared at me, my turn to smile. Fuck, I wanna do her right now on her desk.

Janice said, "There is an undisclosed fee for me to rush the paperwork."

All right, here we go! I bet she will say I have to service her.

I stood up, put my hand on my belt buckle, raised my one eyebrow and asked what the fee would be.

She smiled, put her hand on the top of her blouse and said one hundred dollars, cash up front.

What a perfect cock tease; I reached into my front pocket, and she watched my hand go in, I purposely readjusted my cock before I pulled out a wad of cash.

Her eyes followed my every move, there was so much sexual tension in the room. I have never done anyone close to her age, never even thought about it. And yet right now, that is all I can think about.

I pulled out the cash and peeled off five twenty-dollar bills, then I asked if there is anything else she needs from me.

"For now, just need you to return these papers to me filled out properly."

She handed me the papers with her left hand. I noticed she had a decent size rock on her wedding finger.

Fuck it, time to take this up a notch. "Nice rock, happily married?"

This actually made her blush. She then smiled and walked towards her door, she opened it and told me to have a nice day. I smiled and told her to have a wonderful day also.

Think I will be asking Basil about the dirt on her, man would love to fuck that ass of hers.

I decided to treat myself to a steak and lobster dinner at

Martin's. Sometimes you just have to do that.

As I was eating my steak and chewing away, I realized my life is pretty good right now. All things considered.

Went home and waited for Basil to show up. I found myself pacing, not sure why. Just going to talk business.

He showed up at eight, right on the money. He came up, I told him how much for the dope, all together and individually. I told him the only wiggle room was with the weed as that came from me. But he would have to buy at least ten pounds.

Basil looked at me, shook out his hand and said deal. He asked when he could get it.

I said I need at least an hour. He said he was taking his wife out to dinner with another couple, then drinks.

I reminded him that I will not give him the dope with others around, it had to be him and him only.

He said yes, he remembered my rules and that was not a problem.

Pulled out his wallet and gave me the cash up front. He also said if for some reason he doesn't make it back tonight, can he slide by tomorrow around nine, as he and the Mrs. have church at ten.

I told him that was cool, but she too must stay down in the car.

Fuck, Basil's wife Lynn was a former porn actress. I am sure after confession time; the priest has to go and jerk off.

As soon as he left, I called Steve, said the code word, and waited for him.

The whole time while waiting for him, I am more than wearing out my hardwood floors. Watching every car and person that went up the street. Just in case, I stuck a 9MM down my waist band. I watched Steve and Rick pull up in one of their older souped-up cars. Watched to see any movement out the window before going down and answering the door.

9

The boys came up and took all the different dopes out of a gym bag and put them on my kitchen table.

I picked up each baggie containing a specific dope and had a visual look. I had my scales all set up and I started to weigh each bag.

I said to Steve, "Nothing personal, I just don't want any misunderstandings."

He said he would do the same.

Now, it has been a real long time since a shiver went up my spine and a cold evil shadow was cast upon me. But as soon as I picked up the baggie containing the heroin, that is exactly what happened.

I lost myself while staring at the contents. *Evil, pure fucking evil* were the only thoughts that came to mind. I flashed back to seeing Lucy's lifeless body lying on the couch with a syringe sticking out of her arm.

I had to drop the package, Steve asked if everything was all right with the smack. I just nodded my head yes.

Pulled out the cash, thanked him and asked if they wanted a beer. Both said thanks, but they had shit to do.

After they left, I was like a cat on a hot tin roof. Not worried about the cops or someone kicking in the door and coming to rob me. The fucking heroin was starting to call me. I heard each minute of the clock ticking, and that dragon on my back was starting to shoot fire, fire that only a syringe full of that sweet heroin could put out. I have the syringes for the juice, maybe one small crank. I can hit the one vein in my calf, no one would ever know. Yeah, perfect spot.

For the next hour or so, the demons inside my brain were fighting with each other as to shoot up or not.
Lord knows where the fuck Basil is. So, I decided to make a call. To my grandfather. I really needed to hear his voice. He slays all my demons.

No way will I tell him about me having heroin in the house. Just wanted to tell him that I talked to Rachel, and it looks like Christmas at his house will be a go. He was so happy, his joy made me strong once again.

Ten minutes later, Basil was at my door, alone as I asked. I gave him a paper bag containing his grocery list, that alone was kind of ironic. He thanked me and said he would be in touch.

Time to jump in the shower, have to say I was drenched from my little addiction battle. Glad I won this round, I also made almost a grand in profit.

As I lay in bed that night, I was replaying just how weak I almost became.

Makes me wonder will I have that battle every time I am around heroin.

Did a quick calculation of profit off the smack and I think from now on, I am not going to be put in a vulnerable position. Maybe I can line up a middleman for Basil when it comes to smack.

I fucking tossed and turned all night. Woke up tired, no more moving smack. Not worth losing everything all over again.
***

That morning I jumped on the bike and where do you think I headed? To the graveyard of course. Saw Mom, Pam, and Jake. Then I did a labored walk over to Lucy's tombstone. It felt as if I was bound with thick heavy chains.

I sat down, looked up at the bright sky, shook my head, teared up and said I was sorry. Stayed there for about twenty minutes. Still dragging my ass, the whole way back to my bike.

Fuck this, I am heading home, going to smoke a joint. Pass out, get up and drop my license papers off at Barone's office then I really need to get fucked, big time. Think I will stop by Electric Ladyland and give Mike some deer meat in exchange for one of his strippers.

I struggled to walk to the top of the stairs at my apartment. Once I opened the door, I headed straight for my stash of weed. Grabbed a handful and went into the living room with it and a pack of rolling papers.

Like a Cuban rolling the perfect cigar, I had that joint tight as could be.

I picked up the lighter to spark up when the phone rang. I bet you it is Mindy, yeah, she is supposed to be home today.

Suddenly I had energy, I sprung up out of my seat much like my cock wanted to spring out of my pants and into any body part of Mindy's.

"Hello," was my answer with a seductive tone.

"What the fuck? Is that you, lad? Listen. get down to the bar right now," said a very intense Joseph.

I slowly exhaled, said fuck all, and shook my head.

"Mitchell, are you daft? Did you hear what I said?"

"Yeah, I heard you loud and clear, on my way."

He sounded anxious, not sure what is going on. So, I packed a couple handguns, my Fairburn Sykes knife in my boot. Jumped in the Mustang and headed right over.

As I walked in not sure what to expect. Sandra told me Joseph is in the back with Donnie waiting for me. I asked what was so urgent.

Donnie said, "Glickman is staying in Church Hill Montana. I have the address here. He gave payroll his info so they can give him his final pay by courier. They get paid after every home game. They just played yesterday. So, his final pay will be couriered out in the next day or two."

Joseph said, "I talked to Oscar about flying you two up there, but his jet isn't legal yet to fly. He checked the maps of all airports and just outside Church Hill is an airport in Bozeman. He said daily flights from Montana. You can rent a car, head to Glickman, get my money and rings, and then head back. Sounds like an easy peasy trip to me, boys."

I looked at Donnie who started to laugh at Joseph's statement.

"Easy peasy would be him sitting on a bar stool out front when we go to leave."

"I have total confidence in you boys. Anyways, do your best. Get as much of my money as you can. If he is broke, kill him and take his rings."

Joseph then reached in his wallet and gave us a wad of cash for flights and a car rental. The only thing he ever asks for is travel expense receipts.

Joseph also said he would have Sean Quinn pick us up and drive us to the airport.

I raced home. Grabbed a couple joints, raced to drop off the application licenses at Barone's office. His Mom acting like the true pit bull; growled and said one minute.

Teddy came right out all smiles and called me into his office.

He couldn't care less about the applications; it was the weed he really wanted.

I handed him both and he was so thankful. He promised to call me once he had completed everything.

As I left, I blew his mom a kiss, I think I broke the old broad's face as she smiled, yeah not the exact response I thought I was going to get.

Raced back home and got packed. Two 9MM handguns, eight clips, my knife, of course, and gloves. And yes, the legendary Willie Hertz phony I.D and credit cards that go with it.

I finished that monster joint I rolled up. Downed a couple quick beers and before I knew it, Sean was honking his horn.

Donnie was in the front seat, so I jumped in the back. I had a nice buzz and with Sean not being the talkative type, that was perfect.

"Nice eyes, Strongbow," he said sarcastically. Donnie looked at my slits for eyes and told me to wear sunglasses in the airport.

For the rest of the ride no one said anything. I really wanted to ask how Nyah is doing, but I don't want any bad ju-ju. When I fly, I need all the help I can get.

We got past the security screening; Paul better step up sooner than later. With all these planes being hijacked, maybe the passengers would appreciate that Donnie and I are armed and ready to get into a firefight.

This trip was not a direct flight. As soon as we took off and leveled off, I passed right out cold. Donnie had to shake me to tell me we were starting to descend. Had no clue what he was talking about at first.

We had a three-hour layover before we had to jump into a twin prop DC 3.

Spent my fair share of time bumping around the not so friendly skies while in the army. Just a local run airline. A few of the locals said we should bring our own beer as the pilots are always drinking. Once again, just like in the Army.

Donnie told me *don't even think about it*. He said time is of the essence. We really need to catch an unsuspecting Glickman.
'   "Mitch, this guy has won two super bowls. He comes from some unknown butt fuck town. He will be like a God to these people. They will protect him. I will call his parents' house as soon as we land. Tell him we have a delivery he needs to sign for from the 49ers. He will answer the door all happy. Element of surprise will be the key to our success."

I completely agreed with Donnie, we will be doing a blindside blitz. One thing bothered me though, "And what if his parents are home?"

"Unless they act up, they don't deserve to die. Their kid is a fuck up. Not them. After we rent a car, we need to hit the hardware store. Duct tape, rope, gloves, shovel, small bolt cutters, vinegar, and lime if need be."

Those are our standard tools we always take with us, can't really bring them on a plane and not draw a lot of attention.

The second flight was uneventful and as soon as we landed, we rented a car with our phony I.D.

Then, we headed to a local hardware store where we picked up all our tools of the trade. Donnie also suggested we also pick up some ball caps as Zack knows what we both look like. We got a local map and off we went to a quiet coffee shop for lunch and to also go over the map. Never go into battle without knowing the terrain and how to sneak out of town or make the mad dash out of town if need be.

Zack lives with his parents outside of town. I honestly believe that will work better for us, especially if shit goes south.

The less witnesses the better.

Donnie asked if I was ready, I said sure, make the call.

"Mr. Glickman, my name is Timmy Tucker from Federal Express. Sir, I have a package that needs your signature. Are you going to be home today?"

Donnie smiled, gave me the thumbs up. Told Zack he would be by shortly.

Because of Glickman giving me shots while I wrestled on the ground with Burns, I asked if he minded if I hand delivered the so-called package.

Donnie said go for it, speed will be the key.

I dropped Donnie off about thirty yards from the house. I pulled into the driveway. Put on my ball cap and sunglasses. Made sure to exit the car with an empty envelope, and a whole lot of payback.

I kept my head looking down as I approached the front door. Donnie snuck up to the side of the house. I took a deep breath, rang the doorbell, and was ready for whoever answered the door.

My hearing was magnified as I heard heavy footsteps approach the door. I pulled out my handgun and had it in the same hand as the envelope.

The door slowly opened.

I heard a young voice say, "I have been waiting for this," all giddy.

It was none other than Zack Glickman. I kicked him in the nuts and knocked him to the ground. He looked up in a state of disbelief as I had a fully loaded handgun pointed at his head.

Donnie now came in, closed the door behind him, and asked if there was anyone else in the house.

At first, Zack wasn't sure how to respond, Donnie was pissed and said, "Let me know right now. Yes, or no? I will go room to room and kill anyone I find."

He at first just shook his head no.

"I don't fucking hear you, yes, or no?"

"I am home alone."

"Mitch, keep that gun on him while I sweep the house, your folks will die if you are lying".

Glickman just put his head on the floor, closed his eyes and shook his head no.

After Donnie strolled back, he told me the house was clear.

"Do you know why we are here, Glickman?"

He nodded his head yes. This pissed off Donnie as he now kicked him really hard in the ribs.

"What the fuck is wrong with your voice? I asked you a fucking question, I expect a verbal response."

"I owe people money," he said.

"You owe Joseph O'Reilly money. I don't give a fuck who else you owe money to. Now, where is my boss's money?"

He started to tear up on the floor, my turn for a rib kick.

"Unless those are tears of gold, I suggest you stop it right now. Where the fuck is our boss's money, asshole?"

"I don't have it, but I have a tryout contract with the Lions. They will sign me as soon as I pass my medical, and I will give Joseph my signing bonus cash. And then I will have him paid off by season's end."

I looked at Donnie and raised my eyebrows. Now what?

"How do we know you are not bullshitting us?"

"On the kitchen table is a letter from the Lions; their center is out for the year with a knee injury. I know I will make the team, as long as you guys don't break a rib." He said in a pissed off tone. Donnie told me to go and look for this letter. I found it and started to read it.

Everything he said was true. I showed Donnie the letter. He read it. He looked at our helpless ball player, flared his nostrils, and rubbed his chin as he was deep in thought.

Finally, Donnie said to him, "So here is the deal, and this one is non-negotiable. I want both of your Super Bowl rings for collateral. You will have to pay interest to the Leprechaun. You miss a payment, and it won't only be your life taken, it will be your folks' lives as well." said a stern Donnie who walked over and picked up a five by seven picture of his parents.

"We have associates in Detroit. You will pay them after every home game. You miss one payment and disappear, then Mitchell and I will make your parents pay with their lives. And it will be a painfully slow death. Then my Paper Lion, we will hunt you down and Mitch will skin you alive. Understood?"

Not only tears this time, but full out crying like a hungry

baby looking for his Momma's tits.

Donnie had enough.

"Mitch this fucker doesn't respect you, me, or the Leprechaun. Put a bullet in his head, then put him in the car. Then it will be mom and dad's turn."

He burst out, "O.K, O.K I agree!"

"Rings, give me the rings right now."

He wiped away the tears at first then started to take his rings off. His hands were trembling as he was pulling as hard as he could to take them off.

After a couple minutes he handed me the rings, there was pieces of flesh and blood dripping from them.

Donnie reminded him if he calls the cops, others working for Joseph will make sure the job is complete.

"You won't even hear the shot, or maybe the house will be burnt to the ground with all of you trapped inside."

Once again, he closed his eyes and just bawled on the ground as we left with the jewels and the picture of his parents.

As we got into the car, Donnie told me to head to the airport.

I asked if he thinks we will be coming back and killing the lot of them.

"Gamblers are no different than drunks or dope fiends, guess we will soon find out what means more to him."

We both kept looking in the rear view mirror the whole ride back to the airport.

No sign of the coppers and lucky for us we were able to catch a pair of flights home. Called Joseph as soon as we landed to pick us up at the airport.

He and Quinn showed up within twenty minutes. He asked how it went. Told him about the tryout contract and Donnie passed him the rings which he cleaned off on the plane.

He was happy, thanked us and gave us each five hundred bucks and then dropped us off.

It was just after one A.M., and I was bagged tired. Been a really long day.

I struggled to make it up the stairs. I checked the answering machine as I have the big gun deal going down. Nothing from him, but Mindy called and said her husband is out of town for the next couple days and she is really horny and needs me to be inside of her.

This made both heads smile. I called her and after five rings a groggy Mindy answered the phone.

"Hey baby, sorry. Just got in. So, you are horny. I think I can help you with this infliction."

"Where you out playing with dirty whores?"

Not sure if she was serious or joking around.

"Can't say I was, out of town on business actually."

There were a couple seconds of dead air. Once again, not sure if she is pissed, or has passed out on me.

"You there, baby?"

I heard her take a deep inhale, and then said she loved me and will talk tomorrow.

Then the phone hung up. Has today been so long that I am totally brain fucking dead. I looked at the phone receiver, shook my head and hung up the phone.

I stood there and just stared at the phone and waited for it to call back.

After a couple minutes I said fuck it, I really need a solid sleep. Took the receiver off the hook and headed to bed.

I dropped my clothes like a fireman, right on the floor beside my bed.

Barely remember crawling under the covers. And then I was down for the count. I know I slept hard and was deep in thought in my dreams.

I was woken by the doorbell ringing. I came out of my slumber drenched in sweat.

My gut flipped as I feared Glickman ratted us out to the cops. Then I heard a female yelling, *wake up, Strongbow*. Pretty sure it was Mindy.

I looked down below through the window and sure as fuck it was her. And she was not empty handed. She had something in a paper bag and a tray of coffee.

I answered the door naked which made her giggle as she smiled like a teen seeing a cock for the first time.

"Strongbow, I love that cock of yours!" Said Mindy now staring at my morning wood.

I gave her a kiss and said my cock really missed her.

We went upstairs and Mindy pulled out a couple bagels with cream cheese.

I didn't bother to put some clothes on as we ate, you know the clothes would be taken off right afterwards.

She sat beside me as we ate, she was almost done her bagel when she ran her index finger along the bagel and had cream cheese on that finger. She smiled rather seductively and put it on the head of my cock.

She went, "Oops, guess I better lick it off."

Next thing you know she is on her knees on the ground right in front of me. Her eyes look so serious as she opens her mouth and looks up at you. I mouth *awe fuck* this feels amazing as Mindy is sucking and stroking me hard.

She also taking turns playing with and sucking my balls as she strokes me. She is amazing and after about fifteen beautiful minutes I let her know I am ready to cum, she speeds up her strokes and opens her mouth wide.

Can't hold back and I shoot a full thick hot and steamy monster load right down her throat. The head of my cock is so sensitive, and she is doing swirls with her tongue to make sure the last drop of cum finds its way to her belly.

"Perfect breakfast protein," said a grinning Mindy smiling and proud of her accomplishments.

"You rock me like no other, baby. Fuck that was amazing."

She smiled and said, "I really hope there is no one else rocking you. It would bother me."

Fuck, Donnie was right. Time to see what exactly is going on.

"But you have a husband. Are you saying that you two never have sex? Pretty sure he is rocking you."

She smiled a goofy smile, nodded her head yes. "I hate when him and I have sex, my only way to enjoy it is to think of you. Mitch, I swear, my marriage is more of a business relationship. There is no love for him."

She took a deep breath, put her head down for a second and when her head came up for air, she was crying. She looked me in the eye and said she loves me.

My ice-cold heart was indeed warmed by her kind words, but I had a hell of a lot of scars, Still haven't totally healed from

Charlene, Lucy overdosing will always haunt me, and Natasha, still fucking stings almost eight years later.

So, I didn't want to tell her something for the sake of comforting her. She truly does mean a lot to me, I don't know if I love her or not, so why say those three powerful words. I just hugged her and said I am here for her.

"Know what cheers me up, hon?"

She smiled and shrugged her shoulders.

"Well, if you don't have plans, a long motorcycle ride along the coast. I know this really nice restaurant in Santa Barbara. What do you think?"

"If it means spending the whole day with you, that would make me so happy, yes! Yes, Mitch. Let's do it."

I said I just need to take a shower then off we go. I asked if she wanted to join me. She passed and said she has not carried any makeup with her.

I kissed her and said she was beautiful with or without makeup.

Tears were all gone now. I do care about her, and right now, if taking her for a ride, dinner, and coming back here and spending the night fucking our brains out makes her happy in that miserable life, why not?

Mindy dried off my back, and balls. I then got dressed and asked if she was ready. She came in and gave me a long French kiss and said yes.

We went outside, put on our sunglasses. I fired up the bike and told her to jump on, and off we went.

She held me really tight, DDs and all.

The ride down was outstanding. Nothing better than the open road, sun beating down on your face, and the ocean view.

Every once in a while, I would kick it down and Mindy said nothing at all.

We pulled into the restaurant, and I parked right in front. Nothing sexier than seeing a hot chick get off the back of my bike all smiles and slightly embarrassed as she is readjusting her underwear.

We chose a seat on the patio overlooking the ocean. We finished our beer right away, and as we were waiting for our next round of drinks and our lunch, Mindy spent a lot of time just looking deeply into the ocean.

Normally, I would be pissed and tell my date *hello I am sitting right here* but I know she is really deep in thought. She would look over at me, smile, then go back deep into thought.

Once our meals came, and I gave her a wink, she blushed and said thanks.

We talked about hunt camp, and what I have planned this coming week. I told her I have some friends from out of town dropping by, then I am taking off for a bit.

She smiled and asked if this was hush-hush kind of business. I smiled back and said yes.

I then asked what she is doing. Her eyes went big, and she started to cry. She kept saying she was sorry. I reached out and held her hands, I just said sorry.

She pushed away her barely touched meal and said, "Sometimes I wish Marvin would fall down a flight of stairs or have a heart attack and die. He is smothering me to death. He is so insecure. He asked me all kinds of questions about you."

My back went up and I asked what kind of questions.

"He wanted to know how well I knew you. I said I saw you hanging around Basil. He pinned me against the wall and called me a lying whore. He said he saw the security video of you coming into our building."

My back went up as I clenched my jaw. "Did he fucking hit you?"

More tears as her trembling hand went over her mouth. She then nodded her head yes.

My heart was now starting to pump, and I felt the veins in my arms pop out as if I am getting ready for battle.

"Where did he hit you?"

"He took his belt off and started to whack me with it. I fucking hate him so much."

Her tears were now gone, her face was red with anger. "He forgets that I have friends or make that ex-friends in Vegas that would break his neck and throw him down a flight of stairs. But I am really trying to stay away from them."

My curiosity was now raised. "And who are...or were your friends in Vegas?"

"I used to dance at a club owned by Louis Falcone. He is in

the D'Angelo crime family. I think he was like a Captain or whatever you call them."

Interesting, very interesting.

"I am not sure how they have their shit setup." I sort of know listening to Albert and Sam talk in the pen. But I really don't want Mindy to know all about my other life, my hard core dirty criminal life.

She never finished her meal. I ate most of mine, we had a couple more drinks and as we went to leave, I noticed this car in the parking lot.

A dark colored 1974 Dodge Monaco sedan with all windows blacked out.

Yeah, the hair on my neck went up, something wasn't right. I fired up the bike, told Mindy to get on. I gave the vehicle one last look over, before I put the bike in gear and headed back to San Fran.

Every couple of miles I would check my rear view for this car. Sure as fuck, I would catch the odd glimpse then it would be gone.

Funny, I take her away to wind down and feel good, and now I am the one that is high strung. Not sure if it is a Fed, local cops, or even a private investigator keeping an eye on Mindy.

I had to stop for gas, while filling up my tank, one eye on the hose and one eye on the highway.

Then as soon as we pulled into my place, I closed the gate. We headed upstairs and I kept looking out the window. Mindy asked if everything was all right.

I told her I just had an off vibe.

She now said it was her turn to help me relax. I smiled at her as she walked towards my record collection. She pulled out a Tommy James and the Shondells album *"Crimson and Clover"*. She winked, put the needle on the album and as soon as the first note started to play, she started to dance and strip for me.

She knew how to shake her money maker, that is for sure. Totally teased me and within a minute, I was rock hard. She was rubbing her boobs in my face, grinding her ass into my crotch region.

Eventually she gets on her knees and pulls my throbbing cock out of my pants. She then sits down facing me and rides me while I suck and bite her boobs.

Mindy tells me to spank her ass hard, the rougher I get with her, the wetter I feel her getting. I am now grabbing her ass cheeks super hard as she starts to cum.

She hasn't even caught her breath when I pick her up and throw her on the couch. I need to see those big tits of hers moving around. I mount her missionary style and start to pound her hard. I throw all my weight into her.

We both turn into animals as she digs her nails into my ass cheeks, and I now stick a couple fingers into her pussy with one hand and two fingers into her ass with my other hand. She is moaning and squirming. We both have the most intense eye contact with each other the whole time.

Time to fuck her ass just as hard. I pull my cock out of her pussy. Tell her to get into dogs. Without hesitation she does as instructed and tells me to hurt her.

I ram my cock right into her ass that is now soaked from her pussy juices.

She screams and yells *harder, faster*. I taking turns slapping her ass and pulling her hair.

I also realize that she is also playing with her pussy as I am fucking her ass.

This is such a turn on I can't hold back. The head of my cock is so fucking sensitive that as I start to cum, I shoot one of the biggest loads of my life. Mindy is now shaking her ass making my quivering and pulsating head even more sensitive. My thighs are covered in my own cum. That is how much I shot.

If I was ever to have a heart attack, it would be now. It truly feels as if it will pound right of my chest.

I collapse on top of her. She too is breathing just as hard as me.

She then lets out a sigh and says that was amazing. I can't even talk. I just grunted, "Yep."

It took about ten minutes or so till I got my wind and strength back.

Mindy said she wanted to give me a full body wash in the shower seeing at how I was such an amazing lover.

I said I needed a beer first. She sprang up out of bed and got us each a beer.

She handed me mine; she clanked both bottle necks together and said, "To amazing lovers, and even better business partners."

She had an unusual smile, kissed me. I said cheers and swigged the beer empty in one gulp.

Shower was amazing. She lathered up and washed every inch of my body.

Of course, I did the same to her. By the time we were done she looked deep in my eyes and asked me to carry her back to bed and fuck her hard again.

My legs were like jelly, but I did as she requested.

By the time I finally blew my load on her boobs, yes, her demand, I collapsed once again.

Mindy said she needed to clean up the mess, but before doing so brought me in another beer.

As she crawled back into bed all clean, she curled right into me.

We talked for a bit about how good we were as lovers. She said no one can make her have multiple orgasms like I can.

After a couple minutes, she looked at me and asked if anyone came to mind about killing her husband.

I have never done a personal contract kill. Will need Donnie's advice on this one.

"I can talk to people. Leave it with me. No talk about this over the phone."

Her face lit up and she gave me a long kiss and then said, "Once he is gone. We can have nights like tonight all the time, and all over the world Mitch. I want you to fuck me in every single country on the map."

She was ecstatic, but I had a bit of a nervous vibe. Was Mindy manipulating me through sex, to convince me to kill her husband?

Anyone can say the "L" word. Makes me wonder if this is how she got her husband to rescue her from a life of stripping, lots of hard-core sex, and saying the "L" word.

Between all the sex, and paranoia weighing heavy on my brain, shit, I don't even remember fallen sleep. Crashed really hard. I truly needed my rest; this chick is killing me. So, when the phone rang at 04:30 I wasn't sure if it was in my dream or not. Not even

Joseph would call me at this insane hour. Must be a dream.

I no sooner started to fall back to sleep when the phone rang again. This time the answering machine picked it up.

I looked at Mindy who was snoring away and thought, *do I get up or not?*

Rachel. I wonder if something is wrong with Rachel. I dragged my tired ass out of bed and into the living room to hear the message.

My legs were still jelly like as I staggered to the answering machine.

Fuck me, it was Mad Bill McDowell. He flew out today. He gave me his flight number and what time it lands at. Stupid bastard, never did say if it was California or New York time. I looked at my watch and headed back to bed. This time with the receiver off the hook.

I hung a quick whiz, then headed back to sleeping beauty. Sleeping spread eagle and still snoring. I stared at her for a couple minutes, wondering exactly what is in her head and soul before crawling back into bed and off to dreamland.

Some five hours later I was woken up by some fool ringing the doorbell.

And I know exactly who that fool is. I told Mindy to stay in bed.

I threw on my pants and headed downstairs. Sure, as fuck, it was Mad Bill.

He seemed to be pissed as he came inside.

"Don't you check your phone messages?"

"Oh, I got your message," I snarled back at him.

"Then why the fuck didn't you get me at the airport?"

"You gave me a time, too fucking bad it was New York, and not California time."

He then had that vacant look on his face as he looked down at his watch.

I told him to come up and that I have a friend in my bedroom, so mums the word.

By the time we got upstairs Mindy had made her way to the bathroom as I heard the shower now running.

Bill started to talk about Kevin flying in later tonight. I told him to hang on.

I got up to make sure she was indeed in the shower. Once I saw her behind the shower curtain, I came and sat back down.

"You becoming paranoid, Mitch?"

"Better safe than sorry. She is a civilian, I know you are solid, who knows if she is."

He nodded his head in approval.

"It appears Kevin's flight comes in tonight at 21:00. The boat is arriving tomorrow around midnight. Kevin is showing up with some other ex-SOG soldier."

I asked who, apparently Kevin never did say.

At least now I have correct times and I can make sure that Oscar knows, as do Steve and Rick.

Mindy eventually came out of the washroom and walked into the bedroom wearing just a towel and a smile.

Bill looked at me and said, "Now that is woman."

"That she is," was my response.

I really didn't want to talk anymore until Mindy had left the apartment.

But I did wake up Oscar and told him to drop by as soon as he could, told him company from the North just dropped by.

Twenty minutes later, a fully dressed Mindy exited the bedroom.

She came into the living room glowing and looking like a million bucks.

I did the introductions, but first names only.

She asked when she would hear from me next. I told her a couple days at least.

She gave me a long hug and kiss goodbye. When we broke free Mindy reminded me about her business deal involving her husband. I told her I have been thinking about it since our conversation last night.

Huge smile came to her face. I gave her a slap on the ass and off she went.

I didn't go back up to my apartment. I went inside Pamdora's to see if a certain car that was following us yesterday reappeared. My view was excellent as I saw the street perfectly. Sure, as fuck Mindy was not even a stoplight away when it appeared. It reminded me of a shark just swimming around and looking for its prey.

Janine had a confused look on her face and asked if everything was all right.

I just smiled, said she was doing an outstanding job, wished her a good day, and headed back upstairs.

This matter must be dealt with sooner than later. He is not a cop or Fed, he is a P.I. hired by her husband.

When I came upstairs Bill had a grin on his face. I asked what was going on.

"Your friend is wearing quite the rock. Her husband must love her very much. Obviously not as much as she loves him."

"He tries to buy her love, that I know for sure. Anyways, you hungry?"

He said he was, not sure if he eats breakfast or lunch.

"You are in San Fran, eat whatever you want, man."

I made sure to take him to a place where we wouldn't run into Joseph. So, we headed to this Mexican restaurant that has amazing breakfast burritos.

I asked Bill when Kevin wants the items in the air. He said as soon as they are off the ship. I asked where are we flying them to?

At first, he just raised an eyebrow and smiled, pissed me right off.

"If you guys thought I wasn't solid, you wouldn't have me involved. I want to know where the fuck I am going in case all hell breaks loose when we land. I guess you are not going to tell Oscar also?"

"We are flying to Westchester County Airport. Just outside New York. You don't need to know who the guns are for. Satisfied now?"

"Yep, now you asked me to have extra muscle on the docks and up until the plane is loaded. Do they need to come with us?"

"Not this trip. I know the people waiting for us. They are all solid except this one fucking dick. Angry John Ciccone."

"What is the deal with him?"

"When I was a cop, I busted him for holding up a liquor store. He did a deuce for it. So, zero love between us."

"Are you expecting him to start anything?"

"He shouldn't. He is lucky to be a foot soldier for these guys. He was rising through the ranks with them, but his temper made him a heat score. If that temper is raised with us, we will show no mercy and kill the fuck."

After our bellies were full, we headed back to my place. Once Oscar showed up, I told the boys to make themselves at home as I have running around to do.

I headed to Donnie's shop, now that I knew the exact time. I would need Steve and Rick too. Kind of hoping now that Donnie comes along, at least for the first boatload, his leadership and parts truck will help us.

All the boys were working on bikes. I wanted to talk to Donnie first.

"I need Steve and Rick tomorrow night for that job. Thinking about it, I could use you there also."

He raised an eyebrow, smiled, and asked about the job, and no details left out.

"Shipments of weapons coming in from Asia. Guys I served in SOG with, it appears Cambodia is fallen apart. My contact over there is sending over crates of weapons before they fall into the Khmer's greedy and bloody hands. There is a boat coming in tomorrow night around midnight. We unload our cargo. Drive it to one of Oscar's private airports. Put the crates on the plane and I cut you all free."

"Will there be anyone you don't know personally there?"

"Other than another SOG guy, but I might know him, no."

"What type of weapons?"

"If I knew exactly, I would be lying. I assume you might be interested in buying some?"

"You never know when a war is going to pop up. Been kind of quiet, too quiet."

Donnie went deep into thought. He looked up me a couple times, then back to deep thinking.

"I am in, on one condition."

"And what condition would that be?"

"I want to meet all of those involved."

I know one of the main reasons I want Donnie and his knowledge of the docks and connections that work there. Last time I was involved with any deal at the docks, Jake and I got popped. Mom and Pam were killed as a result, Jake was murdered in San Quentin, So yeah, some really shitty memories, and even worse results.

I stuck out my hand to shake Donnie's hand and seal the deal. Promised him that I will talk to Stokes tonight, if I say drop by for a beer, he should drop by.

That is one knot in my gut gone. Second is that car, the private dick following around Mindy. I think I am going to set him up. Have Mindy over, have the boys sneak up on him. Pull him out of the car, some interrogating, then give the guy the beating of his life.

I came back to the apartment, told the boys that the muscle and vehicle is set.

Also said the one guy is interested in buying some weapons.

Mad Bill was pissed.

"This is to be kept on the hush hush! How well do you know this guy? How do you know he won't rat us out?"

I looked at Oscar and said it was Donnie. He started to laugh and told Mad Bill this guy is solid and scary.

"Who is this solid and scary guy you two laugh about?"

"Donnie Terek, vice president of the Oakland Hell Hounds. He also works alongside us for Joseph O'Reilly. I think that is pretty solid. He has people working the docks."

His face remained red when he said, "No more surprises, hear me? Both of you."

We both agreed.

I said I really don't want to hang around here. Let's go and shoot some pool and check out the strippers.
Titties and beer, Oscar was in. Bill said fine, but we are not getting fucked up.

So, we jumped in my Mustang and headed to Electric Ladyland.

***

Vito the doorman shook my hand and asked how Hunt Camp was. I said great, I have some meat for him, and asked if the boss was around.

He said yes but is in the back with others.

I know better than to ask about others. So, I told him when he gets a chance, let him know that I am here. He said he would. Then Vito escorted us right to pervert's row.

We watched a couple shows and shot some pool when Mike Battaglia made his way out of the back. He was not alone. These real greasy looking fucks in suits came out with him. I didn't know any of them.

As soon as the unknowns headed to the VIP room, Vito approached Mike and pointed out exactly where I was.

Mike came over and gave me a big hug, he heard I had been looking for him and apologized for not being around.

He shook Oscar's hand. Then he and Mad Bill just looked at each other.

"Who is your friend, Mitch? He looks familiar."

Yeah, for whatever reason, no love lost between these two.

"Mad Bill, Mike Battaglia. Both of you would have been in Nam around the same time I believe. Bill was Special Ops."

For whatever reason, neither man stuck out their hand in a gesture of friendship. Can Mike pick up that Bill was a cop? Can Bill pick up what Mike does for a living?

After about a minute of awkwardness, Mike turned to me and asked if I had a package from South Dakota for him and his dad.

"That I do; when can you drop it by?"

"Let's go to your place right now and I will grab it. I will make sure your boys are taken care of."

Bill chalked up his cue and said nothing, Oscar said he wants a private dance with Marie Claire. Mike told Vito to take care of Oscar.

Deep down I think there is something else going on. I hope it has nothing to do with Mad Bill. Especially seeing it was just him and I going to my place, no muscle.

We just pulled out of the parking lot when Mike asked if I was interested in a job.

"What kind of job exactly?"

"I need some people in Montreal taken care of. And I need people that no one else knows specifically, to do the job. I would bring Donnie with you. We need to hit these fucks fast. And it won't be pop pop kills. I need these guys to disappear. Now, here is the ironic part, Mitch. They are fucking around with cash from the building of the Olympic venue there. So much money to be made, and these fucking Calabrian cocksuckers are getting greedy. I want their bodies to be buried in cement in the venue itself."

"Montreal, pretty far away. Will we have solid contacts to help us? Fuck I don't know any French at all. Never been to Canada."

"Don't worry about that. My cousin Bruno will be your contact. What works for you, Mitch?"

"I will talk to Donnie. I am tied up for the next couple days. As soon as I am done, I am good to go. How much for the job by the way?"

"Each soldier I will give you g-note. Martone is the main target, ten grand for him, Bova is his under boss, five grand for him."

I started to think about me being near New York city and asked how far Westchester New York was is from Montreal.

"About six hours. Why? You heading that way?"

"Yeah, will be there Thursday at some point, making a delivery. Would be silly to fly back to California. Can your cousin pick us up there? We can do the nasty deed and fly right from Montreal to home, make sense?"

I find, for whatever reason, when Italians get deep in thought, a hand goes to their chin, and their lower lip sticks out.

"That would be perfect. Sneaking right into the city. No RCMP or Martone's goons at the airports looking for any threats. So smart, Mitchell. When we get back, I will introduce you to Bruno."

I was right, there were sleazy fucks, and I get to meet at least one of them.

Mike stayed in the car as I went up and grabbed the meat for him, his dad, and a package for Vito.

Then back to the club we headed.

Once inside, Mike headed to the kitchen to put the meat back in the freezer.

Then he told me to follow him. I told my guys to give me five. Bill just shook his head.

Fucks sake's, man! You're in a strip club and the owner just sent over a tray of drinks and two dancers, chill out.

Mike and I went into the VIP room and introduced me to this big stocky guy. Dark eyes, real dark eyes.

"Mitchell Strongbow, this is my cousin Bruno Fratoni."

He stuck out his hand and said it was good to meet me. I said the same back.

Mike told Bruno that I will be the exterminator coming to Montreal. His smile was huge, and he said good. Said he was looking forward to working with me.

I told him I will need a ride from Westchester to Montreal, and could he arrange it.

"For you my friend, not a problem. Will you be coming alone?"

"No, my partner in crime will also be coming."

He gave me his number. Said once I am in Westchester to let him know and he will have one of his men come for us. I said good.

Mike told him I am a lethal assassin.

Those dark eyes of his got almost as big as his smile. "Oh, I have heard all about you." Then he started to laugh. "It will be an honor to have you in my city. Whatever you and your partner need, you just ask away."

I thanked him; said I would be in touch. I then went back to see my guys.

Both have dancers in front of them, I told them to drink up.

"For fuck sakes, Strongbow! I am finally starting to enjoy myself, why do we have to drink up?" said an irate Mad Bill.
I looked at my watch, then said, "We have company to pick up."

Bill looked down at his watch.

No way were five people with luggage going to fit in my car. So, we drove back to my place and Oscar also grabbed his vehicle. Then we headed to the airport.

Bill drove with me and asked what was going on with the all the Guiney's.

"Just business. After we do the drop off in New York, Donnie and I will be staying behind." Bill didn't say anything, he just nodded his head yes.

Oscar met us inside where the main flight board is. I asked Bill where they are flying in from. He said Hong Kong. We saw the flight number and it was scheduled to arrive on time. That is a good sign.

The three of us sat and watched the sign now say arrived and headed to the exact gate for the passengers to exit.

One by one, we saw the passengers come out, then the good Captain, Kevin Stokes exited. He still had this glow about him that he possessed back in Southeast Asia. And fuck me, right behind him was Calvin "Crash" Robinson with his flaming, and now long red hair, gnawing on some chewing tobacco.

Holy fuck, he lives. Lucy and I stayed at his sisters when we were on the run, she thought he was dead. Wow, totally blown away seeing him. The ghost lives.

Calvin was always one of those scrawny wired-up guys. Fearless to say the least. When he landed in Nam, they made him a tunnel rat at first. If Charlie was down there hiding, Calvin would head below the surface, find them, kill the non-coms, and drag out the officers for interrogation.

I went over and hugged Kevin and said he still looks like he is not old enough to drink.

Now, I first met Kevin in Special Ops; he was interrogating prisoners we captured. He spoke perfect Vietnamese, Cambodian, Laotian, Chinese, and Russian. The guy is super smart. Graduate of West Point, top five percent of his class.

He was also a scavenger, if we needed something that the army couldn't, or wouldn't get us, he sure as fuck would have it within seventy-two hours. His motto, "Leave it with me."

"Fuck, Strongbow. You are huge, man! Look at the size of you!"

"Eating normal meals and not raw rice and rat meat will do that."

I went in and then gave Calvin a hug. "Brother, have I got a story for you."

"Oh yeah? You have my ear, Strongbow. Spill the beans"

"I met your sister, Uriah." The smile left his face as he shook his head no. That says it all. He doesn't want to hear anymore, have to respect him.

I turned and asked Kevin, now what.

"Well, I have hotel reservations for Calvin and myself at Marvin Towers, you know it?"

I snickered and nodded yes, I know it, one of Mindy's husband's hotels.

"Let us check in. Then, I am dying for a good steakhouse, you know a good one?"

"Yeah, Martin's is the best in town. I am a regular there."

I told Oscar and Bill to go and get us a table at Martin's while I drove Kevin and Calvin to their hotel.

On the drive over, I said one of the guys doing muscle for us is also interested in some weapons.

Kevin asked *guns*? I answered more than likely one or two cases.

This made him smile.

"I said you will meet him tonight if that is cool."

Kevin asked how solid he is.

"I trust him with my life on more than one occasion."

Kevin said that was fine.

As soon as the boys were taken up to their room, I called Donnie and told him to meet us at Martin's. He said that works. The boys put all kinds of stuff in the room safe, then it was off for a business dinner.

It was good knowing all three of us survived the madness of SOG. Kevin and Calvin were both saying how the Khmer Rouge is ripping apart Cambodia. Burning down all the temples, slaughtering tens of thousands of civilians.

They said they were more ruthless than the VC.
I asked about that one temple who nursed me back to health after I was bitten several times by the King Cobra. This is where I met Tamalinda, I know it was him coming to me on the rez.

"Sorry, Strongbow; the walls were painted in blood before they burned it to the ground."

I was pissed and heartbroken. Tamalinda was murdered, as were the rest of the monks. These were peaceful loving people inside of there. They were no threat to anyone. Still not sure how I am supposed to avenge him. Nothing makes sense. I still believe somehow some of Mindy's mushrooms made it into my bloodstream.

We were standing outside waiting for Calvin to finish his cigarette when I could hear an evil roar getting louder, and closer. Sure, as fuck Donnie came around the corner full throttle, loud and proud.

After he parked his bike I did the introductions, I noticed Kevin looking at the Hell Hound stickers on his bike, he just smirked at me.

We came inside and were taken to the table with the rest of the boys.

By the time our stuffed mushrooms and sourdough bread was in our bellies, Donnie and Kevin were shaken hands and had a deal done.

Kevin picked up the tab for all of us, the price of doing business. I asked if he wanted to go to a strip club. Calvin was all in, but Kevin said he was bagged, long flight and he really needed a good night's sleep.

So, I gave them my phone number, said to call me. We can do breakfast. Or lunch if they are really tried.

Before Donnie left, I told him of the deal from Battaglia. Asked if he was interested. He said for the right amount of money he would be.

Once I told him how much we were to be paid, he smiled and said for sure he was in.

Donnie said to keep in touch with times for tomorrow, said I would do just that.

I called the strip club to talk to Mike, I know the phones are all tapped.

"Yeah, it's me, talked to my friend, everything is good. Enjoy the deer meat."

"That is excellent, I will spread the word. And I will think of you as I BBQ up the sausage."

And that was how the conversation went. I am sure whomever is listening in, they will be trying to figure out what the fuck deer sausage really means. Stupid fucking Feds.

After my call, I drove Kevin and Calvin back to their hotel. Then myself, Oscar and Bill went back to my place.

Oscar said he got the phony aviation numbers to fly legit from Paul. Mad Bill told him exactly where we will be landing.

He then broke out maps and started to plot and plan fuel consumption, how many times would we have to refuel and was making sure landing in Westchester was not going to be an issue.

Mad Bill said he just has to call a friend who works in the tower, for a modest fee he will make sure, pardon the pun, we fly under the radar.

On paper everything looked good. I also told Oscar that Donnie and I will be staying in Westchester. He only asked if it was business, I said yeah. If we get in a jam, we will call him.

Oscar had a couple more beers before heading home. I told him to do what he has to do to get the plane ready for tomorrow, he smiled and reminded me it is a jet, not a plane.

Mad Bill and I stayed up a little while longer. As we talked, I was cleaning my rifles, handgun, and patent Fairburn Sykes knife for New York, and yes Montreal.

I was, of course, given a little lecture about the Italians, and their sneaky ways.

He never asked what I was up to, but he knew it was something illegal. He asked if I needed any help. I thanked him for the offer, but Donnie and I should be fine, but if we get into a jackpot, I would call him.

He crashed out in the spare room. He started to snore right away, time to close my door and put on some music.

My brain was racing as my head was on my pillow. I kept seeing Fagan's face, right before I killed him.

I was nervous to be honest; I trusted all that I was going to be doing the deal with, at least down here. Just bad memories. Gun deals caused Jake's life to be cut short.

Eventually I passed out. When I woke up, I was drenched in sweat. Yeah, this is going to be a long twenty-four hours.

I sparked up a joint, then jumped in the shower, I just let the water pound on my uptight neck. Fuck, it felt good.

Bill was still sleeping, so I finished packing my gear for Montreal. Phony ID, I also decided to make up some "Mushroom Bullets" for my rifle. One shot, one kill.

As Bill was dragging his ass out of bed, Kevin asked us to drop by the hotel for breakfast. He also told me to get a hold of Oscar and Donnie. So, I did as instructed. Told Bill he had time for a shower.

Just like the old days with this lot, getting ready for a briefing of an upcoming mission. This time it is over hot chow and yes, the enemy is still very much out there.

The five of us all listened to Kevin explaining how everything was supposed to go tonight.

Latest info shows the ship is still scheduled to arrive at midnight. Calm seas with no moon in the sky, that will help.

Donnie will show up with a truck around twenty-three

hundred hours. Steve and Rick will also be with him.

I will take over Kevin, Bill and Calvin. Oscar will stay at the hangar. He will be all fueled up, and ready to go.

There will be twelve crates in total. They will be marked "Lathe Parts" from, Ankor Wat Machinist from Kampot Cambodia."

Calvin and Mad Bill will jump in the truck with the rest of the boys while Kevin will drive with me to the airport.

Once there, we will unload the crates and put them in the jet. Steve will drive the truck back, and Rick will drive my Mustang back to Donnie's shop.

Then wheels up, we will need one refueling in Iowa. And hopefully will land in Westchester before ten. As soon as we land, Mad Bill will call his contacts and then we wait.

Kevin said next shipment will be November16th. That one will be to Boston; it will also include Donnie's order.

And the one after that is December 7th to Baltimore. The final one for the year will be December 28th. Just a truck for this one as Los Angeles will be the destination.

Then Kevin sighed loudly.

He said, "Things are getting really fucked up in Cambodia. Vietnam is way too hot to move my operations to. Fuck, they will torture and slowly kill any American they find. Maybe Thailand? Laos is too far away from any port. Fucking Khmer are committing genocide. If you boys want to make some good money, come back with me to Cambodia until I get all my weapons out of the country, I will pay you well."

Donnie smiled and said thanks, but no thanks, as did Mad Bill.

Calvin and Kevin both turned their heads towards me.

"When I first volunteered, I did it to pay for my sins over here. It took me a long time to forgive myself. My head is now clear, I guess I will always have some guilt, but not enough to run to the other side of the planet. And you know what? I should have died at least three times. I am past the strike count. Thanks, but no thanks."

Kevin just smiled and said we are all missing out on large cash. He then patted Calvin on the back and said, "More green for us."

Calvin laughed and then spit out some of his chewing tobacco in his empty coffee cup, nothing but class this guy.

By the time we were done breakfast, and our briefing, I was starting to get a really good headache.

Kevin, Bill, and Calvin wanted to do some sightseeing, but I didn't really feel like being a tour guide. Donnie said he was heading back to his shop.

So, Oscar by default became the official tour guide. I gave Bill my spare key to the apartment and said to make himself feel at home.

I headed home, by the time I got there my headache had turned into a migraine.

That greasy breakfast was exiting my ass like a volcano erupting.

I had that throbbing pulse in both temples. Once I was done free basing the puke, I staggered up the stairs. Took a couple Aspirins, got naked and crawled under the covers.

I was woken by Mad Bill calling my name. I was soaked, like I was swimming. Not sure exactly what my dreams were about. That made me nervous, was hoping for a vision or guidance. One thing for sure, whatever it was, I felt like I was being chased. He walked into my room and asked if I was all right as I was a ghastly pale.

"Fucking guts are rolling, how are yours feeling?"

"Mine are good. Drink some coke, it will help settle your stomach. You going to be good for tonight?"

I just nodded yes and headed to the kitchen and grabbed a soda and drank it back like a man dying of thirst. Then a couple glasses of Kool Aid.

Smoked a joint that seemed to get rid of the headache, a nice long hot shower. Toweled off and I felt a hell of a lot better. Smoked another joint and then finished getting all my clothes ready for Montreal.

Nothing with any tags on the inside or names on the outside. Just plain boring clothes, except my leather jacket.

Around six, Bill said we are supposed to meet Oscar, Calvin, and Kevin for dinner at the hotel. He asked if my guts had settled enough.

"They are better, and it is going to be a long night and even longer flight. Yeah, I will have something, just not heavy."

So, we drove to meet the boys at the hotel, I kept checking my rear-view mirror to make sure we are not being followed.

I just had some soup and a sandwich. Easy to digest and guaranteed not to flip my guts. Grease is the last thing on my mind.

We went over the plans one more time. Everyone knew what their function was. Then it was time for us all to grab a couple hours of shut eye.

Oscar crashed on the couch at my place. Once again, I passed out hard. But within thirty minutes I was wide awake. And what exactly woke me?

A dream. No, make that a nightmare. I was back on the straddle ports with Scotty, same fucking storm happening as the night Jake and I got busted.

But this time we were not busted by the cops, no one ratted us out.

Several epic lightning bolts, as if hurled by Thor himself, chased me all over the machine we were working on.

Scotty shook my hand and said it was nice to know me, as soon as he let go of my grip a bolt struck him. Fuck, he was lit up like a Christmas tree.

He had a horrified look on his face as he started to vibrate. Within seconds, he burst into flames, the smoke and stench of him being burnt alive was gagging me, making it unbearable to breathe in such a small cab. My eyes were burning as I reached for the fire extinguisher. I just kept spraying with my eyes closed.

After a couple minutes, I opened up my eyes, that is when things got really fucked up.

Scotty suddenly had his back to me when I asked if he was all right.

He turned around and it was Fagan.

"Surprised, Strongbow? Flames don't bother me seeing at how you sent me to hell."

nine text here.

10

I woke up gagging, I could still smell the burning skin and yep, drenched in sweat once again.

I sat up and replayed the whole nightmare over and over. No way Fagan is alive. No one could survive that frozen lake.

So, is there another rat among us? I know everyone quite well. No bad vibes from anyone. And this is the first shipment to land in the USA. Maybe it is the people in New York I should be concerned about. I know nothing of them. And Angry John sounds like a complete fucking asshole. Maybe he will be seeking revenge on Mad Bill for busting him years ago. I will keep him in my sights at all times. He acts suspicious, I will kill him on the spot.

I grabbed a shower, woke up Oscar and told him I am jumping on my bike and heading for the docks. I just want to make sure nothing unusual is going on. Reassured him I would be home by ten, more than enough time.

The cool air of the open ride on my bike really refocused me.

No bad vibes heading down there, just some nervous energy.

A lot of the areas on the docks were restricted by vehicle. But with working there as a teen, we would always sneak out and smoke weed. So, I parked my bike, climbed a chain link fence just like I used to, and headed to the tallest stack of shipment containers. Climbed to the top, then like a snake, I slithered on my belly and broke out my binoculars and went over every square inch.

Everything looked like a typical night on the docks.

Once I finally felt at ease after my recon, I climbed back down, scaled the fence, jumped on my bike, and headed back home with a smile on my face.

Mad Bill asked where the hell I went. He was pissed at first, but once I told him, he was quite happy.

I made up a pot of coffee, Bill put some whiskey in his drink, I passed. I want to fully concentrate on everything.

The closer to the meet up time I started getting anxious, so I started doing push-ups.

Get that heart and rush of blood to the brain flowing.

The phone rang and I knew it was time to go. I packed up my vehicle with all my gear and off to get Calvin and Kevin.

Both were quiet, rather tense as to be expected. Nothing in life is foolproof but death and taxes, and this job was tax free, that just left death.

Yeah, the only noise on the drive over was Calvin spitting out his tobacco in his cup; it better be in his fucking cup.

We saw Donnie in his truck and pulled up beside him.

All of us jumped into the truck and off to the main gate on the docks we headed.

I had to laugh at Steve and Rick; they had on these black toques like the guys on the docks wear.

They knew I was snickering at them; Rick gave me a punch in the arm and said they were the only two dressed for the part. Security stopped us. Kevin showed them the bill of lading paperwork. He radioed someone, and before we knew it, the gate opened, and we were allowed to drive in.

The ship was a massive saltwater freighter, or as we called them, a salty.

All of us piled out as Kevin and Calvin approached the dock foremen.

I recognized him so I stayed in the shadows, I actually told Donnie I was going to do a little recon, he said to take Mad Bill with me as he now went to make sure there was no issues with us getting our cargo. Maybe the foreman is his contact.

I looked for anything that wasn't normal for a night shift. Sounds, too much manpower, and of course, anything visual.

After about thirty minutes I heard a car horn. Shivers went up and down my spine. I pulled out my 9MM and was ready for the battle when Bill said the truck is loaded and running, let's split. We double timed it back to the truck and jumped in.

Donnie asked where we went.

"The last time I was on these docks is when Jake and I got busted. Was making sure that would not happen again."
He looked right at me and nodded his head yes, then said good boy.

We drove off the docks. Then Bill and I jumped in my Mustang and off to the airport.

Both vehicles drove the speed limit. I knew that if a cruiser happened to pull us over, the truck would keep going. If the truck were pulled over. Well, that would have been the cop's last shift.

We made it to the airport in under a hundred minutes. This is good to know, should have actually done a dry run.

Before we started to unload the cases, we did a perimeter sweep. And you know with five of us being in Special Ops and four of the five of us in SOG, all was sparkling clean.
Fuck, Mad Bill and I even helped to load up the jet. I just want wheels in the air and off to the second half of this mission.

Once the cargo was all aboard, Donnie gave Steve and Rick their cut, and I gave Rick the keys to my Mustang. Told him to be careful. He reminded me his toque was also NASCAR approved, smart ass.

We all jumped aboard the jet that was now ready for takeoff as soon as the tower gave us the green light.

For me, I didn't fasten my seat belt until Oscar said we are clear for takeoff.

I kept looking out the window looking for bandits, or cops. I will tell you one thing; it would be an interesting shootout if it came down to it.

Three or four minutes later, Oscar said those magical words, we are clear to take off. "Fasten your seat belts, gentleman. Air America is set to take off once again."

I closed my eyes, took a deep breath, slowly exhaled, and grabbed the arms of my chair nice and tight.

We went racing down the runway and off into the pitch-black sky.

Once we leveled off, Oscar said we could take our belts off.

The whole Mindy proposition of killing her husband was still on my mind.

So, I called Donnie over and told him exactly what she said to me.

He looked at me, thought about what I said, and nodded his head.

"The thing that might come back to bite you in the ass is if she's ever had anyone else attempt to take his life. If so, there would be history and she would be the prime suspect. And how solid would she be? She lives a very pampered life, I am sure if it meant her spending the rest of her life behind bars, or her ass sitting in an electric chair, she would chirp like a canary. And then there is making it look like an accident. Enough of an accident to fool the cops and the coroner. Not sure about this one, Mitch. Sorry. If you do make it look like a robbery, she might have to be shot too, not sure about security systems where they live. Tell Mindy to give him an Espresso and fuck him to death, she seems to me like a girl who loves sex."

"Fuck, Donnie; she loves sex. I swear, a couple times my heart was going to explode. That is actually not a bad idea. Maybe give him some uppers and get that heart racing.
The coroner will find speed in his system, just strong coffee and even stronger sex."

I thanked him for his advice and honesty.

Before we knew it a deck of cards was out, and a poker game was taking place.

I played a couple hands till I was down a yard, fucking Stokes; he talks the whole time, and he just knows when you are bluffing or have a solid hand.

I decided to keep Oscar company. He told me to have a seat, he asked what I thought of his jet.

I looked at all the instruments and said one word.
Outstanding.

And as powerful as a full moon looks during a night flight, no moon in the sky lets your imagination run wild.

We were starting to descend to our refueling airport when a sensor went off. It was just a simple flashing light with a low sounding alarm.

But when Oscar said *not good,* I said nothing. Took a deep breath, fastened my seat belt, and then asked what the problem was

"The cabin's oxygen sensor just went off."

Oscar yelled for everyone to fasten their belts as he is going to do a fast descent.

He then called the tower and said he had an oxygen sensor going off, can he get a runway right away.

The tower acknowledged his request and told him what runway would be cleared for him.

I know he was concentrating to getting us down fast, but I had to ask what was going on. Remember the last time I flew with him, we had to crash land.

"If this sensor is right, we are losing oxygen in the cabin of the plane. If I don't get us low enough, we will all die of hypoxia, won't even now what hit us. We will all fall asleep; I guess a peaceful way to die."

I notice that he is also tapping the sensor, and sure as fuck, it stopped buzzing.

"Maybe Strongbow, just maybe it was a faulty sensor, you don't feel tired at all do you?"

"Fuck, Oscar! My heart is racing, and my eyes are huge, anything but tired."

He said good, as we continued our fast descent.

We landed safely this time, thank fuck. Took a couple minutes for my ears to clear, damn.

Oscar and the one mechanic from the airport crawled under the plane, I too crawled under, and you know why? Marvin Matheson would be the reason.

What a perfect way to kill that fuck. Mindy says he has his own private jet.

All checked out underneath the jet, then they went in and dicked around with the censor. The mechanic pulled out the malfunctioning fuse, and that was the culprit.

We all boarded the jet once again, and off into the wild black yonder we flew.

Kevin looked at his watch and said we should be getting in right around sunrise. We went over our game plan.

Bill would make the call and then wait for them to show

up. Calvin, Bill and Kevin would meet them. Make sure all was good.

Donnie and I were there just as a show of force, or if shit hit the fan, to react accordingly.

Hopefully a smooth transition, and if that happens, Donnie and I would be taking a taxi to the Carvel Inn hotel in Westchester, call the Italians in Montreal, and wait to be picked up, and head north.

That is the plan, but as you know, it doesn't take much for the best laid plans to get all fucked up. Improvise to all situations, all of us are excellent at that.

Well, the rest of the flight was smooth, I really like this jet.

We touched down at 06:35. Went to a hangar that was reserved for us.

Mad Bill went and made his phone calls. He came back and said they are on their way.

The three Amigo's waited outside for the buyers, while Donnie and I hung inside the hangar, and yes, we were armed and ready for battle.

Twenty minutes later, the three Amigo's came in with the buyers. Four in total.

As they walked towards the jet, two of them sort of looked familiar, I just couldn't picture from were. They were big guys, big Irish guys, they had to be the muscle.

Third guy was dressed to the nines, lots of jewelry, he must be the boss.

And the fourth guy was a miserable looking greasy fucking goof, toothpick in his mouth and walking like King shit on turd island. This has to be Angry John.

One by one he would stop and eye us up and down. He is a fucking punk, is he really trying to intimidate me by doing this? The other two guys I can tell can handle themselves. Angry John is a fool, a pretend tough guy.

He looked at Donnie, then me and asked Mad Bill if we were also ex-cops, or maybe Feds, maybe this is nothing but a set up.

I just growled at him; does he have a death wish? If this was my deal, I would put a bullet between his eyes.

Before Mad Bill could answer, the two big guys walked

towards Donnie and said it had been a while, they shook his hand and gave him a hug.

The one guy, a big red head looked at me then asked Donnie was this the kid that the Leprechaun sent to New York about ten years ago.

Bingo! That is where I know them from. Donnie said yes. Then they came over and said I have grown quite large.

The big redhead told their boss that we work for Joseph O'Reilly. We are anything but cops.

Their boss seemed to relax. He turned to John and told him that his big mouth, has always gotten him into trouble in the past, zip it.

I just smiled at him, like the cat who caught the canary. This pissed him off even more. His face was now going beet red as he was pointing his middle finger up at me.

Fuck him, I blew him a kiss.

"Fucking Wahoo!" He screamed out as he now charged towards me.

Everything went into slow motion as I saw him reach around his back. Well, that is where I keep my one gun, I am not taking a chance with my life.

Timing is everything, right now he is a QB trying a Hail Mary pass and I am that freight train of a linebacker. I closed in so quickly he has no time to bring his arm out. I do a flying drop kick right to his gut and knock him to the ground.

He hits it hard and is gasping for air. I jump on top of him and start to land punches while yelling at him asking him how tough he is now. The toothpick he was chomping on, is now impaled in his chest. I pull it out and ram it right into his eye.

His face is a bloody mess, as I watch his eyes roll back in his head with the toothpick still stuck in his eyeball. I also believe he has now pissed his pants. The moisture snaps me out of my rage.

I stay on top of him and look around. Everyone is in shock at what just happened.

I apologize to Kevin and their boss. I explain he was reaching for a gun.

Yeah, things are now starting to get tense once again.

Their boss asks me to get the fuck up off him, and not the

friendliest tone of voice.

I look at Kevin, then Donnie, who nods yes.

So, I stand up, and back away. The big red head is ordered to roll Angry John onto his back.

Their boss calls him a fucking asshole, as we can see a handgun in his right hand.

He is beyond pissed. He apologizes and then asks to see the weapons.

I stand over Angry John while they are doing their deal. I want to see this fuck take his last breath.

Looks like both sides are happy with the weapons and the cash. The crates are loaded into a cargo van.

There is now only one last thing to deal with, not-so-angry-now John.

I never should have taken him in, says their boss. The big redhead asks what they should do with him.

"Lay the boots to him, then we will get rid of the body," said their boss.

I respectfully asked him if I could join in on the fun. He smiled at me and said of course.

I could hear his ribs break; I was kicking him with such force.

After a couple minutes he was dead, the smell of shit and the death rattle confirmed that.

They picked him up and threw him in the back of the cargo van, and off they went.

Donnie and I went back into the jet to get our gear. Kevin shook our hands and then paid us our cash for the job.

Said he would be in contact with us. I wanted to say sorry, but I wasn't sorry. No one treats me like shit, I knew dead John had zero respect from his boss or peers.

I gave Calvin a hug and said I was looking forward to the next shipment.

Calvin and Kevin got aboard Oscar's jet that was now refueled.

Mad Bill had his car in the parking lot and said he would drive us to the hotel. He even said he would buy me breakfast for killing douche bag John.

On the drive to the hotel, a puzzled Donnie asked Bill if he was a cop at one point.

"For five years I was. I even made it to detective."

"Never got the cop vibe from you at all. Why did you leave?"

"Between the shit pay, the courts and seeing scum walk and I mean the lowest scum, the rapists and child molesters, my brain said fuck that bullshit. Seeing at how we are all honorable criminals, my eight-year-old niece was assaulted by an animal. Courts felt sorry for him, said he was not mentally fit for trial. The bastard had a rap sheet as long as my arm. So, I went into Bellevue as a cop, said I was taking him in for questioning for another case. Somehow, he managed to get out of my police car. He hasn't been seen since."

Bill then had this big smile come to his face; I know this smile. Pure fucking evil, love it.

After breakfast we said goodbye to Bill, said we would see him in a couple weeks or so.

Checked into our room. We were both bagged, big time tired and needed sleep. So, I made the executive decision to call Bruno Fratoni after we woke up. The last thing I want to do is hunt humans half asleep. I have a solid criminal reputation starting to grow you know.

I guess I did have a clear conscious about killing dickhead John as when I woke up. It was jet black out. I looked at the time and it was almost nine o'clock.

Decided to wake up sleepy head Terek before I made my call. Yeah, snoring Donnie would not be a solid sign.

He too was shocked at how long and solid we slept for. Hope the boys made it back to San Fran O.K.

I called the number Bruno gave me. It was some Italian sports lounge.

Of course, the guy on the other end of the line has attitude and asks who I am.

You never want to give too much info up over the phone, but I am positive the cops up there will have no clue who I am, but why take that chance.

"Tell him it is his friend from California."

It is a big state, should keep the coppers guessing if anything. Sure, as fuck wasn't going to use my first name.

"My friend from California, how you doing?"

"We are doing good, staying at Carvel Inn, Westchester. When can we expect you?"

"Too late tonight, thought you might be in earlier," he said a bit annoyed.

"Had some jet issues." Hey, I wasn't lying.

"Will meet you in the lobby at say twelve noon, sound good?"

"Sounds excellent, see you then."

I told Donnie what was going on. He said good, let's go for some beer and grub. Don't have to twist my arm.

There was a corner bar a block away, as long as it has cold beer and decent grub, I will be very happy.

We walked into the bar, and everyone stopped what they were doing and just stared at us.

Donnie and I were the outsiders all right. Both of us had lots of hair, mine was long and down my back. Donnie had the big afro happening.

Everyone in the bar had short haircuts as if they belonged to the Cleaver clan.

And they were mutant looking fucks. There has to be a nuclear power plant really close as they have been drinking the water.

Donnie and I grabbed a seat at the bar.

The bartender came over and said, "You boys are clearly not from around here, are you?"

"Not at all," I said.

Donnie looking rather intense said, "Is this a cop bar?"

The bartender said, "Yep, I won't refuse you service, but I think you two should find another bar to drink in."

Donnie said, "You don't need to say any more than that."

The next bar, a couple blocks down, had a couple bikes parked out front. Donnie checked them for club stickers, bad enough walking into a bar full of cops, walking into a bar full of Thunder, that would be even worse.

No stickers were found, so we walked into this smoke-filled loud bar playing Black Sabbath on the Juke box.

Both of us smiled and walked in and grabbed a table against the wall. Ordered a pitcher of draft beer and four shots of

Jack.

The beers and shots were downed right away, a big belch and we started to relax.

Ordered another pitcher, went to order more Jack when Donnie reminded me the Italians are coming for us tomorrow. If they weren't happy with us checking in later, they sure as fuck won't be happy with us hungover.

Made sense, so we ordered some grub. Then we finished our beers and headed back to our hotel.

**

The next morning, we went downstairs and ordered breakfast. While waiting for our food, Donnie went into the lobby and bought a map of the area that expanded a hundred miles in each direction. It was for me, another lesson from the master.

"Whenever you are in a town or city for the first time. Buy a local map. Always know how to get in and out, just in case, Mitch."

Certainly, made sense to me. Montreal will be a bit overwhelming as some streets are in French, whole different culture. But I am looking forward to the challenge, and yes, the pay once the job is complete.

We chilled until the Montreal connection showed up. Bruno and his driver-muscle, Yves, a born and raised Montrealer. First impression of him was good, quiet guy. You could tell he lifts heavy.

We threw our stuff in the trunk of the car and off to Montreal we headed.

After being on the road for only thirty minutes, Yves' chain smoking was getting on my nerves; I swear he would light a new cigarette with one he was about to put out.

Of course, it was blowing into the back seat. Had to say something.

"Yves, you look like you are in pretty good shape."

Bruno boasted at how he was a mister junior Quebec bodybuilding champ.

"Then why the fuck do you smoke like a chimney. Do you know why us Indians gave you whites tobacco?"

Donnie looked at me and smiled. No one said anything in the front seat.

"We gave it to the whites to kill them slowly. Now, I don't want to die slowly. Would you mind not smoking while we are in the car?"

Yves just looked in the rear-view mirror at me. Bruno gave him a smack in the back of the head and told him to get rid of it. Bruno then turned around and looked at me. I said thanks to both as soon as he flicked it out the window, even though he sighed. Fuck him.

We stopped for a piss break about an hour before the border. Light one up, Yves. Yeah, he was pissed, and if he starts, I already killed one loudmouth this trip.

Me and Donnie then asked Bruno if there had been any updates from Mike.

He said no, everything is still a go.

Donnie asked who will be going along with us making sure we have the right targets and who will help us to get rid of the bodies. Bruno took a deep breath and said Yves.

"Can he be trusted?" I asked Bruno. And I meant fully trusted in the aspect of killing someone, getting rid of bodies and most importantly, solid with regards to the cops and the people we are going after.

"He is one of my most trusted soldiers. I am married to his sister. I watched him strangle someone to death with his own two bare hands. Yes, he can be trusted. I give you my word."

Both of us looked at Bruno and said good to hear. Bruno also said we will be staying at Yves' house.

Donnie started to snicker while looking at me.

"Mitch, you can't tell a man in his own house that he can't smoke in it."

"I don't plan on spending much time in there. I want to kill these fucks and get back home."

Bruno told Yves to pull the car over in Glen Falls so we were all on the same page regarding Donnie and I coming into Canada.

Good thing he did, as we told them the aliases we were using.

The story is that we are coming up for a hockey game. To watch the Habs play. The dreaded and hated Broad Street Bullies aka the Philthy Flyers. I haven't saw much hockey, but what I have seen, I've really liked. A fast-paced sport with grace, finesse and brutality all rolled into one.

As we approached the border, I got a few butterflies. I thought about me taking Lucy across the Mexican border and back into the USA after Jansen had raped and beat her.

There was a big sign that said *welcome* in French. And when we got to the border the guard spoke to Yves in French and to us in English.

He asked the typical questions but kept staring and Donnie. He asked for our identification then spoke in French to Yves. Both the guard and Yves turned around and looked at Donnie and laughed.

He then gave back our I.D. and Donnie asked what the fuck that was all about.

"The guard says you look like John Wensink from the Boston Bruins, he wanted to shoot you."

"You Canadians take your hockey too serious," said Donnie as he shook his head.

I am stopping and looking for a picture of this guy now.

Originally, Bruno was going to take us to his Italian sports bar until Donnie asked if the cops watch it. He said yes. Donnie said that is a no. Find us a quiet diner and we need two maps of the city.

Yves was told to go to Teddy's, and that is where we went.

There was a corner store beside it and that is where Bruno went and got us the maps.

We took an end booth, grabbed something to eat, a pot of coffee and off to work we went.

Donnie was the ultimate pro. He wanted to know where the two bosses lived, where they hung around, what they drove. Any normal routines that they followed. Any weakness either drugs, whores, or booze.

Bruno said after they have their weekly meetings on a Thursday night, they like to hit a strip club called Chez Kitty on Saint Catherine Street.

I asked about any loyalties with the strip club and them.

Bruno said they pay them protection money, and a couple bouncers have been used for muscle in the past.

It would be such an easier job if we could just shoot them

as they are entering the strip club, or in the washroom or any private rooms.

This whole making their bodies disappear is going to be a pain in the ass.

Where are exterminators, not magicians.

Donnie took a deep breath; he must have been reading my mind and asked what we are doing with the bodies afterwards.

"Mike wants sweet revenge. Their bodies are to be put into the columns at the Olympic Stadium. Then they will be buried alive in cement. See, the irony has to do with them refusing to share the wealth and having their union guys fucking up jobs at the Olympic Stadium."

Donnie said for now, let's drop off our gear at Yves house. Then head to Chez Kitty around the same time they would normally show up at. Donnie wanted to check out the lighting around the club and also the streets or alleys near it.

For yours truly this would not be my first kill out front of a strip club.

And even though I was a full-fledged heroin addict, the way I killed General and Gifford was flawless. Truly a masterpiece.

Donnie told us we were there to scout, not to get pissed. Bruno then looked at Yves who took a big breath, I picked up on it as did Donnie.

He turned to Yves and asked if there were going to be any issues with what we are specifically there for.

"I don't drink, or make that, I *can't* drink. I have had several legal issues regarding booze, the crown said they would keep me on probation on the condition I take Disulfiram."

I looked at that and asked what exactly that is. Before he could answer me, Donnie smiled and said that is how we will take everyone down.

Still at a loss as to what the fuck this is exactly.

"It is supposed to stop people from drinking. You have any liquor on it you will become violently sick. You have any of those pills left?"

"No, I have to go to the hospital daily and take it."

"Suppose you tell them you are going fishing for a week. You think they will give you a week's supply?"

"I don't know, I will find out at 9 A.M."

So, Donnie and I split up, Yves and Bruno stayed together as we went in the strip club.

No perverts row for me, I took the west side of the bar while Donnie took the east. Yves and Bruno took pervert's row.

I have to say, all the waitresses were hot. Better looking than Battaglia's. Maybe he should make a trade, that actually made me snicker, throw in a few g-stings and a couple bear rugs as part of the deal.

And French-Canadian strippers, beyond fucking hot. Mike must come up and look at these chicks. I gotta fuck me one.

Oh yeah, back to our recon mission. So, the bathrooms are right by the rear exit. That will help us. I have an idea and once we go back to Yves to debrief, I will give my two cents.

Two drinks were enough. Donnie left first, that was the cue for the rest of us to leave. We met at Yves' car and then headed back to his place.

Once inside Bruno asked what we thought, both Donnie and I said it can be done.

Donnie asked his young apprentice, aka me, how I think we should do it.

"Get Yves' waitress pal to spike their drinks. I think Donnie and I should have seats by the washrooms. Their goons head to the washrooms, we wait for them. Knock them out and put them in a stall. Once our two intended targets come to the washroom, we need a diversionary tactic. Yves, you start a fight near the stage, so the bouncers must leave the door. We will have duct tape ready. Mouth gag and bind their hands. Knock them out cold. Carry them out of the bar. Everyone will be watching the fight, bring some more muscle with you and scrap the bouncers if need be. We have vehicles out back, throw them in the trunk and off we go to this Olympic Stadium venue. Bruno, we will need another car and driver. I don't think you want to be seen with us throwing the bodies into the trunk of a car."

I looked at Donnie and asked how I did.

"Fucking beautiful, Strongbow. You get an A+ for that one. Yeah perfect, but a van would be better, pull up with the side doors facing the club. No one on the street sees anything."

Donnie asked Bruno if he could make our plan including

the van happen.

Huge smile as he said of course. "I have to say, I really like the way you two work. Truly professionals, very impressed."

We called it a night, Donnie told Bruno he wants a drive by where both Martone and Bova live tomorrow in the light of day. We needed to know where they hang around in case the bar kidnap is scrubbed.

***

Yves had a two-bedroom house, that meant I had the couch, lord knows I have slept in worse spots.

The air was cool, I kept the living room window open, it also aired out the smell of cigarettes, I swear I was back in San Quentin.

The next morning, Yves dropped off Donnie and I at this restaurant while he went to the hospital to hopefully grab some of those pills.

As we were eating Bruno came in and joined us. After breakfast he asked if we were ready to see what Donnie asked for last night. Always ready for intelligence gathering. But first, I needed to stop off at a bank. Bruno asked which one. I said any kind that won't hassle me for opening a bank account. Bruno smiled.

Funny as I talked about starting to hide money. Why not have some hid in Canada?

Only issue I had was the language barrier. But it went well for Mr. Willie Hertz.

Recon time. Both lived in an upscale neighborhood and both houses had these huge iron gates in front of their houses. Martone owns a driveway resurfacing company that is in an industrial area, easy to kidnap if need be and Bova owns a janitorial company which he is never at, not so easy.

We went back to Yves' place where he scored the Antabuse pills.

So, we all went over the game plan. Yves said he will talk to Josee tonight. He said she will drug them for the right price, plus she said they are cheap tippers and are always grabbing her ass. She has no use for them.

Bruno said he has no problem paying her, if she will remain solid as she talks shit about everyone. Yves said he would vouch for her.

Donnie then suggested that him and I get out of Montreal as soon as the kidnappings have taken place.

Bruno was deep in thought. "Fully agreed, you get Martone and Bova to the stadium, I will cut you guys free. It will be a pleasure killing those two. Yves, you think Josee will get the boys across the border, for a couple yards?"

"Josee will do anything for money." Yves started to laugh. "I will make sure she gets you across the border."

"Yeah, if she can drive through the Cornwall border, way less a heat score and then drop us off in Massena that would be great. I will get us home from there." Said Donnie.

"Sure thing, Donnie, I will talk to her tonight."

Donnie reminded him to talk to her in person and not on the phone.

Yves smiled and said that goes without saying.

Well, we had the whole night ahead of us. So, I asked Bruno if he could get us tickets to see this hockey game we were supposed to be at.

He said yes, he can. I asked Donnie what he thinks, he said why not.

Then I asked Yves, can he get Donnie and I a day pass at his gym?

Once again things were a go. This must be a positive sign.

Bruno said he will pick us up around four, take us out for a monster steak and then drive us to the game. I asked about Yves, but he hates the Habs, he loves his Nordiques who play in another league.

Didn't even know there was another.

"San Diego would be your closest team. The WHA is more for the players, the NHL is more for the greedy owners, fuck them."

You learn something new every day.

Bruno went home for a bit and Yves spent the rest of the afternoon explaining the rules of hockey to us. Man, he was such a huge fan, he could not speak fast enough and with his accent, a little hard to follow.

Before we knew it, Bruno was back. We jumped in his Caddy and out for a steak dinner.

On the drive over I was really taken back by the heritage of some of the buildings, almost feels as if you are in the 1800s in France.

The churches were huge and very Gothic looking, very cool.

But you know what was even cooler, this 8-track that he was listening to.

I know my music and didn't recognize the singer or guitar player.

"A Canadian group called Rush. Caress of Steel is the album."

Totally blew my mind. I will be picking up this album as soon as I get home. I can see smoking a fatty and buzzing right out to it.

Of course, Donnie and I didn't have any suit jackets and there was a suit jacket policy, but that is for most people, not for guests of Bruno Fratoni.

We sat in a different part of the restaurant, normally where guys bring their mistresses as not to be seen.

I asked Bruno what they are known for, he said the prime rib.

So, I ordered the full portion, medium of course, Donnie was rare, he wanted to hear it mooing.

Bruno said he expects lots of blood to be spilled on the ice tonight. The Flyers are a very dirty hockey team who try and brawl to win.

Turns out he is going with us after all. Good as there are some rules I am still confused about.

Dinner and conversation were really good. I asked if he thinks a war will start after they realize Martone and Bova have been killed and aren't just missing.

"I think the D'Angelo's have to look at themselves in the mirror. They don't give a rat's ass what happens up here as long as they get their cut. Martone and Bova have been pushing their weight around way too much. Making lots of enemies including the cops and people who have been solid with the D'Angelo's. If we need extra muscle, would you two been willing to come up? I pay very well. And it will be killing on sight. No kidnappings."

Donnie said just make the call. If we have nothing on the

go, we will entertain what the offer is on the table.

This made Bruno smile. He looked at his watch and said we should get going.

On the drive to the Forum, he said he was able to pull in a few favors and our seats are in a private box with a full bar service.

I just smiled and know he is truly wining and dining us for future endeavors which is good, I guess.

I really liked the atmosphere once inside the arena, you could feel the raw emotion building, almost like a summer electrical storm off in the ocean and heading to shore.

The warmup was pretty cool, these guys can move pretty quick and shoot a puck pretty damn hard. What a great way to torture someone. Take slap shots on them, of course wearing no equipment, specifically a jock.

Once the game started, I was surprised only a couple guys wore helmets and this was a pretty hard hitting and violent game.

A few of the Flyers, when they touched the puck, the fans booed. Bobby Clarke and Dave Schultz who is their tough guy. I would knock him out in two seconds. Clarke was pretty dirty; I saw what he was doing with his stick.

I only had one drink as did Donnie. Bruno said the bar is on him. But Donnie said we have an interesting day tomorrow in which we need all our wits and strength. Being hungover would lead to an epic failure.

Bruno smiled and said, "Fucking pros, I love you both."

The game ended in a hard fought 2-2 tie. Hockey, you just gained two more fans.

Because we stopped drinking there was no bar, or another strip club after the game.

Donnie also told Bruno he is best not to be seen at the strip club tomorrow.

So, we said we will see him at the Olympic Stadium.

Donnie also said he needed proper clarification, "If all hell breaks out and everything goes in the shitter, we can kill them right on the spot, correct?"

Bruno took a deep breath and said, "Only as a last resort."

Let's hope it doesn't come to that. We shook his hand and said we would see him tomorrow night.

As we walked into Yves' house, you could tell he had a

female in his bedroom, a very loud female I must say.

So, we sat down and turned on the TV, took a few turns of the channel dial until we found an English-speaking station.

After about twenty minutes the moaning had stopped, thank God.

The bedroom door opened and out came a fully naked, smoking a cigarette Yves, and an older blonde with a bad dye job and big sloppy saggy tits and stretch marks, puffing away on a cancer stick.

She was horrified to see us as she raced back into the bedroom muttering some profanity in French.

Yves sat on the couch naked and asked how we liked the game.

"I am totally hooked; I think Donnie is as well."

This made Yves smile and laugh, "I told you that you would love it. Even if it is the asshole Habs."

The blonde came back out of the bedroom, but this time was fully dressed.

Yves went to introduce us, but no way did I want her knowing our real names.

So, I introduced us as our alias names. And her name was Josee, the same Josee that will be spiking the drinks, then driving us to Massena. She sure as fuck wasn't the model for Josie and the Pussycats, more like Muttley, guess that makes Yves, Dick Dastardly.

"So, you two are the big bad ugly hired American killers. I still don't know why Bruno just doesn't let Yves murder them. He is certainly a lot stronger, and better looking than you two."

Donnie was pissed. "Looked you stunned cunt, you do your job, and we will do ours, understood?"

"Fuck you two," she said before she kissed Yves goodbye and told him she would see him tomorrow night.

Once she slammed the door and left. A very pissed off Donnie asked Yves did he trust her a hundred percent?

"I trust her ninety nine percent; I don't even trust myself one hundred percent. I am sorry she spoke to you guys like that, trust me, she is like that with everyone."

I looked over at Donnie, who just smiled and nodded to me, a devilish smile at that.

We stayed up for a couple more hours and went through our game plan tomorrow and over every single *what if*.

Then it was lights out, once again the couch for me, I was so tired I didn't care.

It seems crazy dreams are not limited to take place in the USA only.

Had a dream I was playing for the Habs. Opening face off and I was lined up against that goof Dave Schultz. But my dream also had some reality to it. We are both trash talking each other. He goes *once the puck drops, we fight, tough guy*. I tell him I am more than willing and able. Then I realize I have never been on skates before, and I have zero balance. How am I supposed to fight someone when I can't stay upright? For the first time in a long time, I actually am afraid going into a fight. Donnie is also on the ice; I look at him and he says he can't skate. Fuck it, this guy is a bully. Anything goes. So, I spit in his face to blind him and then I use my stick, that had been holding me up, and with all my might I lifted it up between his legs. Total asshole move on my part, who cares. He hit the ice in pain, and I fell on top of him and started to smash his head into the ice.

I woke up drenched in sweat, as I was driving my pillow violently into the couch. It took me a couple minutes to clue in where I was, and that it was just a bad dream.

Could really use a joint about right now. But that is not going to happen.

So, I sat up for a bit and went over our game plan tomorrow until my eyes started to burn. The whole house is like an ashtray. Can't wait to get back home. Even my clothes reek.

I guess I crashed pretty hard as the boys had to wake me up and say breakfast is on the table.

Chowed down, then off to the gym we went. Yves was able to get us a day pass as our assess plan on being stateside by the next morning.

I asked Yves what he was working on today, he said chest and back. I love the push and pull routine. Donnie said he was also in.

We started off on the bench after some warming up. I know Yves' kind. He is going to show us Yanks what he is made of, I would do the same and that is exactly what I plan on doing.

We started off with a single plate to get into it. Then another plate for set two, another plate for set three.

Donnie said he is not going any higher, 310 pounds is good enough for him.

Yves looked at me and asked if I was also giving up. Fuck no was my response.

Yves added twenty-five pounds per side and struggled. Only two reps.

I put on a full plate making it an even 400 pounds. I was able to bang off three reps. I got up off the bench and told Yves he is up.

He smiled and then laughed and said he is done.

Yves was stronger than me when it came to back strength though, and I let him know this. After all, we are brothers in arms.

Then back to Yves place to go over things once again. Donnie asked if he had guys lined up for the diversionary fight tonight. He said they will be there for eight.

Donnie told him he doesn't want to meet them. "The less people know of us, the better of us getting away with it." Yves fully agreed with him.

We all agreed that Josee is the key. She must drug them. Yves once again reassured us she will come through.

I cleaned all my weapons, made sure all our gear was also packed. Then it was time for an afternoon nap. A rested body and brain are the key.

Donnie woke me up and said it was time. I put my knife inside of my boot.

Put one 9MM in my back, and one in my side pocket of my leather jacket designed for carrying such a weapon and last but not least, my brass knuckles in my front pocket. Yep, all set for the battle.

Yves drove us over in the van that we will use to transport Martone and Bova. Still not sold on leaving their bodyguards in the washroom. Maybe we will get lucky and Martone and Bova will throw up first and head to the bathroom.

We got to the strip club just after eight. Donnie and I walked in first. As per our game plan, I took a table near the washroom on the left side, Donnie took right side.

Yves came strolling in after parking the van. He headed

right to the washroom and put a roll of duct tape on top of the condom machine. Then he went and grabbed his seat on pervert's row.

Josee came over and asked what I was drinking. I said rye and ginger. I asked if she was ready, she snapped and said, "Of course. Do you think I don't know what I am supposed to do?" With her thick fucking douche accent. Cunt.

The bar had two doorman who hung at the back. They had a perfect view of the whole bar from there. Both of them looked like bikers for sure. Not sure what gang affiliations they have up here, or just a homegrown Montreal gang.

Both guys were big and solid, could be a good battle, hope it doesn't come to that.

Shortly before nine, four muscle heads walked in. I recognized them from the gym as they were Yves' pals.

Everything seems to be falling into place. Now we just wait for the Italians.

As I was watching this blonde on stage show us how she can almost go down on herself, I felt a pressure change, then I heard a lot of noise as the doors opened. My guts told me that these were the parties we have been waiting for.

Four loudmouths coming our way. I looked at Yves who gave us a quick nod.

As the four walked past us, this one ape turned around and looked me up and down, then looked over at Donnie and did the same. The guy was pure evil, but what put a little shiver up my spine, this guy was fucking huge. I am 6'3" around 280 pounds, this guy had to be close to 7' tall and close to 400 pounds. I am not sure the meds would have any effect on him. The second ape was also a monster, couple inches on me and you could tell he was a huge steroid user. His neck was bigger than my thighs.

After they took their seats, I looked big eyed at Donnie. He too just raised his shoulders and shook his head. Could use Kantonescu tonight.

Josee strolled over to their table and was laughing and making conversation with them. You sit back and observe everything, look for any intangible you never thought of. Then you weigh out everything as to whether or not you go to the backup plan. Or you adapt and just make things work.

Really wish Yves and Bruno would have told us about this size of the bodyguards.

After about five minutes I saw Josee bring them over a tray of drinks include the shots of whiskey that those meds were dropped in. The dark rye will disguise the drugs. And shots go straight down the hatch. She also dropped down a tray of beer.

Twenty minutes later, Josee has four more shots of drug induced whiskey and more beers.

Martone and Bova are who I had my eyes on. They had their eyes on the girls on stage. The two monster bodyguards were watching everyone in the bar.

I will give them kudos; they are solid that way. Sitting that close to the stage and seldom looking at the strippers.

I noticed when round three of the drinks came to the table Martone said no and waved his hand over his glass. This is a good sign, a really good sign. Bova was now starting to get a vacant look on his face.

I know that look, that is the look I get before I throw up.

My heart was now starting to race; I clenched my jaw as my battlefield brain was racing a thousand miles an hour.

Bova started to spray puke everywhere including nailing some of the guys with Yves. I look at Yves and give him the nod; I look at Donnie and mouth *show time*.

Yves and his guys now stand up and start to yell at the four Calabrian's.

The bouncers head right to the commotion, make that three of them, as Bova is now racing to the washroom, staggering with his hand over his mouth as is Martone. But the giant is ten steps behind him looking angry and fit as a fiddle.

Time to improvise. I tell Donnie to take care of the two Italians and I will take care of the giant.

We really wanted to keep this low key easy and just a kidnapping, but then again if it was easy, they wouldn't haven't hired Donnie and I and flown our asses all this way.

I pulled out my 9MM, the one with a silencer on it, and headed towards the giant.

He looks at me and with a real ugly scowl on his huge mug; he growls and tells me to get the fuck out of his way.

I shake my head no, do an insane smile, and then I empty

the whole clip in his upper body. But he doesn't collapse or die like any other human should.

He has slowed down a bit, but his momentum is now drawing him to within steps of me.

I slip on my brass knuckles and as he reached for my throat, I land several hard body shots. I hear him grimace, and then I see his face turn pale as he drops to his knees. My knife in my other hand has cut his groin wide open and he is now bleeding to death.

Time to finish off this giant. I ram my knife right into his throat, I drive it as far as it will go.

I can feel the moisture of his warm blood seeping through my gloves.

His eyes roll back in his head, and I get out of his way as this mighty oak tree is about to hit the ground. *Timber*, and down he went.

I hear the death gurgle and then head right in the bathroom. Donnie has both Martone and Bova tied up and knocked out cold.

I tell him to go. I put another clip in my 9MM and head out the washroom door first. The brawl that Yves and his guys started is still going strong, we have to flee as you the cops must be on their way.

I head right to the van and pound on the side door. Within seconds Pierre opens it wide, I tell him to start the engine as Donnie throws Martone in the back. I go back in for Bova, while Donnie covers me.

Like a sack of potatoes, I throw Bova in the back beside Martone.

We both jump in and tell Pierre to haul ass out of here.

Once we were a mile or so away, Donnie tells Pierre nice and easy to the drop off point. "Let's not give the cops any reason to pull us over." And with that, Pierre backed off on the accelerator.

It took us about twenty minutes to show up at the construction site.

The guard on duty looked at Pierre and said to drive through. I kept my head down, one less person to recognize me, which means one less person to rat me out.

We drove around for about five minutes; this place is

fucking huge. Pierre stops the van and says we are here.
If I have learned anything in my three plus years of being a criminal, never trust anyone.

I have my gun in my hand as does Donnie as I open the side door of the van.

As the door opens up, I can barely see two big drums with fire coming out of them. A snow flurry has now started. I now squint my eyes as I exit the van and see several bodies standing around the fire.

One approaches me and I realize it is Bruno. He asks how it went as he is now staring at the blood covering me.

"We have Martone and Bova in the back. The blood is not mine; it is this fucking giant bodyguard of these two fucks that I killed."

Bruno pulled his head back, his eyes got big, and he said, "This is the blood from Gilles Doucette?"

"No idea, he is about seven feet tall, four hundred pounds, crazy hair?"

"Yes Doucette, is he dead?' asked Bruno with a nervous smile.

"Yes, he is dead, I emptied a clip in him, gave him shots with brass knuckles and then I castrated him and sliced his throat open. Is there a place I can change these bloody clothes"?

Bruno stuck out his and hand congratulated me. Fuck, I think he is just as happy that Doucette is dead as us kidnapping Martone and Bova.

"He is the one person in life that gives me nightmares, they say when he was in prison, he was jumped by three other cons, he broke all their necks. Mitch, this makes me so happy. Thank you. Yes, there is a completed dressing room that is heated and has running water."

He showed me where it was, then he came with me as we threw Martone and Bova out of the van.

Then Bruno truly looked like the cat that swallowed the canary. He told his men to take control of our prisoners.

Bruno asked if we wanted to watch us torture and kill them. Both Donnie and I said we will pass. We will wait for Josee and then head back home.

Bruno said that is fine, he pulled out his wallet and paid us the arranged price.

He also gave us each an additional five hundred for killing Doucette.

Shook our hands and said it has been a pleasure. I told him if he needs us again, just go through Mike.

He seemed happy by this which is good. I asked if he could get rid of my bloody clothes, he said not a problem.

I then went and got changed, washed up and handed my clothes to him.

Then I went back to the van and waited for Josee with Pierre and Donnie.

11

Twenty minutes became an hour, so you wait by the fire. Luckily Pierre had some hash. Now that hit the spot, great way to wind down.

Waited about another forty minutes before Josee showed up. She got out of the car and just eyed Donnie and I up and down with disgust.

She then spoke to Pierre in French; we just know by the tone she is slamming us.

Donnie is pissed and asks her what the fuck she is saying. She doesn't answer him, so he asks Pierre what she is saying. She then mouths something to him once again in French.

Donnie sternly tells Pierre to speak up, or he will kill him right on the spot.

Pierre looks at Donnie, then Josee, but when Pierre heard a clicking sound, the sound of a 9MM being cocked and a bullet in the firing position, well that got Pierre's full attention.

"She says the bar looks like a bloodbath, she had to walk through blood."

He then looks at Josee and says, "She feels sorry for Gilles, he has a brand-new baby at home, he was always kind to her, we shouldn't have killed him. Fuck you two assholes, find someone else to drive you."

I don't trust this cunt. She is a loose cannon.

"Donnie, maybe we should ask Pierre if he wants to drive us instead of her."

"Three males crossing the border late at night doesn't look

good."

I can't believe the balls, or is it stupidity, of this broad.

Donnie starts to walk away, and I am kind of shocked to tell the truth. I ask where he is going.

"I am going to have a private conversation with Bruno."

I just nod at him and stare at Josee who is chain smoking once again and acting like a cat on a hot tin roof.

After about fifteen minutes Donnie comes back with Bruno, and he is pissed and gives her a smack.

"You have a job to do, you agreed to it, I feel you are ripping me off, is this what you are doing, Josee?"

As pissed as she was at us, she was more scared of Bruno. "No, not at all. I will drive them."

Bruno pulled her in, gave her a hug and said *merci*.

We then shook Bruno's hand and said thanks.

We packed all our gear in her vehicle and headed to the next stop, Cornwall Ontario, and the USA border.

I sat in the front with her while Donnie sat in the back. He told her no speeding, signal every turn, nice and easy.

She didn't talk much other than muttering under her stinky breath, and of course, she chained smoked. I was surprised it only took us around ninety minutes to get to the border.

Donnie told her the story line is we are going to a friend's house in Massena.

He would ask her to confirm what he said, she mumbled in French. I looked in the rear-view mirror and Donnie was not happy at all with her, what a stunned cunt she is.

We pulled up to the American side, and the guard asked where we are we headed. I said Massena. He asked our citizenship. Two Americans and one Canadian. He asked how long we were in Canada for. We said two days, did the hockey game. The guard seemed to be picking up on something, he then asked if we had any drugs, alcohol, tobacco or firearms we are bringing into the country. We all answered no, but Josee, I put my hand on my pistol, if she rats us out, I will kill her.

The guard had a quick look in the vehicle, then said we were good. Fuck that was close, too close.

As soon as we were a minute into New York state, Donnie once again reminded Josee she has twenty-five more minutes till we bail, and she can head back to Canada. No speeding, stay in the yellow lines, don't do anything to draw attention to us.

She threw her arms up in the air, said something in French, and lit up another smoke. I saw Donnie look back at me in the rear-view mirror. She was certainly trying his patience, no doubts about that.

We were now about fifteen minutes from the border. Donnie said he had to piss and for Josee to find a secluded area for him to use. She mumbled something once again, and down a side road we went.

I too had to piss, she asked if Donnie and I were going to shake each other's cocks after pissing.

Glad she found humor in what she said. She started to laugh, and cough at the same time. Guess Donnie had enough of her and chopped her, open fist, right in her throat.

Donnie pulled her out the driver's side window by the hair and started to pound her in the face. At first her legs were kicking, grasping for air, after about eight punches, her legs stopped moving. Her face was now so swollen, you couldn't tell if it was a male, or female.

He then asked for my knife and asked how sharp it is. Will cut paper was my answer, he said perfect.

Donnie now starts to cut off her fingers, one at a time. I am positive Josee is still alive as I hear faint whimpers.

Time for a history lesson from Professor Terek.

"Mitch, do you know who Edmund Kemper is?"

I knew the name, but not sure from where.

"Edmund is a serial killer. He would kill females, eat part of their bodies, cut them up, some real fucked up shit. Now what I am doing here, is if they were to find a murdered Josee, the coppers would realize it is part of the murders in Montreal. We, or should I say yours truly, cut her up, and I mean mutilation to its finest, well they will think there is another Edmund Kemper on the loose. And let's be honest, this cunt is getting everything she fucking deserves."

Donnie wasn't fucking around. Not only did he cut all her fingers off. He cut her breasts off, cut out her cunt, and the piece de resistance, cut her head clear off.

This whole going down this side road was part of Donnie's plan. We threw her body parts, and Donnie's now bloodied clothes in the Grass River.

I had a question for him. "When you went looking for Bruno at the stadium, did you tell him what you planned on doing, or you just that you had enough of her disrespecting us?"

"All the above really. She is the weakest link, the loose end. She was too hot headed. She felt sorry for you killing Doucette. The thing with these Italian gangsters, especially Captains and up, they are all about you giving them respect. I explained my serious, and logical concerns to Bruno. He gave me permission to take her life."

"I am curious, what would have happened if he said no?"

"I still would have killed the cunt, I am sure, or hope you had the same concerns about her as I did."

"One hundred percent. It took everything in me not to kill her before we left Canada, but I am not sure how to even get to Massena New York, or even where the airport is."

Donnie laughed and said, "Massena was just a front. We are actually going to drive to Buffalo New York, jump on a plane there to get us home. I am sure the cops will be looking for any clues within a 100-mile radius from Montreal. Buffalo is nice and quiet, about a five-hour drive from here. We can keep a low profile there until we fly out."

Now, that may not seem like a long drive, but the kidnappings, and murder of Doucette were such an adrenaline rush. It really did us in physically and it was mentally draining. And I was starting to get a wicked headache from that cunt steady chain smoking and just plain disrespecting us.

Donnie drove first, so I jumped in the back to get some shut eye.

Before I knew it, Donnie was waking me up. I told him to give me a minute to fully wake up before I start to drive. He told me we are already in Buffalo at our hotel.

Far out was my only response. I got out of the car to stretch my legs, and something really stunk. I asked Donnie if he just let a killer fart go.

"That is the smell of slag, we are about three blocks from a steel mill."

The hotel he chose for us was some dump, in the shit part of town. But he assured me they make a great breakfast, rooms are clean, and we would fit right in. Is there any city in North America that Donnie doesn't know something about?

Well, he was bang on with the breakfast and the room. We went and checked in and grabbed a room with twin beds. Donnie said I have one job and one job only, to call the airport and see if I can line us up with the next flight out of here to get home.

So, while he crashed for much deserved sleep, I went back to the restaurant, had another coffee and made my calls and got all excited reading the sports section about a hockey game in town tonight. That will give us something to do, beats sitting in a shit hole bar.

It turns out the next available flight for us is tomorrow at 7 in the morning. I grabbed us two flight tickets, then headed to the Buffalo Aud to get us tickets for tonight's game between the Sabres and Rangers.

Donnie was snoring loud as ever. I turned on the air conditioner to try and drown him out, note to self, bring several pairs of ear plugs next time we go on the road together.

Donnie woke me up a couple hours later. He was happy seeing the flight tickets home and asked if hockey was my new addiction. I answered him with one, and only one word, violence. This made him laugh.

He told me to bring a gun, he said Buffalo can be rough once the sun goes down.

***

Dinner was excellent, Italian joint that was a short walk to the arena.

As soon as we walked in, just like in Montreal, once I smelled the ice, I got butterflies.

The game was lopsided, Buffalo destroyed the Rangers. Hell, they didn't even score a goal.

We hit a bar close to the arena, had a couple drinks before heading back to the hotel. With an early morning and long flight, including a couple hour layover in Atlanta. Needed to rest up, even though we just sit there and hope the pilot does the rest.

Woke up the next morning to a couple inches of snow on the ground, really hope they don't ground our flight.

I asked Donnie what about the van.

"You wore gloves every time you were in it correct?"

To the best of my knowledge, I said yes. He said to give it a wipe down, just in case. Then he would drop it off a couple blocks from here in this ghetto, leave the keys in the ignition, it will surely be stolen by the time the sun goes down. No longer our problem.

We grabbed a quick bite at the airport before we boarded. The flight took off on time and off to Atlanta we headed.

Can't say I have ever been there before. Would like to see some of the civil war stuff. Maybe one day.

The flight was good, a couple minutes of turbulence, but after my last couple flights, no complaints.

We had a couple hours to kill before our plane left for San Francisco. That meant bar time.

Also, in the bar were a bunch of stewardesses and a couple pilots, all in uniform, I hope these are not our next pilots as they were catching a good glow.

And for yours truly, you know what a woman in uniform does for me.

I noticed this one tall blonde kept looking over at us and smiling. Hmm, I know this look all too well, wonder if she knows a secluded place, I can fuck her. Her smile is getting bigger as she gets up off the bar stool, she now walks towards us. Yes, going to score in Hot Lanta.
Man, she is all legs, gorgeous long blonde hair, no wedding ring. And a huge smile. She has a very confident walk, I bet you she also does modeling.

I tell Donnie to watch the master in action.

The blonde Goddess stops at our table, looks at me, then Donnie and says, "Pilots bore me, I like the bad boys." Wow! Is this chick crossed eye as she said that while looking at Donnie, and not me?

Donnie smiles and shows his wedding ring to her.

"Are you sure I can't convince you take it off?" she said.

"Sorry, I love my wife way too much."

"Your wife is a lucky woman, and I respect you for your loyalty. Very admirable quality these days. Well, if you change my mind, you know where to find me, big guy." She then turned around and walked back to the bar, by the way, her ass, out-fucking-standing.

Donnie smiled, looked at me and said, "What where you

going to show me Master Bater?" Then he burst out laughing.

We had one more beer before heading to our next gate, and yes, he teased me the whole way.

As soon as we were airborne, Donnie fell fast asleep. I guess a non-guilty conscious will do that. Not complaining as I didn't to hear him teasing me all the way back home, that would be a long flight.

It was a long day, ten hours in the air, two hours in between flights. So, by the time we landed in San Francisco I was bagged.

Donnie called Jeannie who came and picked us up. When she got out of the car, that happiness or I guess love between them was genuine. It was like they were still teens madly in love with each other. I hope one day I find someone that would give me enough strength to stay loyal to them. Must be one hell of a magical and powerful spell. Till then, I am staying loyal to myself, and myself only.

Jeannie dropped me off right at my front door, I thanked her, and Donnie for being a great traveling companion.

And what is the first thing I did before I even put my key in the door? I made sure my Mustang was there and looked spotless. Now I can go upstairs.

Once inside I take out all the cash from the Montreal kidnappings and put it in the safe. Put away my weapons, took off my clothes, that smell of smoke is still strong, and put them in the hamper.

I get myself a beer, roll and nice tight joint and then check the answering machine.

Rachel called, which is normal. She said her and Pat are having a party tonight if I am interested. Mike Battaglia phoned saying his dad thanks me for the deer sausage. A couple calls from Mindy, two of them were very sexual, those ones I will keep. And Joseph called asking if I wanted to work tonight at the Drunken Leprechaun. He said my friends the Stuarts are playing there tonight. Jerry also said the club is having a party if I am around. Nice to feel wanted.

I weighed out all my options and decided to do something I have never done, something I really wanted for myself. I need solo time to wind down. This past week has been pretty fucked up.

So, I called Donnie and asked if I could slide by and pick

up my canoe.

At first there was dead air, and then he asked if my canoe was part of some late Halloween costume.

"You know what; I just want a couple days away, under the stars, back to nature."

I know he was waiting for a punch line and when none came, he said he will leave it on the front porch as he is heading to the Clubhouse shortly.

I thanked him, said I would be coming back Sunday night, if he wants to slide by and throw a line in.

I grabbed a box of beer, an ounce of weed, the rest of my essential camping gear. Hit the grocery store for some food, ice and off to Donnie's I went.

As promised, the canoe was on his front porch. I picked it up, put it in the box of the truck and off I went.

It was already dark out, kids darting back and forth all hopped up on sugar and the thoughts of each house being a score for them.

Once I saw the last of the city street lights in my rear view mirror my shoulders dropped.

Popped the Magician's Birthday in the 8-track player. Lit up a joint and just got mellow. Fucking right, this is exactly what I need to wind down.

I pulled up to Ford's bait shop. I said, "I will take some uppers and a container of worms."

He laughed and said he had both.

Then it was off to my site. About a twenty-minute drive, zero lights coming from any lifeform as far as the eye could see, just my headlights.

I pulled in and kept the lights from my truck on until I could gather up wood for a fire. Once that was lit, I pitched my tent, put my cooler in it and had my sleeping bag all set up inside.

I cracked a beer and sat by the fire, looked up at the millions of stars in the sky. I wonder if Katrina ever looks at the stars the same time I do.

One of the first places I would take her would be to grandpa's place. She must learn the Strongbow way. Learn all about the Sioux, not just that Jew bullshit.

I take a deep breath as I feel my blood pressure starting to rise, then I saw a brilliant flash in the sky. I look up and it is the North star. I guess dad is telling me to relax, either he will deal with it, or in time, I will have Katrina in life. I look deep into the fire, and I see it, I know it.

After a couple more beers I take a deep breath, fuck I love it out here. I swear to God, between Yves and Josee smoking like a chimney on fire, it will take a month for my lungs to be clear.

I wonder if any fallout has happened up in Montreal. Was a real learning trip, damn I have a great teacher in the professor, aka Donnie Terek.

Before you know it, I was getting pretty tired, between the fresh air, the long flight home I was ready for bed before midnight. I crawled into my sleeping bag and was out cold faster than a patient on anesthesia.

Now, I can't remember the last time I slept in my bed. With being on the road and different beds, and yeah, a couch. I had no idea where I was when I opened my eyes. But once I realized that I was in a tent, on my own property and was going to spend the day fishing, I was happy.

Well sort of true, I was also pretty horny, could use Mindy right about now.

I fired up my breakfast, put my beers in the lake as the water was cold. Took the canoe out of the box of the truck, put it in the water, grabbed my fishing gear. And off I paddled and paddled. I just felt like exploring the whole lake. I broke a good sweat; fuck, I felt so alive with my heart pounding strong, I will get all that nicotine out of my system. I smelled my arms, yep it was coming out of my pores.

I spent the rest of the day on the lake with my line in the water and thinking about all the woman I have ever truly loved. Then I start rating them in bed, top three, Lucy, Mindy and Charlene. God damn, Charlene; I go back to seeing her at Herschel's wedding. Every hole she owned was being fucked. Next thing you know I am starting to jerk off in the canoe. The vision is so clear, I can hear her moaning and looking at me with her big blue eyes. I know the sex was more for me, my kink being full filled by a pleasing girlfriend. As I start to cum, I am now shooting on my jeans, I move my leg quick, maybe too quick as I now capsize the canoe.

It takes me what seems an eternity to come back to the surface. I am choking on water, but once I realize I am not going to drown, I look to see how far I am from land. Maybe a mile, so I grab onto the capsized canoe and try my best to swim to shore with it.

If paddling the lake was a workout, this was the ultimate exercise routine.

Once again, I am taking it one stroke at a time and ironically, that is what also caused me to capsize.

By the time I reach shore, my arms and legs are burning. My legs are shaking as I am getting out of the water and flipping my canoe over.

The cold air now has my whole body shaking. Fuck, this was also my only pair of pants, no towel, so I strip down to nothing, start a fire to dry off my clothes and use my sleeping bag to dry my drenched body off.

As I sit by the fire I am shaking like when I was coming off the heroin. Once I stop shaking and the initial shock has worn off, I realize I have lost all my fishing gear, and my dinner that I caught. Good thing I left most of the beer and weed here.

Yeah, then I start to laugh at what went down, then I think about her and Burns, fuck you Charlene, still haunting me.

The thrill of fighting for my life totally drained me, tonight I was in bed by ten. Was thoroughly exhausted, guaranteed my lungs are cigarette free now.

I slept super solid, in fact I woke up still tired twelve hours later, and once I crawled out of my sleeping bag, every single muscle in my body ached, holy fuck.

I smoked a joint for pain relief, then struggled to put the canoe in the back of the truck. My neck was seized, this is going to be an interesting ride home.

Even turning the key in the ignition was a challenge. I felt like I was eighty-five years old the way I was driving, felt every bump on the road. I really hope Donnie is home as getting the canoe out of the back will be even harder than getting it in.

Lucky for me, when I pulled up, there were half a dozen bikes out front.

No way am I telling the boys the truth, I will say I was pissing over the side and the canoe tipped. They find more drowned fisherman with their zippers down than up.

Jerry, Steve, Rick, John Kantonescu and a couple other club guys are sitting on the front porch.

I take a deep breath and open the door; I struggle to get out of the truck without falling flat on my face.

Donnie asks me what the fuck is wrong. I tell them the piss story, and instead of a mile out swim, let's tell him it was mile and a half.

After telling my story, Steve and Rick took the canoe off the truck for me.

Jerry then says if I am not too sore, they are doing a run to Sacramento if I want to join them. I thanked him but say I am going home for a long hot bath and stretch.

Didn't even feel like a beer, I wanted to keep moving, felt like the Tin Man from the Wizard of Oz. I used all my strength to crawl back in the truck and headed for home.

As I pull in, I know I have another battle. The stairs are going to be a challenge and a half.

I put the key in the door, said Rangers lead the way and tackled the steps as if I was climbing Mount Everest. Now, one thing that Sir Edmund Hillary ever had was a phone, mine started to ring halfway up the stairs. No way am I moving any faster to answer it, well that was until I heard that it was Mindy, saying she is all by herself. All of a sudden, a miracle happened, my cock gave me the strength to move a little quicker.

I called her right back fully out of breath. She laughed and asked what I was doing. I said nothing yet, perhaps she should drop by, and we can work on both of us getting out of breath. She laughed and said she would be over in twenty.

Well, I hope she is feeling rather energetic. Only muscle on me that isn't hurting is my cock.

Twenty-one minutes later my doorbell was ringing, fuck I have the door locked. It will take me an hour to climb down the stairs and back up again.

So, I walk over to the window, I open it and see that it is Mindy, I tell her I will drop the keys down and to let herself in.

After I drop the keys, I see that car that was here last time drive by nice and slow. The boys are all out of town, but next time I have Mindy over, I will have them waiting for this fuck and give him a royal beating.

A concerned Mindy makes her way up the stairs and asks what happened. This time I change the story a bit. I tell her I was beating off thinking about her.

She blushes and says I am naughty, and to not do that again in a canoe of all places. I then ask would she have gone away with me. Absolutely was her response.

"Nothing better than fucking under the stars, Mitch."

She then told me to sit back and relax, she is going to run me a hot bath, then she is going to give me a full body massage. Hell, she even went and got me a beer out of the fridge while waiting for the bath to fill up.

She helped me into the bathroom, undressed me, saw that I was fully erect, smiled, gave it a little kiss, and said she loved that thing. I told her that thing fully loved her just as much.

She helped me get in the tub, she then told me to move forward as she also got undressed and joined me. Those magical hands of hers started to rub my neck. After a couple minutes I had full range back. Then she worked on my traps and back.

As she is digging deep into my muscles, she asked what exactly I was thinking about to get so horny and jerk off. So once again I substitute Charlene's name and lust for hers.

"Was thinking about you taking on a couple guys at once."

At first there was silence as she continued to massage me.

She then reached around started to play with my cock and said, "You want to hear me sucking some other guy's cock as I am getting fucked in the ass, is that want you want to hear?"

She reached around, gave my cock a little tug, kissed the back of my neck, and said, "In time I will tell you some stories. But right now, your hair smells, would you like me to wash it for you?"

I can't tell you how damn erogenous it was with her washing my hair, her nails gently digging into my scalp, total combination of turn on, and total chill.

After the tub I was pretty loosened up, enough to mount Mindy and give her a payback orgasm for her taking care of me.

About fifteen minutes later, Mindy put her head on my chest and asked if I had talked to anyone about getting rid of Marvin once and for all.

How I answer her will truly be life altering, not just for her, but for me. Mindy will be a prime suspect if the murder isn't perfectly executed. She is used to a very lavish lifestyle; would she give me up to the coppers?

Once again, I listened to Donnie's advice and asked her questions, specific questions, and those answers will dictate whether I decide to take on the job or not.

"The people that I have talked to want you to specifically answer some questions first."

She smiled, took a deep breath, and assured me she will answer every question truthfully.

"I know you will, baby. Have you ever talked to anyone about having Marvin killed in the past, and we are even talking about joking around?"

She said not as far as anything serious, but also said every couple jokes around about killing their spouse. I thought about her answer and agreed with her.

"Have you, or Marvin changed your wills lately, that is a huge red flag with the coppers."

"Not at all. Marvin wanted a prenup agreement drawn up before we were married. He has two other children from his first wife. In the event of his death, his assets are to be divided three ways between me and his bastard children, they are evil, Mitch. Ruthless. They tried everything to break up Marvin and I before we were married. Said I am nothing but a Vegas whore call girl, a jezebel."

She teared up as her face and neck went beet red. I hugged her and said she is anything but that. Her heart and soul are honest.

"My people have said there will be a lot of planning going into this kill, some high-end people will be used, not just thugs with a gun. If you suddenly withdrawal a large amount of cash, that too will be a red flag with the coppers."

"I have a couple bank accounts under my maiden name, but I hear you with the cash issue. I also have cash on hand in a couple safety deposit boxes in several banks. How much money do you think it will be in total?"

"He said because this is a high risk, and complex murder, he wants fifty grand."

She looked deep into my eyes, thought for a moment, then

finally said, "When, and how is this going to take place?"

I told her it will involve his jet. So, I needed lots of intel, I needed to know where he stores it, the identification number on it, and his travel plans for the next thirty days. With her being the client, I don't want to give up too much information, and I also had to make sure she was in one hundred percent with this.

She looked at me and said she is fully in. She promised she would get me all the information I need. She then asked me what my fee is.

My turn to smile, "I will start off with your ass, and a story. As far as cash goes, surprise me."

She smiled and said that is fair, but first she was hungry, and with me moving slower than molasses, we ordered in a pizza.

We ate, had a couple drinks, she was in a pretty good mood.

After our food had digested, Mindy said, "So you want to hear a story, do you?"

Butterflies started to flutter, my heart skipped a beat, and I nodded my head yes. She stood up and said let's talk about it in the bedroom. Suddenly the only muscle that wasn't aching was my cock, and that was throbbing. I had to promise that I wouldn't judge her. After everything that I have done in my life, I am definitely the last person on the earth to judge anyone.

"When I was dancing in Vegas, Marvin would be a regular. He would always ask for me for private dances. What started off with me stroking or blowing him in the private rooms turned into him asking me to visit him in his suite on my off time. I was struggling to pay for my apartment, never mind putting food on the table. So, he basically paid me to spend time with him. The pay would also include him fucking me, and eventually he said he would pay me a month's salary if another girl from the club could join us. I guess I was always a little bi-curious, I know this girl quite well, so I said sure. Now please don't laugh, but Marvin believes in past life experiences. He believes he was a plantation owner. This was also part of the kinky side of him. After I left the club and he kept me as his mistress at one of his hotels, we went on a road trip to The Poconos in Pennsylvania. Have you heard of the Penn Hills resort?"

I just shook my head no.

"It is a swinger's club. And at that club, he wanted to fulfill his past life kink. He wanted his young blonde mistress to be with not one, but two black bulls. Now just like me being bi-curious, I too wondered what the big fascination was with being with a black guy, never mind two of them. And being a mistress for Marvin, meant you had a fully furnished suite, a brand-new car, top end jewelry, clothes, the whole deal. So, I guess two fantasies were crossed off that night. The two black bulls come in the room; I was wearing a see-through nightie. Both guys were muscle bound, they looked like they played football. They started to play with my breasts as Marvin sat in a chair, watched while stroking his dick. His eyes looked possessed. I pulled out both their cocks and started to stroke them, they were rock hard. And as soon as I put one of those throbbing black cocks in my mouth, I heard noises coming from Marvin. Mitch, he came, I mean he shot all over the place. I even asked if he was all right, he could barely speak, I thought he was having a stroke, pardon the pun. Now I wasn't sure what to do next, I was so horny for these guys, but Marvin was done. The two guys looked at me and said now what. So, I asked Marvin should they continue, he nodded his head yes. If he said no, I would have told them to continue anyways. He had me worked up all week for this. The three of us fucked for around two hours, and yes Marvin jerked off and shot one time, then once the guys had shot all over me, well he got on top of me and fucked the shit right out of me."

What a fucking story, I seemed to be as worked up as Marvin as I shot a monster load in her ass, damn. I can totally envision this.

After we took a well-deserved shower, we sat in the front room, both naked, smoking a joint, drinking a beer, and eating cold pizza. I was curious; I asked how long they swung for.

"Right up till we got married, nothing since. We seldomly even have sex now."

It killed me as she had a tear rolling down her cheek now.

"Are you fucking serious? You are beautiful, baby. You have an amazing sex drive, and nothing is taboo, maybe he can't get it up anymore?"

She went deep in thought, her whole face changed, it got angry.

"He still gets it up; I think he is fucking his one lawyer. She always goes with him out of town on business trips. She is young, beautiful and I see the way she looks at me with disdain."

"You are still young and fucking beautiful, he is a goof."

"Thank you for saying that, Mitch. That is very kind of you."

"I mean every word, hon; I swear on my daughter."

She leaned in and kissed me, nodded her head yes then said, "Marvin is actually having a 40th birthday party for me this Saturday. Would you like to come?"

"I am not sure about that Mindy; you don't think it will raise all kinds of flags for Marvin? I am honored you asked me, but shit I come within ten feet of you, I will want to fuck you right then and there."

She smiled and said maybe I was right.

"But this is what I want you to do, Mindy. I want you to act as if you are madly in love with him, hang off him all night. Make sure everyone hears how sweet a husband he is to you. Thank him for hosting this party for you. The more people hear what a loving couple you are, the better it will be once he is found dead."

"Mitch, that is awesome advice, I will put on an Oscar winning performance."

"Excellent, baby. But seeing at how I will miss your birthday, I would like to take you to dinner this week, what day works for you and when is your exact birthday?"

She pulled out her day planner, went through the pages and said, "Wednesday I am free, Friday is my birthday."

"And I assume you are here because Marvin is on the road, when is he back?"

"Yes, he is in Los Angeles until Friday. So will you come and get me Wednesday, or should I come here?"

"Come here. I think right now more than ever, I don't want any doorman, or video showing me at your place, I hope you understand?"

"Once again you make perfect sense. Thanks for thinking of me."

Mindy kissed me for my actions. Damn straight I was telling the truth, but I also had another ulterior motive. I want the boys to pull that P.I. out of his car, give him a beating and find out exactly what he is up to. And any notes he has on me, I want to read them, let's see how deep his intelligence goes.

Mindy spent the night. Then the next morning we went out for breakfast. Sure, as fuck the car drove by as we took our spot in the diner. I was starting to get really pissed; a huge part of me wanted to sneak out and pull him out of the car myself. But not in broad daylight, and right now, my body is hurting more than yesterday. Legs are like jelly.

After breakfast, Mindy went on her way while I went to the gym to get a much-needed full body massage.

Then it was off to Donnie's shop to hire someone to take care of this fucking prick that is following Mindy around.

The boys said I was walking a little better, I said thanks to Jen the massage chick at the gym.

I came right out and told them the whole story about the guy following Mindy. I just want to know what he is up to, throw a scare into him.

Donnie said he is not interested, but for a hundred bucks each, Steve and Rick said they were in.

I told them all the particulars on the car, where I have saw him parked, and what time Mindy is going to arrive, what time we will be heading out for dinner. I said once she and I are back at my place, it will be dark, and then do what must be done.

By Wednesday I was moving normally. I had reservations for Mindy and me at Martin's Steakhouse for six.

She showed up just after four; I had a dozen red roses ready for her upstairs. As I presented them to her, you would think this was her first set. She was so happy, and that made me happy.

And what do you buy a married woman for her birthday that won't draw suspicions? Well, I bought her a full day at a high-end spa. Never anything tangible.

She actually cried once she opened up the gift card, I went in and hugged her real tight and said she is so special.

Fuck, it was such a good feeling, really good.

Dinner was amazing, drinks went down really easy and before you knew it, we were back at my place.

We ripped our clothes off each other and headed to the bedroom like teens.

I have to say, Mindy may be turning forty in a couple days, but man she sucked and fucked like a twenty-year-old. In fact, she must be in the top three sexual females I have ever been with.

After we were done round one, I was catching my breath when I heard the doorbell ringing like crazy. Something is not right. I told Mindy to stay in bed as I went to the intercom.

"Mitch, it is Rick. You have to let me in," he said with horror and desperation in his voice.

As I opened up the door, I looked at Rick's face that was a bloody mess. His nose was swollen, fat lip and looked like he was missing a front tooth.

As he came in, Mindy was now at the top of the stairs asking if everything was all right.

I told her everything was cool, go and grab a shower. I don't want her hearing shit. I told Rick to come up as Mindy now had the water running.

"Fuck man, what happened?" I asked him. "That fucker was tough as nails. He wasn't going down, he was actually winning so Steve had to shoot him, he had to empty his clip into him." Fuck, this changes everything.

"Where is Steve and the dead dick right now?"

"He is in the alley, we put the guy's body in the trunk of his car. Steve is a mess. I think he might have a broken jaw."

"O.K. We have to get rid of the body and the car. Let me get dressed."

I told him to grab a beer as I went in and told Mindy I have to take off. She was concerned and asked what was going on. I obviously can't tell her.

"Best you don't know. I am sorry, baby; I will make it up to you."

She nodded her head yes, came over and gave me a kiss and told me to be careful.

I called Donnie and told him we have a situation, asked if he could come by immediately. He said would be over in twenty.

Rick and I walked over to where Steve was, his jaw was starting to swell really good. His eyes were also starting to glaze over.

I told him to pop the trunk as I wanted to look at this guy. He was a real stocky guy, looked like a linebacker, crew cut and a square jaw.

I told the boys lets go back to my place and I will get ice

for their injuries and a beer or shot to kill the pain.

Mindy was horrified to see the boys so banged up. They each did a couple shots before Donnie showed up.

We went outside to talk, explained the situation, and asked Donnie for guidance.

He said we should get him out of here as soon as possible.

"We will take the car to your dad's scrap yard. Mitch, this is your mess, you will be driving the car. No one speeds, no one draws attention from the cops, understood?"

I put on my gloves and the death caravan drove to Korab's scrap yard.

The man still growls at me for the way things ended with Daphenia and me.

I was the second to last car, Donnie was to be the distraction and bait car if the cops got too close and decided to pull me over.

We pulled up, Rick got out and opened the big gates. All four vehicles drove in, and which car did those junk yard rottweilers come charging at while frothing at the mouth? Mine of course. I swear Korab has trained them to kill me. Zero love.

I waited for Steve to put them in the pen before getting out. They maintained eye contact with me and should me their massive teeth the whole time.

We all went to the trunk, when I opened it, Donnie laughed and said, "Fuck you, Big Joe Trombone, he was a fucking prick."

I asked Donnie what the story with him was.

"He was a cop in Oakland, real bad ass, he didn't care who you were, he would lay a beating on you. He rose up the ranks by doing a lot of dirty work like planting dope, guns, anything illegal on people the cops wanted to take down. Made it to detective. Did the same, he had one of the highest arrest rates ever. Then, one day he was watching some grass dealers in some shit hole ghetto project. He goes in and starts laying beatings on everyone in the house for information on some missing girl. This one kid gets mouthy with him, Joe isn't going to let some long-haired punk kid get lippy. Joe beats the kid within an inch of his life, turns out the punk was the mayor's son. That was the end of Joe's career. I heard he was doing P.I stuff."

Donnie growled then did a Moe move and drove two

fingers into the corpse's eyes.

"That is for jumping me when I was leaving The Rusty Nail back in '69 you bastard. I know a lot of people will be happy knowing this fuck is dead, but this secret stays with us, boys."

We took out his wallet, took all his cash. I found his notebook, read it and sure as fuck he had been spying on Mindy for a while now.

Yep, there is my name, each place we visited, how long she spent at my place.

I also see he is supposed to meet with Marvin Friday night. Pretty sure that is not going to happen.

I decided to keep his notebook. I want to go over it in more detail. I want to know what else is in it about me.

Donnie decided to keep his gun. "I will have payback with this cocksucker. I think I will do some planting of my own."

They kept him in the car as they crushed it. As this was happening, I reflected on Getz and wondered if there is even an honest cop out there. Wilson, I know in my gut is also corrupt. At least he has backed off, for now. I know he will be an issue in years to come. But fuck him too, he can be crushed into a square cube of metal.

Before we left, I told Steve and Rick to give me the medical bills and I would take care of them. I gave them each two hundred bucks for the kill, and Donnie a hundred for showing leadership.

By the time I got back home, Mindy was fast asleep in bed. So, I kissed her on the forehead, grabbed a beer and started to go through the notebook. Fucker had a whole two pages on my history.

Ex con, did 2 years in San Quentin for the overdose death of his girlfriend. While in there killed two members of the Thunder motorcycle club. Several assault charges since being released. One victim due to testify has gone missing, associate of the Hell Hounds motorcycle club. Close ties to the Battaglia family and Joseph O'Reilly. Never married but has a child, never sees the child. Mother of the child filed a restraining order against him, since dropped. Owns a t-shirt store, owns his own building. Works part time at the Drunken Leprechaun. Father killed in Vietnam, mother and oldest sister killed by disgraced police off Barry Getz, brother

Jake killed in San Quentin, youngest sister and sole surviving member of immediate family, she is a lawyer living and practicing in Sacramento. Very violent temper with a short fuse, highly respected in the criminal underworld. Now that put a smile on my face. Yeah, he knew of all my vehicles. Address, and the writer states, *Mindy spends the nights; I am sure they are not up playing chess.*

I think I better hide this.

I have a couple more beers, a couple joints and a few shots of Jack. I find myself rereading my adult life story. Fucking Tash put a restraining order on me, cunt.

When I finally crawled into bed with Mindy, I woke her up. I tried to be quiet, but I had a pretty good buzz happening.

She asked if everything was O.K. I said things couldn't be better, in fact, I told her I would be going to her party if the invitation still stood.

"Of course, it does, of all the people I know, you are the one I wanted there the most. You make me so happy, Mitch. Thank you."

She was so thankful she wanted to reward me, but I was done. I asked if I could take a blow job rain check in the morning. She said of course I can.

We kissed for a bit, then I was out cold.

I woke up the next morning feeling good, was surprised consider how much I drank, like binged drank before bed. Then I realized why I felt so good, Mindy kept her promise and was going to town on my cock. Her big beautiful green eyes dancing as her mouth, lips and hands did their magic.

I swear every stroke I was ready to cum, but I didn't want to as it felt amazing. Then she started the lick the under shaft of my cock, I couldn't hold back, I gave her a warning that I was ready to cum. She then started to suck me even harder. I even moaned out her name as I started to cum. Surprised, I didn't shoot right out of her nose. She took the whole load down her throat; she even tongued the last drop. That was fucking amazing, God damn!

We went out for breakfast, and then she went her way. She told me to drop by SOL and she can give me my invitation there. I said fine, would see her later on today.

Then I hit the gym, another massage. Then I did something

even braver than last night's body disposal. Grocery shopping, yep with the all the crazy housewives.

I was pleasantly surprised, I had several flirt with me, and two gave me their numbers. Never thought this place would be a pickup joint. Sadly, all four were married. I am already banging one married chick; she takes pretty good care of me. So, I took the phone numbers, and threw them out once I got home.

Later, I jumped on the bike and headed over to SOL records to pick up my invitation to Mindy's 40th birthday party. Suddenly, I don't have a good feeling about me going. Is she having me there just to piss off Marvin? Never make a promise when drunk and stoned, always go with your sober head. How ironic. I am talking about head and that was my reward for saying yes and going to the party.

I pulled up on my bike, looked at the outside of building and still had that bad vibe.

So, I parked my bike and headed to Basil's office first. I want to see if he acts any different around me.

Basil's flirty secretary always gets a little bubblier when I am around. She always has a sexual pun and tries her best to cock tease me. I believe Basil said she is just recently divorced.

And today was no different; she asked me when I was going to take her for a ride. "Sorry, Carol; I didn't bring an extra helmet with me."

"I didn't mean on your motorcycle, Mitch." She then undid a button on her blouse. One day I should just fuck the living shit right out of her, throw her down on her desk and have her pussy take a royal beating. What a brilliant cock teaser she truly is.

She then had that look a dog gets when he thinks it hears something.

Carol asked me what I was doing Saturday night. Mindy would freak if she knew Carol was asking me out.

"I am not sure; I think my sis is coming down. Why what's up?"

"Listen they are having a party for our vice president, Mindy Matheson. I need a date, what do you say?"

This might work out better, I have no interest in fucking her, but it would give me a legit reason to be there.

I asked what time she is working till today, she said five. I said I would get back to her. She then wrote down her home phone number in case I miss her at work.

I went in and saw Basil; my whole thought process is to see how he reacts around me. He seemed relaxed, we talked about the Stuart sisters and how Lesley who works part time for me is showing lots of talent and promise. That made me feel good.

I asked him how things are around here. He said good, told me about Mindy's birthday party. I told him I just got invited, he didn't ask if it was Mindy, that too is a good sign. He asked who. I told him Carol. Basil laughed and said my name has been brought up on more than one occasion.

He asked if I plan on going. Said I wasn't sure.

"Mitch, please go; I know the majority of the people coming are going to be from "Squares Ville", but booze will be high end stuff, food will be awesome, I am pretty sure you will score with Carol."

I just smiled at him and said I am fifty-fifty right now. I asked him to call Mindy and tell her I am here with something for her.

He was curious as to what. I said I brought her a couple joints. He laughed and said sure.

I don't trust Mindy's secretary; in fact, I really don't trust anyone in here.

She told him she would be right down.

When Mindy walked in, she was wearing a one-piece white jumpsuit, showing just enough cleavage to make my tongue hang out like a dog.

She acted all surprised and asked what brings me down today.

"I have something for you."

She smiled and said, "oh yeah?"

I reached into my pockets and pulled out her weed. She thanked me and she then asked Basil to give us a couple minutes alone as she wants to ask me something in private. Basil said of course and left the room.

She came in and kissed me and said she was so happy to see me. She thought I was going to flake on going to her party, I then told her I have a better idea, but she must promise me she won't get mad. She said go ahead.

"Look, Carol asked me to go to your party as her date/"

Mindy's whole face changed; it went red as she now squinted her eyes.

"That fucking whore, I should fire her ass."

"No, this is actually better. Since she asked me, this will not draw any suspicion at all, especially if Marvin asks what I am doing there. And I have zero interest in her."

She tapped her toe the whole-time making eye contact with me.

"You and I both know what is coming, more so now than ever, we have to play the game, a game to win."

She nodded her head yes, stuck out her pointer finger and reiterated no fucking that whore Carol.

I did an x over my heart and promised her, no fucking Carol.

She agreed, she gave me a kiss and said she will get me the info on Marvin's jet and his travel plans. She said that she is dreading him coming home tomorrow.

I told her it will be over soon, please be patient.

She gave me a hug and kiss and said she will see me Saturday.

I gave her a smack on the ass and said she was sexier than Raquel Welch.

She said I must be drunk and stoned; I told her stone cold sober.

Mindy left the room, Basil came in and asked if everything was good, I said yeah, all good. Told him I had to get going, and I will see him Saturday.

He was happy to hear that, and when I went out and told Carol I will go with her, she was more than happy. I told her I would pick her up.

She gave me a big hard hug, wrote down her address and said four works as cocktails start at five, and dinner starts at six. I said I will see her then.

I left and headed home, better put my suit in to be cleaned.

After I did that, I stopped by Donnie's shop to see how Steve and Rick are doing.

Rick had a broken nose and Steve had his jaw wired shut. They handed me the bill, and as promised, I rolled out a wad of hundreds and paid for their medical care and some extra cash for pain and suffering. Donnie asked if I had heard from Pat since we have been back home. I said no, but I plan on heading there right after here.

Finished my beer, then I headed to Sacramento and see what my beautiful sis is up to, and what her boyfriend, our business partner is also up to.

I was on the other side of the Bay Bridge when I saw cop's sirens light up behind me. A million things are now racing through my mind, all criminal thoughts of course. Good thing I gave Mindy my last couple joints.

Then I wondered if I was being pulled over for something more serious. But then the apprentice criminal realizes it is just one cop car, if it was anything serious. It would be several cars.

So, I pulled off to the side of the road, shut my bike off, and waited for him to approach me.

I looked in my mirror and saw there were two of them. I snickered as one of them was Wilson. The other guy was stocky, flat top brush cut. He has this smug look on his face.

Both of them stared at me, yeah, no love for yours truly. I looked at his name tag, T-R-O-M-B-O-N-E. God damn, this must be his offspring.

My turn for the smug look as I ask if there is a problem.

Trombone points right at me and say I am the problem.

"Wilson, your boyfriend seems mighty intense, too much sexual tension. You better suck his cock. Wilson, you are good at that."

Trombone stuck his chubby fingers and said, "The only cock sucking will be done by you, Strongbow. I am sure you gobbled enough dick in prison."

"You take a couple lives in there, you get space. Speaking of space, why are you in mine?"

We both glared at each other, I firmly believe if he didn't have the badge on, we would be throwing them.

"I have heard a lot about you, none of it good at all. Heard what you did to Wilson's fiancé, just thought I would introduce myself. You ever hear of me?"

I know exactly what he is up to, I was born at nighttime, just not last night.

I looked at his name tag.

"Trombone, never heard fuck all about you, why? Did we serve together in Nam?"

He stopped for a minute, thought about what I had asked, and then said, "I was in the Marine Corp from July 69 to July 70, yourself?"

I knew he was a fucking Jarhead.

"506th infantry, 101st Airborne, 75th LRRP. And I went in fall of 67, came out in 71."

He once again just stared at me for a couple minutes before saying, "Watch your speed."

They headed back to the cruiser, and I started my bike back up and headed off to Rachel's. As I'm driving, I'm replaying the whole conversation. I noticed Wilson said fuck all. I still think Trombone is fishing, I think he hasn't heard from his dad. I also believe his dad got all my info from his son being a copper.

See how Trombone starts to act or react when he finally realizes his dad is more than AWOL.

The rest of the ride was good, the cooler fall weather really clears your head. Makes you feel alive.

Good thing the coppers didn't hold me up anymore then what they did. As I pulled into her work, I saw her heading towards her car. So, I opened the throttle and raced into her parking lot. Everyone stopped in fear to watch this maniac driving with reckless abandonment. Everyone but Rachel, she turned around, put her hands on her hip, stuck out her thumb as if she was hitchhiking. I raced towards her and did a fish tail stop.

She was laughing and shaking her head. Rach then came over and gave me a big hug and asked what brings me to town,

"I miss you sis, think that is a good reason to come visit."

"I miss you too, so glad you are here, I am meeting Pat for dinner, want to join us?"

This works out well as I definitely want to see Pat and see how our deal goes.

"If you both don't mind, that works for me."

Rach said of course he won't mind. She told me to follow her, I said I hate that. Give me the address and she can meet me there.

She smiled and said it is on. Time for an old-fashioned

Strongbow race. Two wheels versus four wheels.

Of course, I took the early lead, no way would I be fair in the race, after all this is her turf.

I caught the next three lights green, go old fashioned American motorcycle beating the snot out of her German sports car.

I finally hit a red and look in my mirror and Rachel was darting down a side street, why would she do that?

My mind is now starting to race; the car behind me honks his horn as the light has turned green. Fuck my current route, I switch to where she is heading, maybe there is construction that she knows about, and I don't.

I burn rubber, I now hang a right and within thirty feet I am stuck in construction traffic.

I hear another horn honk, fuck it is Rachel driving past me back to the street I was just on. She duped me; she knew I would follow her. Great play, sis.

Five minutes later I can turn around and by the time I walk in the restaurant she already has her martini half drank, bitch haha!

Pat had a beer waiting for me; he said one more minute he would have been forced to drink it as it must be warm and flat by now.

I congratulated Rach on her out thinking me. This meant next round of drinks was on me.

After we ordered our dinner, I asked Pat if everything was still good with the apartment deal.

Even before he answered me, I could tell by his facial expressions that not all was good.

"Contact has been limited, and their responses have been kind of confusing. I have my lawyers looking at it."

Hmm, must be serious to bring in lawyers. Rach put her hands up and said she has nothing to do with this one.

I told him any issues let me know. I am sure Donnie will want to know what is also happening. Don't be afraid to keep us in the loop.

Pat apologized and said he would, but even right now he is confused, so he can't really give us a straight answer.

My stomach wasn't sitting well. In my world, if someone is fucking me around, they take a royal beating, or worse, a bullet in the back of the skull.

He said our other businesses are doing quite well, good profits and what would I like done with them. I told him I don't have a clue, what does he think is best.

"Well, if you don't need the cash, I have some other strip malls in prime locations. A few businesses, two restaurants, one bar and one gym, much smaller than Popeye's. What do you think?"

Right off the bat the gym interested me. But I would want Jerry to have a look at the books, location and see what he thinks. Popeye's is a legendary success.

Then I remembered to tell Rachel that mom's house is up for sale.

She asked if I would be interested in buying it for myself.

"I have so many amazing memories in there, but the sad memories outweigh them all."

I looked at both and wanted to tell her how I almost committed suicide after Mom and Pam's death in the living room, how I even had Dad's revolver down my throat, good thing Grandpa called and saved my life. But I couldn't, not now, maybe one day.

So, I told Pat let's check out these places next weekend. I will bring Jerry along and will look at the gym.

He broke out his day planner and wrote it in. He will get as much info as he can. I also asked him to look for stuff in the Bay Area. He said he has a solid contact there. And I would like the look of her.

Rachel asked who, he said Olivia Sanchez, Rachel just rolled her eyes.

I laughed and asked her what that was all about.

She said no, Pat will tell me the story.

"I took her out a couple times, nothing serious."

Fuck, I can tell my sister is jealous. And Pat's face is going red.
You know a part of me wants to shit disturb, but I don't like seeing Rachel upset.

"Give her my number, ask her to call me. Does that work?"

Pat looked at Rachel, once again another eye roll. Pat said he will do that tomorrow.

I was asked back to Pat's for a bit, but I have a busy day tomorrow.

Pat promised to let me know as soon as he heard anything more.

I gave Rach a kiss goodbye. Jumped on my bike and headed back home.

The ride out to Sacramento I used to clear my head and it worked. Now I am driving home with it even more cluttered. No way can I tell Donnie about the apartment deal. He will be pissed, and I like Pat, and knowing Donnie the way I do, yeah, Pat's health would be greatly affected.

When I got home, I checked the answering machine, I had three voice mails from Mindy, one by one she was sounding more upset. She told me to call her as soon as I got in.

So, I gave her a call not sure what to expect. Within three seconds of our conversation, she went from being upset, to a jealous rage. She was asking me where I was tonight. I told her I met Rachel and Pat for dinner. Dead air at first, then she asked if I was out fucking Carol. For fuck's sakes, really?

Mindy was also slurring, so I asked how much she drank tonight.
She started off as crying, then angry.

"I broke a couple toes tonight, and I really needed you to be here for me. My personal physician met me at the hospital, he gave me some codeine, I am not drunk, I am medicated under Doctor Gaffenberg's orders."

Once again dead air, except this time no sobbing. Then she started to apologize.

"I am so sorry, I am in pain, and Carol is such a slut, and the thought of you with her was eating at me all day, I had to take a couple Valium to settle my nerves."

I promised Mindy that tomorrow will be Carol be my one and only date with her; I also said to her that I have zero interest in fucking her.

Once again dead air, then she said she was coming over to make sure I have no sexual desires for Carol tomorrow.

God damn, I am more than game, but I said I couldn't come by and pick her up, she knows why. And I certainly didn't want her to drive over that stoned. We want Marvin dead, not her. So, I told her to grab a taxi and I will wait for her outside. She said that works, and she has a surprise for me.

As soon as I hung up the phone, I could hear Donnie's voice telling me that Mindy had fallen for me hard and this is a dangerous game I am playing with her. But I am also falling for her big time, so, not really a game.

Within twenty minutes I see a yellow taxi pull up with Mindy in the backseat.

Her eyes are definitely glazed over, she also has a goofy smile on her face.

"I am horny as hell, but you are going to carry me upstairs if you want to get fucked."

I laughed and said, "Your chariot awaits, m'lady."

When I looked down, I noticed she has a shoe on her left foot, while her right foot is bandaged up. I asked what the hell happened.

Her face went beet red, said she accidently kicked something, and now she has broken her big toe, and also the one beside it.

Not fucking good. Time to put some pleasure back into her life.

I smiled at her, carried her up the stairs and right into the bedroom. Told her I would be right back after I run back down and lock the doors, I also told her she can certainly start without me.

Now, just when you thought Mindy couldn't raise her sexual game any higher, well fuck me, she certainly did.

As I came into the bedroom, a fully naked Mindy, had now resting between her legs a black dildo. Playtime just got elevated.

I couldn't rip my clothes off fast enough, and once I did, I was rock hard, and where did that rock hard cock of mine go? Right into Mindy's eagerly awaiting mouth, while I slowly penetrated her with the toy.

She was soaked as her muff made those funny funt sounds. What is a funt you ask? It is like a fart noise coming from her cunt. Time to experiment. I wonder if her pussy could fit me and her toy at the same time?

Well God damn, it was tight, but she took us both like a champ. Her face looked different, I could tell it kind of hurt her, but I could also tell that pain was part of her kink.

The tightness and her moans made me build up to an orgasm quicker than I would have liked. Time for some coordination as I am not sure whether she came or not.

So, I pull my throbbing and ready to explode cock out of her soaked pussy and start to shoot all over her boobs, while still trying to best to get the dildo to bat her home.

Mindy now laid back to catch her breath as I went to get a beer, and a cloth to wipe my cum off her.

When I came back into the bedroom Mindy was drinking something, at first, I thought it was an airplane bottle. I asked if she wanted a drink, she said just water.

So, I asked what she was sipping on. She said her liquid codeine medicine.

I know she has had an emotional day, I respect that, but her husband is coming home tomorrow. She can't be a total zombie, especially with her 40th birthday party the next day.

The only sure-fire way to get it away from her was to ask for a sip myself. This made her smile and she said sure. Now, I only pretended to take a sip before putting the bottle out of her reach, and on to my dresser.

After I wiped away my mess, we laid in bed and talked, yes talked about the bigger picture, and her jealousy of Carol.

Right now, more than ever before, Mindy must have total confidence in me. If she truly doesn't, I will cancel the hit on Marvin.

As I am explaining once again why me taking Carol is a good thing, Mindy had her eyes closed the whole time.

I asked if she was listening to me.

Mindy struggled but managed to open her eyes and said, "Enough talking about that cunt Carol. I want your cock in my ass, and that toy back in my pussy. Fuck me hard, Mitch; treat me like the whore I am, your whore!"

She certainly knows how to get a rise out of me, in more ways than one. And yes, I clued in what her game was. She wanted to make sure I had no mojo left in my cock, at least for Carol.

Mindy got on all fours as I lubed up my cock. I spanked her ass a couple times pretty solid before I put the toy back in her pussy.

Aw, those sweet moans, now it's time to hear those sweet

groans as I slowly guided my cock into her ass.

My God her ass was tight, like an anal virgin. Is it because there is a toy in her pussy, or from the codeine?

I truly struggled to get any rhythm going. I can only imagine how much this is hurting her. Fuck, is she this jealous, or insecure?

Five thrusts later, suddenly Mindy collapses onto the bed. And I mean she drops.

I called her name at first, nothing, then I shook her and nothing. My gut flipped and my heart started to race, fuck did she have a heart attack, or end up overdosing on the codeine?

Panic, pure fucking panic set in. I can see Lucy with that fix still sticking out of her arm. That horrible haunting feeling that I wouldn't wish on anyone, has now kicked down the bad memory door for me.

My throat was starting to close as full-blown panic was now setting in.

I roll her onto her back, touch her jugular, and can't feel a pulse, I stick my head on her chest and can't hear her breathing. *Fuck, fuck, fuck. Is she dead?*

Do I flee the scene just like with Lucy, but this time, not heading to my grandfathers, instead straight to Canada? Did I know deep down opening that bank account in Canada would pay off this quick?

District attorney will have my ass fried, not one, but two girlfriends will have died of overdoses around me.

Just like an air raid siren going off, I have seconds to decide to hunker down, or bug out.

BOOKS BY TIM FORD

1 – SANTA DIES ONCE AGAIN

2- SUMMER OF LOVE, FALL OF HATE

3- A JUNGLE IS STILL A JUNGLE

4- CRIMINOLOGY 101

5- CHASING DRAGONS, SLAYING DEMONS

6- INSIDE LOOKING OUT

7- FREEDOM

8- DIABLO RETURNS

9- FOOL'S BETRAYAL

10- THE GHOSTS THAT HAUNT ME

11 – FORBIDDEN, OR WORSE *

12 – CARINI INC *

13- STRONGBOW'S REVENGE *

Coming Soon = *

Shop at www.pandamoniumpublishing.com/shop